In the Blink of an Eye

#253179460

Anthony Fields

Lock Down Publications and Ca$h
Presents
In the Blink of an Eye
A Novel by *Anthony Fields*

In the Blink of an Eye

Lock Down Publications
P.O. Box 944
Stockbridge, Ga 30281

Visit our website @
www.lockdownpublications.com

Copyright 2021 by Anthony Fields
In the Blink of an Eye

All rights reserved. No part of this book may be reproduced in any form or by electronic or mechanical means, including information storage and retrieval systems without permission in writing from the publisher, except by a reviewer who may quote brief passages in review.
First Edition June 2021
Printed in the United States of America

This is a work of fiction. Names, characters, places, and incidents either are products of the author's imagination or are used fictitiously. Any similarity to actual events or locales or persons, living or dead, is entirely coincidental.

Lock Down Publications
Like our page on Facebook: Lock Down Publications @
www.facebook.com/lockdownpublications.ldp
Edited by: **Lashonda Johnson**
Book interior design by: **Shawn Walker**

Anthony Fields

Stay Connected with Us!

Text **LOCKDOWN** to 22828 to stay up-to-date with new
releases, sneak peaks, contests and more…
Thank you.

In the Blink of an Eye

Submission Guideline.

Submit the first three chapters of your completed manuscript to ldpsubmissions@gmail.com, subject line: Your book's title. The manuscript must be in a .doc file and sent as an attachment. Document should be in Times New Roman, double spaced and in size 12 font. Also, provide your synopsis and full contact information. If sending multiple submissions, they must each be in a separate email.

Have a story but no way to send it electronically? You can still submit to LDP/Ca$h Presents. Send in the first three chapters, written or typed, of your completed manuscript to:

LDP: Submissions Dept
P.O. Box 944
Stockbridge, Ga 30281

DO NOT send original manuscript. Must be a duplicate.

Provide your synopsis and a cover letter containing your full contact information.

Thanks for considering LDP and Ca$h Presents.

Anthony Fields

In the Blink of an Eye

CHAPTER 1

"Deep throating is a form of oral sex. A type of fellatio in which the whole erect dick is taken into the mouth. Check this out." Rhoda grabbed the remote off the coffee table. With a push of a button, a sixty-four-inch plasma screen came to life and showed a pretty brown-skinned woman giving a man head. "This bitch is the epitome of a real nasty girl. Her name is Ménage and she can deep throat the dude's dick she's giving head to. His name is Mandingo, and his dick is about thirteen or fourteen inches long. Watch how she does it."

After a few minutes of watching the porn star in action, Rhoda clicked off the T.V. and took center stage. "Me I'm not on her level. Just watching her do that shit makes me wanna gag. Since the average erect dick is longer than the average mouth is deep, the art of deep throating requires the suppression of the gag reflexes in order to partially swallow the end of the dick. In order to perform this oral act, the dick recipient, that means you ladies, control all the muscles in the back of the throat and flattens the tongue. While gradually inserting the dick completely.

One way to learn how to deep throat your husbands or boyfriends is this. Lie back, face up on your bed, with your head hanging over the edge. This is called the *'upside down'* position. This position ensures that the throat and mouth are lined up and aids the penetration. However, because mouth and throat struc-tures vary from person to person, some of you may prefer the *'upright'* position. Meaning, you on your knees, ladies; upright and him sitting or lying back. Does everyone follow me so far?"

All six of the ladies' present nodded their heads. Rhoda al-most laughed out loud several times throughout the session. She couldn't believe, she'd let one of her male friends talk her into teaching his wife and five friends how to properly suck a dick. When Nadir 'Smoke' Mahdi first mentioned it to her, she had done just that...*laughed*. But, when Smoke pulled out several wads of cash and handed it to her, that wiped the smile off her face.

"Okay," Rhoda continued. "In front of every one of you is a dick. You might call it a dildo, but either way, you look at it, it's a dick. These are new; they are made of a synthetic composite that is made to imitate real skin. They make fake legs and arms outta the shit. The veins and everything has been added to make them more life-like. I took the liberty of purchasing you all a seven inch. You can thank me later. I want you all to get down on your knees, ladies. Thank you. You too, Ms. Yvette. You ain't too cute to get your knees dirty."

Yvette Williams laughed unabashedly. "I know that's right, girl."

"I also think it would be easier for you if the dick was lubricated. There's a water-based lubricant on the table that tastes like watermelon, for those who want it and need it. Okay, let's proceed, then. Take the hand that you use to eat with and gently massage the dick, up and down, slowly. Feels real, doesn't it? I told y' all so. Close your eyes and imagine that the dick your sucking belongs to your husband, boyfriend, lover, thug on the side, or whoever."

Rhoda coached all the women through their inhibitions and fears. All the while struggling not to laugh at them for being on their knees, sucking rubber dicks.

"Ms. Buchanan?" one woman said as the dick plopped out of her mouth.

"Call me Rhoda."

"Rhoda, I saw the D.V.D and all that, but can you please demonstrate to me the proper way to do it? I'm sure I speak for all of us when I say that we'd love to see a professional at work."

This bitch ain't said nothing slick to a can of oil. Rhoda thought. Aloud she said, "No problem. Give me a few minutes and I'll be right with y' all." Grabbing her cell phone out of her purse, Rhoda made a phone call, thirty minutes later, the doorbell rang.

"Let me get that," Rhoda said to her audience as she headed to the door. Opening it, she let a man in. "Ladies, let me introduce you to my friend Dexter. Dex, these are the ladies."

"What's good, ladies?" Dex said.

"Dex, come and sit in this chair right here, for me, please." Rhoda kicked off her heels and fell to her knees. "Ladies, I'm sorry, but I don't do rubber. I only do the real thing, now watch and learn something."

The ladies in the room looked on in awe as Rhoda pulled Dexter's eleven-inch dick out of his jeans. She slowly licked the length of his dick and then spit on the head. Rhoda gave the dick a few customary strokes to spread the saliva all over it. Then she put her head game down for everybody in the room to see. When her lips finally touched the base of Dexter's dick, Rhoda heard the collective gasps from the audience. She never stopped or slowed down her assault on Dexter's dick.

Several minutes later, he grabbed her hair and held her down on his dick. Rhoda felt the twitching in his dick and knew Dexter was about to cum. The grip on her head forced her to stay on the dick and accept every drop of his seed. It wouldn't be the first or the last time she would swallow his babies, so like the real bitch she was, Rhoda relaxed her throat muscles and used them to coax all the cum from Dexter's dick. As she gently rubbed on his chiseled stomach, warm and thick cum coated her own stomach. Rhoda knew that her work was done. *Message received, money earned.*

For visual effect, Rhoda continued to suck and stroke the semi-hard dick in her mouth. Then she raised up off it. As the last remnants of cum rushed to the tip of Dexter's dick, Rhoda made a show of licking the cum off and moving it around on her tongue before swallowing it. *Job complete*; she stuffed the dick back into Dexter's jeans, slipped on her heels, and stood up to face her audience. "Thank you, ladies, for your time. I hope you enjoyed today's session. I wish I could stick around and teach y' all some more tricks, but I have a plane to catch."

Outside by Dexter's Escalade, Rhoda raised up onto the tips of her toes and kissed him. She palmed Dexter's dick and said, "Thanks, for coming and then cumming. I'ma call you when I get back and get Rock settled."

Rhoda walked away briskly and got into her forest green Maserati. She put the car in gear and headed for the airport.

In the Blink of an Eye

CHAPTER 2

Ronald 'Rock' Blackman walked the track inside the walls of the federal penitentiary in Terre Haute, Indiana. His story had come to an end, it was bittersweet, but bitter nonetheless. Rock was excited about regaining his freedom after almost twenty-four years. The bad part was leaving his co-defendant and partner Beanie Caldwell behind. When they first came to Terre Haute seventeen years earlier, someone had disrespected Beanie in his block and he stabbed the man several times in the head and face. The federal court in Terre Haute, sentenced Beanie to an additional thirty-six months to run concurrent to his life sentence. An oversight by their trial attorneys two decades ago allowed them both to give their sentences back in the Supreme Court. So, Rock was going home and Beanie had to stay an extra three years. That hurt Rock deeply.

"Don't worry about me, big fella," Beanie said to his partner as they walked the track together. "I'm good. All I gotta do is two more years and I'll be out there with you. I know how you feel and believe me; I love you more than I love my own blood. But, you gotta go out there and get shit ready for me, for us. You know you've always been the smarter one. Go ahead out there and deal with the growing pains so that I won't have too. We rich all over again, slim. You can afford to live it up out there young nigga style. With no pressure. No more throwing bricks at the penitentiary wall. Go pop some bottles, fuck some young bitches, and wear them tight ass pants like them young niggas on TV."

Both men laughed. Beanie knew how much Rock hated the 2000's. He was a traditional old head that yearned for the days of old. The days when there was honor amongst men and not the 'get down first, tell on your mother and father' new millennium.

Every time Beanie and Rock decided that there was no hope for the younger generation and that it was filled with down low brothers, faggots, dykes, and rats, they remembered the greatest young dude that came out of the new generation. *Roscoe.*

11

Roscoe Sanders had come to Terre Haute in the early 2000's, a young and thorough kid with eighty years to life. Rock and Beanie liked him and were eternally grateful to him because he came in for killing the rat that put them behind bars for life. Having a little knowledge of the law, together they poured hundreds of hours into finding a loophole in Roscoe's case. They found it and that loophole freed Roscoe a few years later.

The men in Terre Haute had grown to love Roscoe and the kid reciprocated that love from the streets. He and his cousin single-handedly moved more drugs in one year than the city had ever seen. Then they paid almost three million dollars to lawyers for Rock and Beanie. But, they never lived to hear that the old heads had finally found their freedom. Tragically, the next year Roscoe was ambushed and blown up in a club he owned. His cousin had been killed a couple weeks earlier. Roscoe's death crushed all the good men in Terre Haute but, Rock, Beanie, and Foxboro-Bey were inconsolable. Knowing that the person responsible for Roscoe's death was the Latin drug kingpin Carlos Trinidad, made getting their freedom that much more bittersweet. Rock promised Beanie and Fox that he would put into action the events that would lead to Carlos' demise. And that was a promise he intended to keep.

"I'd rather die than emulate the dudes of today. I'ma take it back to the good ole days. Crocodile, Ostrich, and all that shit. You'll see. I'ma fly them flicks up in here."

"I know you are old timer, I know you are. Monday is the big day, huh?" Beanie asked already knowing that it was.

"Yeah. I can't believe it. Bean, I just don't feel it, yet."

"Don't worry, you'll feel it Monday when you walk through them gates and leave this hellhole. You'll feel it when you climb into a real bed with that fine ass young girl you got. You'll feel it when you put those street clothes on you keep telling me about. What the fuck was that name anyway...John Var...who?"

Rock laughed. "It's John Varvatos. Some kinda designer shit that Rhoda put me down with. She says it'll look good on me."

"Well, you'll feel freedom once you put that shit on. You'll feel it..."

"Okay, okay. You've made your point. I'll feel it soon, I got you."

"Good. Now, let's go find Fox so he can get his quality time in with you before you leave. I wanna see if his tough old ass is gonna shed a tear."

Both men laughed and walked towards the inside of the prison.

Anthony Fields

CHAPTER 3

"Ma'am, would you like something to drink from our beverage bar?" The stewardess asked Rhoda as she placed a pillow behind her head. "Something to eat maybe?" *That's why I love flying first class. They really know how to treat a bitch.* Kicking off her shoes for the second time that day, Rhoda reclined her seat and got comfortable. "No thank you, boo, I'm straight."

Rhoda closed her eyes and focused her mind elsewhere. It had been about three months since she'd last taken the flight, but this one would be her last. She was heading to Indiana to welcome home the man that she loved. As the jumbo jet found its comfort zone thirty-five thousand feet in the air, Rhoda reminisced about the first time that she'd met Rock Blackman...

That day started off early on a Friday, Rhoda and Cinnamon had been told that they were going to a prison out of town to sex some incarcerated ballers. Her and Cinnamon had argued incessantly over who was gonna wear the black Isaac Mizrahi wrap around skirt. The skirt belonged to Vita but, they didn't care. Vita owned all the most fly gear that was in style and she regularly loaned all her pieces to her girls. Rhoda knew how good the skirt fit her shapely curves and wanted to impress the out of towners. Incarcerated ballers became free ballers eventually and she wanted to be kept in mind when they did shine.

Cinnamon must've felt the same as Rhoda, thus the long argument about the skirt. Vita, who had been relatively quiet morning, got tired of the argument and took the skirt back so that no one would wear it. And just like that, the argument was over. Cinnamon and Rhoda knew that if Vita was going through the trouble of going out of town to a prison to sex dudes in a visiting hall, they had to have money. Money and more money was the only thing that motivated and moved Davita Allen.

Rhoda ended up rocking a tan Escada skirt with a matching blouse and Dior heels, getting her corporate look on. Cinnamon settled for the hood rat look in a multicolored Mchunu ensemble that accentuated her cinnamon complexion and freckles. Her whole outfit screamed, "I'm from Southeast D.C." Being the thoroughbred that she was Rhoda didn't care what the dude she was going to sex looked like. What she did care about were the two-thousand dollars she was making that weekend. She could get around looks, that was easy, and dicks didn't have faces, they looked exactly like another, just different sizes, girths, and colors.

But to her surprise, the man that she ended up pairing with turned out to be gorgeous. He was a hair under six feet and around one hundred eighty or ninety pounds. His hair was cut into a skin fade with enough waved in his head to make the ocean jealous. His goatee was well trimmed, and if it wasn't for the gray hair that started to sprout, he would've looked thirty years old tops. When he grabbed her as if they were old friends and hugged her, that sealed the deal. She was gonna fuck him into a coma.

He slowly released her and said, "What's up love? My name is Rock."

It didn't take long for Rhoda to see why he was called Rock. His body was chiseled like granite stone and his dick stayed rock hard. Just like that Prudential Insurance commercial, she got her piece of the Rock. For two straight days, they went to the federal prison in Terre Haute and sexed Rock and his friends. The thought of him never left her mind. Even as they drove back down I-70 and argued all the way, Rhoda remembered everything about Rock. Apparently, the feeling had been mutual because a few weeks later, Rock called her house. He told her that he had gotten the number from his man Roscoe, who got it from Vita.

In the end, Rhoda was glad that he took the initiative to get in touch. For one, she liked him and for two, it wasn't hard to tell that Rock was the epitome of old drug money. Fucking with him had to be a come up. As they racked up phone minutes, Rhoda discovered that Rock was a good conversationalist. That was what she had lacked in her life. She had yet to meet a dude that could hold her attention for five minutes after sex.

16

In the Blink of an Eye

In the Blink of an Eye

With Rock so far away, their friendship was built on good ole fashioned getting to know one another. In time, he was the one that opened her eyes. Before meeting Rock, she had been content with tricking for next to nothing. As long as she had a bottle of Remy, a bag or two of sticky green, the latest outfits, and a few dollars she was good. Orgasms were non-existent and she didn't care. Vita did all the planning and thinking for her so Rhoda rarely cared about much. That was the way Vita wanted it. She had been either too high or too drunk to realize that on her own. With her looks...five-five, one hundred and thirty-seven pounds, tight and in the right places, toned abs, hazel eyes, big breasts, and a pussy print that resembled a lion's paw...she knew she could pull any dude and hold him. The fact that she was more than willing to go all the way sexually, kept her in high demand. Rhoda figured that she had to have been worth a fortune money wise, but she never even saw eighty percent of the money Vita did.

It wasn't the fact that they didn't know that Vita was pimping them, they had agreed to it. In the beginning, Vita started calling herself and two other girls, Dominique, and Carolyn, the Pomeroy Road Good Pussy Clique. But, when other chicks started biting and calling themselves names like The Pussy Pound, The Nothing Butt Ass Honeys, and others. Vita decided that it was time for a name change. One that she said would separate the real bitches from the imitations. Where she got that idea for No Holes Barred was anybody's Guess. Maybe she watched too much wrestling. The No Holes Barred Crew became an instant hit. The name alone drew attention. Any woman in those days that put it out there publicly that she was willing to take it in any orifice on her body, demanded respect, and attention. Bitches were getting fucked in the ass behind closed doors and loving it but they kept it secret. The No Holes Barred name told you up front that you could serve it up anyway that you wanted to and the crew didn't care who knew it.

Vita went to all the parties and go-go promoting the No Holes Barred Crew. It was her aim to put Dominique and Carolyn on

17

the market to be ravished anally, vaginally, and orally by the highest bidders. After a few dates, Dominique bucked. She was being fucked every which way while Vita reaped all the benefits. She decided to bounce and she took Carolyn with her. Having thoroughly marketed the N.H.B.C., Vita was then a pimp with no hoes. With clientele on standby, she had to literally put the workload on her back and stomach. Quickly tiring of so many degrees of penetration, Vita recruited Cinnamon, whom she'd grown up with. Then they approached Rhoda after a few blunts were passed around and Rhoda was high as a kite, she agreed to join the crew. She loved to fuck anyway. The rules to the crew were simple. Fuck and get money, but pay your dues to the house lady...Vita.

What Vita did was hook up over ninety percent of the dates, provide a place to do the deed...her townhouse...and then collected the money. Your average every day Joe was cool from time to time, but Vita targeted the hustlers. The Tony Lewises, Cornell Joneses, Michael Frey's, Cliff and Roy Cobbses, Blackwell's, Tommy and Tony Edelin's, and Michael Howards. They represented D.C.'s elite. They had the money that rubber bands couldn't hold. Vita's philosophy was simple... "snag the niggas with the long money, suck their dicks until they cum in your tummy, and a real bitch's pockets would never feel funny."

Rhoda's introduction into the crew had been Vita strapping on an eight- inch dildo and breaking her ass in. When Rhoda had protested vehemently, Vita simply said, "We're the No Holes Barred Crew, stupid ass girl. Not the One Hole Closed Crew." She lubed up and repeatedly introduced Rhoda to the wonderful world of anal sex. After learning their lessons well and knowing their role in the crew, came the other girls, Jamie, and Pebbles. Then came Quanda and Sparkle and lastly, Billie.

While she continued to take orders and dates from Vita, it was Rock who constantly dropped jewels for thought on Rhoda. "You have to use your brain, boo, as well as your body...slow down on the alcohol, it will damage your liver...drink plenty of water and eat right, you'll live longer...the greatest gift that God ever gave to man was a woman..."

18

Then tragedy struck, two years later, Vita and Cinnamon were shot and killed as they slept in a hotel out Virginia. While on a date with a friend of Roscoe's, somebody picked the locks on their hotel room door, walked in, and killed the dude they were with and them too. The N.H.B.C. WAS crushed. The loss of their leader and sisters was devastating. All the while the girls grieved, it was Rock who comforted Rhoda. He became her constant source of strength. It was then that she fell in love with him.

With the deaths of Vita and Cinnamon, Rhoda knew that she was the heir apparent. Somebody had to galvanize the team and lead them forward. Rhoda stepped up to the plate and with Rock's guidance, changed everything. Rhoda urged all the girls to move out of their apartments and move into the townhouse that Vita owned. They needed to comfort each other and they would save money in the process because the townhouse was paid for. Rhoda took Vita's Cadillac Escalade and Lexus 460H and sold them to the highest bidders. That money went to Vita's parents. The money that came from Vita's safe went to the bank. Rhoda opened a business account in the name of N.H.B.C. Enterprises.

Everybody in the crew wasn't happy with the changes. There would always be differences of opinions, especially in a clique of females. Pebbles and Jamie had never thought too highly of Rhoda, so her taking over for Vita didn't sit well with them. They eventually decided to go in a different direction. Down to four members...Sparkle, Quanda, Billie and herself, it was time to ride or die. Rhoda encouraged everybody to go and open personal bank accounts. They would always need rainy day money. Instead of paying weekly dues to Rhoda, as they Vita, all dues went into the N.H.B.C. business account. Where Vita had them getting by, Rhoda, at Rock's insistence, wanted to make them rich. She advised them all to go back and finish school if they hadn't. They enrolled in college courses...well, everybody except Sparkle, who was already college educated.

They all went and got health insurance as well as life insurance. "Let Vita and Cinnamon's deaths be a lesson to you." Rock always told Rhoda. Applying for and receiving secured credit cards helped to build all their credit histories. Newly independent and established in the game, next came the cars, trucks, and jewelry that they always wanted. One year after the deaths of their sisters, the No Holes Barred Crew was back and better than ever. No longer thinking small, they invested big and charged more for dates. Hustlers would always be the meal of the day, but the ballplayers, politicians, musicians, and C.E.O.'s became their desired dishes.

"Ma'am, please buckle your seatbelt, we should be landing shortly." The stewardess said, then added. "And I love your tattoo."

Rhoda glanced at the tattoo on her chest, above her breasts. It was a picture that Vita had drawn and then forced all the girls in the crew to get. *"The mark of the beast,* she called it. "Thank you."

A voice came over the intercom and announced. "We are now at ten thousand and descending. The weather at Marie Hollman Airport is overcast skies. It's sixty-seven degrees, we hope you enjoyed your flight."

Rhoda stared out the window and watched as the ground below quickly came into view. It had been over four years since she'd first met the man; that she was now coming to welcome home. It didn't matter at all to her that, that man was old enough to be her father. Rock Blackmon was her man and she'd do anything, including, changing her lifestyle to keep him. She had been introduced to him as a young girl. He groomed her into a young woman. Monday morning when the United States Penitentiary-Terre Haute released him, she'd be there waiting to bring him home in style.

20

CHAPTER 4

"You gotta hold still, baby girl." Tay the tattoo artist, said exasperatedly. The squeamish young girl in the chair was starting to wear out his patience.

'Star' gave the tattooist one of her famous, *'You must be crazy'* looks and jumped again as soon as the tattoo gun touched her skin. She looked over at Quanda, who was near tears with laughter. "Ain't nothing funny, Quan! This shit hurt like a mutha-fucka.

Knowing exactly what Star was going through, Quanda tried to stop laughing, but she couldn't. She had been nervous and jumpy over four years ago when Vita had brought her to Off Da Hook Tattoos to get her membership tattoo. Quanda stood up and looked in the mirror at the tattoo on her chest, above her breasts. The image of a naked woman squatting on several stacks of cash, holding a chain necklace stared back at her. The chain necklace ended with a pendant attached. That pendant read, enlarged for all to see, N.H.B.C.

Quanda instinctively glanced at her left arm and saw the tattoo that she had gotten nine months ago. It was a tattoo of two tombstones protruding out of the ground on a moonlit night. The writing on the stones read 'Rest in Peace Vita and Cinnamon'. As always tears threatened to fall down her eyes as they always did whenever she thought about her two slain friends.

"Ooow! I can't keep still! This shit hurt, boy!"

Quanda turned in Star's direction and laughed. Tay was trying to ease the young girl's fear. He wasn't having much luck. Before she could open her mouth to say anything. Quanda remembered Vita cursing her out for being so squeamish when she got her tattoo...

LaQuanda Jasper was twenty years old then and just happy to be associated with a crew of bad bitches like Vita ad her crew. She met Davita Allen, at the Tunnel nightclub one night in the VIP section. She had heard a lot about Vita and the No Holes

Barred Crew. They exchanged numbers after Vita told her how pretty and sexy she was. After talking to Vita on the phone every day for a couple of weeks, she was invited to come over to Vita's townhouse on Pomeroy Road. That ended up being a night that she'd never forget.

Her brother Mike had dropped her off on Vita's doorstep and kept her car. Ringing the doorbell, she didn't know what to expect from Vita. Quanda thought that they'd just drink, smoke, and chill out. She was wrong. Vita answered the door dressed only in a black thong with a thick towel wrapped around her hair. "Come in", was all that she said. Quanda didn't consider herself gay or bi-sexual, but she couldn't keep her eyes off Vita's apple bottom shaped ass as they walked through the living room. "Follow me", Vita said, more a command than anything. Quanda complied like a person awestruck. She followed Vita up some stairs and down a hallway, into a large bedroom.

"Sit," Vita said and disappeared into an adjoining bathroom.

Hearing nothing, but water running, Quanda wondered what Vita was doing. A minute later, Vita stuck her head out of the bathroom and said, "Take your clothes off, Quanda. I wanna see what you look like under all them damn clothes." Then she disappeared back into the bathroom.

A mild panic attack set in as she untied her retro Jordans. Somewhat, of a tomboy, Quanda wondered what her body would look like to Vita. Was it ugly? None of the dudes that she been with had ever complained. After pulling off her socks, Quanda wiggled out of her Diesel denim. When she pulled the t-shirt off bearing the image of Michael Jordan, that was as far as she was going.

Exiting the bathroom and without even looking at her, Vita crossed the room and said, "The panties and bra too, Quan."

Reluctantly, Quanda did as she was told. With some sort of remote, Vita dimmed the lights in the room and turned on a stereo. Majic 102.3 had Leona Lewis' whole CD playing. Quanda, watched nervously as Vita grabbed the cordless phone on her dresser and took it off the base. Then she did something to her cell phone.

"How can you see me with the lights so dim?" Quanda asked, but received no reply. Instead, Vita walked over to her and bent down until their faces met.

"Be quiet, okay? We'll talk later. For right now, just relax and go with the flow." Vita said. And then she kissed her.

"But…Vita …I never…" Quanda started to say, but Vita's mouth was on hers again. She felt a wet tongue part her lips and enter her mouth. The kiss was warm, powerful, and passionate. It didn't take long for her juices to start flowing. When that happened, Quanda threw caution to the wind and returned the force that she was receiving. When their lips finally separated, Quanda had to breathe deeply to stop her heart from pounding.

Then she felt Vita's mouth all over her breasts. First the left one, then the right one. It felt so good that all she could do was throw her head back and prop herself up from falling back. Quanda moaned and bit down on her bottom lip as her nipples were sucked on and lightly chewed. Next Vita's fingers found her soaking wet pussy. Loud moans escaped her mouth as she was pushed back onto the bed. Before she could protest, Quanda felt soft lips, and a tongue replaced the fingers. As Vita's tongue danced around her clit with the grace and skill of a ballerina, Quanda could do nothing but reach her hands above her head and grab the bed sheets.

She slowly grinded her pelvis in circles as Vita ate her and Leona Lewis sang her into a peaceful, comfortable, erotic place. Vita's tongue felt like it was at least three inches long as it moved in and out of her. Quanda couldn't hold back the rivers of ecstasy that she was trying to hold inside. With a mirror shattering scream, she climaxed all over Vita's face and mouth. Vita never came up for air. Slowly, methodically, she brought Quanda to many more orgasms until she finally had to beg Vita to stop.

Stop was evidently, a word that was not in Vita's vocabulary because Quanda ended up on all fours with Vita eating her ass. Her body eventually collapsed from exhaustion and too much pleasure. Vita left the room and let her recover for a while. The next thing Quanda knew or felt was a dick slipping into her. Alarmed, she looked over her shoulder to discover that Vita was back and she had strapped on a dildo.

Over the next couple of hours, Vita fucked her in every position possible and even made her cum several times anally. Anal sex was something that she had tried but hadn't enjoyed before that night. With Vita, it was different...better. She had been shocked when she found herself begging for it deeper, harder, slower. After they showered together and lay in bed together, Vita had simply said, "You will do nicely." Then she fell asleep.

The next morning, she was introduced to all the girls, although they already knew each other. Two days after that, Vita took her to the tattoo parlor on Pennsylvania Avenue and got her initiated.

Quanda laughed to herself as she put herself in the chair that Star now sat in...

"Ouch!" She had whined every time the dude tried to start working. "Owww!"

"Hold on for a minute, Paul," Vita said to the man holding the tattoo gun. To Quanda, she said, "Shut the fuck up, Quan. You're killing me with this crybaby shit. You like to fight and all that stupid ass shit, but you scared to get a tattoo. Sit still so the man can start and hurry up and finish. You act like somebody is tryna kill you. He ain't even touched you, yet!"

"Vee, I changed my mind. I don't want no tattoo. Why can't I be down with the crew and not have the stupid tattoo?"

"Stupid tattoo? I got your stupid tattoo. You can't be down with my crew without shedding a little blood for the cause. It's the ultimate sacrifice. That shit ain't shit. Your threshold for pain has to be higher than what I'm seeing now, I know. All I ask is that you be branded with the mark of the beast. Is that too, much to ask? Huh? Is it? After this, you are officially one of us. We are identified by our tattoo. You are joining an exclusive club of top flight bitches. Do you know how many chicks wanna be with us? I turn bitches down every day. But, you wouldn't know that, would you? Because if you did, you wouldn't be sitting here acting like a little ass girl. I chose you; you need us. So, stop moving, shut the fuck up, and get the stupid tattoo!"

And reluctantly, she had done just that. Quanda felt a sense of Deja Vu as she watched Star go through the same thing as her. That's what made it so hilarious.

Then another thought hit her. *Whoever said that 'what makes you laugh, will make you cry' had never lied.* Thoughts of Vita threatened to overwhelm her. Quanda often wished that Vita was still here. She missed her scathing criticisms, direct bluntness, her humor, and her sex. But, not particularly in that order. Rhoda was doing a good job of keeping everything together; well maybe even a better job than Vita, but she wasn't Vita. There would never be another person to touch her life like Davita Allen.

Quanda glanced back at Star and noticed that she had settled down some and was getting the tattoo. That was a blessing. Then she sat down in the waiting room lounge chair and thought back to the day when her world almost stopped spinning...

It was 4 a.m. when she got the call from Rhoda. They had all partied like rock stars at Roscoe's new club called Immorality. Quanda left the club with a dude named Kevin Grover that had just come home. His pockets were on swoll and that's all that it took for him to be lying next to her in the middle of the night. When the call came through. She had started not to answer it. Quanda had shared her every hole with Kevin and was tired. Giving a dude the H.A.P. treatment (head, ass, and pussy) wore the body out. She had welcomed the blanket of darkness as sleep overtook her. But, then the phone wouldn't stop ringing. She had to answer it.

"Hello?"

"Quanda, where is everybody?" It was Rhoda.

Her patience thin and her eyes half closed, Quanda spat, "Rho, how the hell do I know? Them bitches is somewhere getting money, I hope."

"Quan, I got bad news..."

It was then that she noticed that Rhoda was sobbing on the phone. Quanda became instantly awake. "What bad news? Are you okay? What's going on, Rho?"

When Rhoda didn't respond right away, Quanda became more afraid. "Rho, you are scaring me! What the fuck is up? Why are you crying?"

"Vita...Cinnamon..."

Getting out of the bed, Quanda paced the floor frantically. As her eyes watered, she hollered, "What's wrong with Vee and Cinn?"

"They...gone, Quan. They gone."

Tears openly fell down her cheeks now. "What do you mean, gone, Rho? Gone where?"

"Somebody shot them...they're dead..."

At the sound of the word 'dead', Quanda dropped the phone. She felt hands on her shoulders but all she heard were the sounds of her own screams. When her throat gave out and her screams quieted, Quanda could hear Rhoda still on the phone saying, "Quan?! Quan answer me! Quan!"

"Noooooo!" she cried repeatedly. It couldn't be. Vita and Cinn couldn't be dead. She had just left them. They had just partied at the club. How could they be gone...?

"Till death do us part." Vita had once said to her after a wild night of drinking, smoking, and sex. Back then she never knew that they would part ways sooner than later.

Make sure you keep those tattoos moist. Use some type of gel and keep them covered for at least two weeks." Tay said to Star.

If looks could kill, the one that Star gave Tay in return would have done just that. Quanda paid the eight-hundred-dollar tab and lead Star out of the parlor. It was starting to get dark outside. They walked up the street to Quanda's convertible BMW 645ci. Quanda noticed how tacky Star looked. "You hungry?"

"Hell yeah!" Star replied. "Where are we headed now?"

"Olive Garden. First, we eat, and then we shop. You can't be ripping the baddest bitches in D.C. while looking like a hood rat."

In the Blink of an Eye

The sounds of *French Montana's* new song *Don't Panic* filled the car as they headed to Interstate 66.

Anthony Fields

CHAPTER 5

At the airport, Rhoda walked into a Heritage Rental and drove away in a 2014 Mercedes Benz ML 550. She drove down Wabash Valley Avenue and pulled into a Comfort Suites Hotel. It was the same hotel that they'd stayed in when Roscoe first brought them to Indiana. A little while later, she was undressed and relaxing in a Jacuzzi. Rhoda periodically glanced over at her cell phone. She had given Rock the timetable for her flight and arrival in Indiana. *Why hadn't he called yet?* Rhoda tried getting her mind off Rock and his impending release. *"Don't worry yourself."* Her conscience said. Getting out of the water and drying off, Rhoda clicked on the TV. She channel surfed for a while, before settling on a movie…*Gladiator.* It was a good flick and she thought the white man that starred in it, *Russell Crowe,* was kinda sexy.

Having already talked to most of the crew, for some reason Billie couldn't be reached. Usually, she would have worried, but Rhoda knew Billie well. When Billie was with somebody she enjoyed sexually, she always turned her cell phone off. What was unusual was the time of day, Billie rarely went out before 9 p.m. Laughing, Rhoda realized that in many ways she had become like a mother hen to the girls. She didn't know if Vita's affections for all of them was sincere or just money related. They would never know, but her affinity for them was real and sincere. Especially with Quanda and Billie. They were closest friends.

"Billie was a mess." Rhoda thought. Billie was the most flamboyant person in the crew. She always needed to be seen and heard. And the girl knew everything about everything and everybody. Nobody could tell her anything, Billie was a lovable comedienne that missed her true calling. Standing 5'4 barefooted and weighing one-hundred-forty-six pounds, she was a brick shithouse. She was the spitting image of the legendary blues singer Billie Holiday, thus the name Billie. Her café latte skin complexion looked like a never-ending waterfall of coffee. Billie's best features were her smile, her eyes, and her jet black wavy

sometimes curly hair. The girl could work, sexually Billie had the whole beat hands down. Rhoda had seen her in action enough times to give her the *'Just like Vita'* award of the decade. Billie loved her work, she lived for it, actually. No matter what length or width of the dick, Billie could work it. Watching her fuck one man or three, it was like watching a young *Vanessa Del Rio*.

One particular day always stood out in Rhoda's mind. They, her, Quanda, and Billie were entertaining three Washington Wizard basketball players. Not the star players, but a couple of dudes off the bench. One of them in particular, a young kid that had just been drafted out of Prep school, was all over Billie. That day, Rhoda learned that the myth about niggas over six feet, with big feet, wasn't true. The dude she was with was six-eleven and not packing at all. His fingers were longer than his dick. That caused her eyes to wander around the room as he humped her. Rhoda's eyes settled on the youngster that Billie was pleasuring. It was unbelievable. When Rhoda saw, Billie swallow his dick until her face rested in his lap, it made her gag. The young boy's dick had to be at least twelve inches. She couldn't believe that little ass Billie had the whole dick in her throat. It was amazing. Rhoda knew then why Billie booked more dates than anybody else in the crew.

Rhoda remembered that tall light skinned dude that had Quanda bent over the couch that day. By the look on Quanda's face, his dick was in her ass. That was vintage Quanda. Everybody in the crew indulged in anal sex, to be in the crew, but as far as Rhoda knew, nobody enjoyed it as much as Quanda. Quanda was, to Rhoda, a little rough around the edges. Meaning she was only a few steps removed from being a chicken head.

People say that you can take the girl out of the streets, but you can't take the streets out of the girl. That's definitely true in Quanda's case. All of them were from the streets, but the rest of them had made the transition over to respectable, high-class hooker, easily. But, Quanda had not. Girlfriend got real mannish when provoked. It didn't take much for her to pull out the Vaseline for her face, tennis shoes, and a scarf for her head when it was time for drama. But for all the female etiquette that Quanda lacked, she made up for it with heart and beauty.

Quanda was by far the most attractive girl in the crew and everybody knew it, except Quanda. She was a dime piece on any scale. Where all the other girls were MAC cosmetic hounds and beauty salon regulars, Quanda didn't need any of that stuff. Her natural beauty and big breasts were her greatest assets. At five foot five inches in height, she wore her curves well. Quanda's skin was flawless and the color of creamy tapioca pudding. Her hair was naturally curly and she often kept it in a ponytail. The ponytail accentuated her forehead and almond shaped eyes. Quanda had those eyes that seemed to be staring straight through you. The gap in her teeth gave her a playful appearance, but that was a trick. If you stroked her right, she'd purr like a kitten, but when crossed, she became as deadly as poison.

Having seen Quanda in action several times, Rhoda knew that oral sex was something that she did for the money, but her heart was never into it. Giving head was only her forte when it involved a woman. When on the receiving end, she didn't care if the giver was woman or man. Whether Quanda was bi-sexual before she met Vita was anybody's guess. But the fact remained that Quanda loved sex with women more than men. Over forty percent of her dates were women. Whichever way the wind blew, Quanda was there with a jacket on, ready to get busy for that paper.

Now on the flip side of that coin, Sparkle hated anal and girl on girl sex. She wouldn't indulge in either unless the date paid extra for it. To Sparkle, anal sex hurt way too much, it was uncomfortable and just plain nasty. For the life of her, she couldn't understand all men's fascination with fucking people in the ass. It was the exit tunnel of human waste. On one occasion, Sparkle told Rhoda that when things had gotten messy literally that her date had gotten upset. She said she lashed out at him and said, "What the fuck did you expect to happen when you shove a yard of dick up a tiny asshole?" When the man complained further, Sparkle told him, "You and I got the same thing…a shitty deal.

You paid for it, I'm still in pain, so get over it. Go and wash your dick off and let's continue."

Even though she had her moments, everybody in the crew knew that Sparkle was all bark and no bite. An ex-ballerina and modern dance addict, Sparkle was the most athletic, limber, and creative girl in the crew. Sexually, she did things to men that could've been taught and paid for by thousands of women. Being with Sparkle was like going to school, majoring in Acrobatic Sex 101. Rhoda had seen dudes literally limp out of the room after experiencing Sparkle.

Katia Reed was nicknamed Sparkle because her father said her eyes lit up so bright they sparkled. Out of all the girls in the crew, Sparkle was the most educated. She was a dark-skinned beauty who resembled Naomi Campbell. Sparkle had deep dimples and pretty white teeth that were squeezed together by silver braces. Sparkle loved weaves and braids. She was a regular fixture at the African hair galleries. The tallest member of the crew at 5'9, Sparkle, had less body and curves than everybody else. But it didn't matter because she wore clothes well. Her gait was graceful and catwalkish. Sparkle's whole swagger was that of a model. She could turn heads and stop traffic with the best of them any day. The only thing that turned Rhoda off about Sparkle was her propensity towards lying, her suspicions of everybody, and her argumentative nature. Sparkle was a compulsive liar that lied for no reason at all.

If you didn't know her, it would be hard to tell when she was lying, but the girls of the N.H.B.C. did know her and they knew when to pay her no mind. Well everybody except, Star. Star, was the new girl, Quanda sponsored her into the crew. Rhoda had all about thirty minutes to spend with Star before having to rush off to meet with the wives. But from what she could see, the pretty young girl definitely had what it took to be down with the crew. When she returned home she'd have to find out what Star's sex rated on the *'cold slut scale.'*

"What's is your name, Gladiator!"

"My name is Maximus..."

Rhoda, glanced at the TV and then clicked it off, the jet lag was starting to set in and it was time for bed. Looking at her watch, Rhoda checked her phone again for any missed calls. There were none. *Why hadn't Rock called her, yet?*

Anthony Fields

CHAPTER 6

"A new girl is always good for business, Spark," Billie said as she immersed her feet into the portable hot water foot massager. "It adds more spice and variety.

"What the fuck are we a kitchen cabinet? Spice and variety? I ain't talking about a married couple in the bedroom. I'm talking about our house. Our crew." Sparkle responded.

"Either way, variety is the spice of life. Why do you think Baskin and Robbins were so successful? Because they offered thirty-one flavors of ice cream. On the real though, Spark, I don't give a damn if Star joins the crew."

"Well, I do." Sparkle pouted.

"Well, why didn't you voice all this shit to Rhoda and Quanda before they left here?"

"Because Rhoda, has her head so far up Rock's ass right now, she has to wipe shit out of her ears before she can change her mind. And you know how Quan is. She's gonna swear that I'm just hating on Star. Like I really got a reason to hate on that little girl."

Billie laughed at that. "On some real shit, it do sound like you hating, though, Spark. No bullshit."

"*Hating*? Billie answer me this. Where did Star come from? I mean, damn, girlfriend just showed up out of nowhere. Who the hell knows her? Nobody, I know does. And now Quan wants to put her down with our crew. She could be with them 'Young, Black, and Sexy' bitches or the Hell Razors Honeys. Out of all the girl cliques in D.C., why she gotta be down with us?"

Billie laughed Sparkle out, it was all she could do.

Annoyed, Sparkle asked her, "What the fuck is so funny? I'm serious."

"Naw, my bad, Spark. I was just picturing in my mind, Rhoda and Cinn asking Vita why you had to be down with them.

Billie wondered what was really eating at Sparkle. As long as they had been friends, she had never known Sparkle to hate on another chick. It couldn't be trepidation due to competition because Sparkle had dates lined up for months. She decided to dig a little deeper and see what was on Sparkle's mind.

"What does it matter anyway, Spark, where the girl comes from? She's from D.C. ain't she?"

"That's my point. I don't know. We don't know. And that matters to me, even if it matters to nobody but me. All of us know each other from somewhere, schools, clubs, parties, and all that other shit. Vita hooked up with Dominique and Carolyn because she knew them. They knew each other. They started it all. When things went south and they bounced. Vita rebounded with Rho and Cinn. Two people that she knew. Follow me?"

"Yeah… I think so."

"Okay. Rhoda brought in Jamie, right? A friend of hers. Then Jamie brought in Pebbles. They were half-sisters or something. Vita approached me and then we both stepped to you. Then Vita put Quan on. The common denominator is…we all knew each other. Nobody knows Star. Quan just met her."

"So?"

"*So*? So, who the hell is she and where does she come from? How come nobody has ever seen her around? Come on, Billie, D.C. ain't but so big."

"Look, Spark, all I know is that she and Quan have been hanging out for a while. Quan says that Star is good peoples, so that's good enough for me. I trust Quanda's judgment and anyway, she says that Star comes from down Good Hope Road somewhere. Down by the deli on 14th Street, I think she said. I don't know why we've never seen her or why nobody knows her. Maybe she came off the porch late. Or maybe she partied with a younger crowd. Either way, I'm still tryna figure out what the hell is the big deal. You act like we are a secret society or something. What's really bothering you, Spark?"

Sparkle lifted both of her legs and put them under her. She shook her glass of instant iced tea to make sure that the sugar that sat at the bottom of the glass floated around as she drank. "I'm just not as trusting as I used to be, that's all. It's been awhile since

36

we welcomed anybody into the crew and according to Quanda, she's gonna be living here with us. Is it a crime to want to know who I'm living around? Even apartment buildings and shit do background checks before they let people move in. It's been what...almost two years since Vita and Cinn were killed, right?"

"About that, Spark, but I..." Billie pulled her feet out of the massager and inspected them. She wanted to make sure that the solution, she put in the water to soften her feet wasn't eating at the polish of her French pedicure.

"What do we know for sure about their deaths?"

"What the hell does all that have to do with Star?" Billie responded vexed.

"Nobody has ever been arrested for their deaths. How do we know that whoever killed Vee, Cinn, and Ping, didn't just kill Ping because he was there? All this time we have automatically assumed that Ping was the target and Vee and Cinn were innocent victims. What if it was the other way around and Ping wasn't the target."

Billie couldn't believe what she was hearing. She felt like she was on an episode of the Twilight Zone. "Sparkle, baby, have you been smoking dippers on the low or what? No bullshit, boo, you are cracking up. We are still grieving in our own personal ways, but boo, you lunching like shit. Are you tryna imply that whoever killed Vita and Cinn are still out there and they might wanna kill us, too? Is that what you're saying? Are you saying that Star might be down with the killer or killers? Is that what you're saying to me?"

"All I'm saying is..."

"I hear what you're saying, loud and clear. There's no need to repeat that. I've been listening to you for the last forty minutes and this shit is crazy Spark. If somebody wanted us dead, we'd all be cold as fuck right now lying in the ground. We've been all over the country in the last twenty months. We are high profile bitches in the city. We fuck the big boys and get paid well to do it. We advertise that. Think about all the niggas we been with. It ain't like we hard to kill. We ain't been hiding anywhere. Why would it take almost two years to kill a bunch of bitches? It wouldn't. All a nigga gotta do is book a date with either one of us or all of us. If that money right, you know damn well we'll all get our gang bang on. And besides, what is Star gonna do living with us that she couldn't do not living with us?" Billie stood up and unplugged the massager. "I swear to God, Spark, for you to be so smart, you say some of the stupidest shit. Pump your brakes, boo, it really ain't that serious. Now if you'll excuse me, I have to go and get ready for my date."

Sparkle looked at her watch, "Date? With who? It's awfully early for a date, isn't it? At least for you, that is."

Billie picked up the foot massager and headed for the stairs. "Same old Sparkle. Some things never change."

"What's that supposed to mean?"

"You still noisy as shit, that's what it's supposed to mean. But if you must know, I have a date with Chico."

"Chico? What Chico? Is Chico Debarge back in town?"

"Girl, Chico Debarge is broke, you ain't heard? I'm talking about Chico from down Paradise."

"Didn't he just come home last week? How can he afford you?" Sparkle asked curiosity piqued.

"See, boo, you have been so worried about where Star comes from that you haven't been paying attention to the streets. Don't you know that Block got back on appeal about a month ago and he back on like a muthafucka? Block and Keith Holmes are Chico's men. We both know that Keith's tight ass been rich for years. Either they breaking Chico off or that nigga still spending money from the eighties. He just copped a 2013 big body Lexus, and that joint is the same color as his hazel-brown eyes. Now mix light brown with canary yellow diamonds, I'ma be wearing, and me fucking him until he turns blue. What do you get? Green. The color of that big face money. My favorite color. Chico is in the halfway house and he gotta be back by midnight. It's a little after seven now. That gives me about thirty minutes to get dressed, ten minutes to meet him, three hours to suck and fuck him, and five

minutes to collect my money. I would love to stay here and indulge you in your conspiracy theories, but I gotta go, I gotta
leave, so please don't make it hard for me." Billie sang the last
line of the song as if she was *Vivian Green* as she disappeared up
the stairs.

Anthony Fields

CHAPTER 7

"Yes, Whistle. We're still on for tonight, Whistle. I told you I'll be ready by twelve. If you let me go now, I can take my nap and then be ready to see you later. Yes, Whistle. I know, Whistle, Bye, Whistle." Sparkle ended the call on her iPhone and lay across her bed.

Artinis 'Whistle' Winston was the newest kingpin in the making in Southeast D.C. he controlled Valley Green projects and everything that surrounded it. Whistle had the whole Southside on smash with some new exotic drug called 'Ghostface Killa'. It was rumored to be every drug rolled all into one. Sparkle, hooked up with Whistle at least once a week and made him pay five thousand dollars per visit. Sometimes when she felt extra sluttish, she'd try out a rack of new shit on him and charge him ten grand. A wise old man once said, *"A fool and his money will soon be parted."* Sparkle knew that that adage was true when it came to Whistle.

Closing her eyes, Sparkle let herself relax completely. What Billie had said to her moments ago replayed in her head...

"What's really bothering you, Spark?"

She had told Billie that she just wanted to know where Star was from. And that she was just concerned and curious. All of that was true, but she left out one thing. Sparkle was positive that she had seen Star somewhere before. She just couldn't remember where to save her life. The first time that she had laid eyes on Star, there was a glint of recognition in her eyes as well. The fact that Star acted as if they never saw each other before and didn't mention it, sparked suspicion. The girl know as Star was up to something, Sparkle could feel it.

Alicia Keys' *'Woman's Worth'* ring tone severed her train of thought. Sparkle, picked up her cell phone and saw that the caller was calling from somewhere in Maryland. For a second she contemplated not answering the phone but answered it anyway. "Hello?"

"What's up, Kay?" a male voice said.

Instantly, recognizing the voice and the nickname, Sparkle cursed herself inside for not going with her first instinct and ignored the call. Baltimore Vito was the only person in the world that called her Kay instead of Sparkle. One day after they had fucked, her wallet had fallen out of her purse and she didn't know it. When she came out of the bathroom, Vito had the wallet in his hand, reading her driver's license.

"Katia Reed, huh? 2520 Pomeroy Road..." He never got the chance to finish the rest of her address because she ran across the room and snatched the wallet out of his hand. But it was too late.

"What do you want, Vito?" Sparkle said into the phone with a lot of attitude.

"Damn, yo, that's the tone I get? After all, we been through? All I get is, what do you want, Vito? That's foul, Kay. I thought we were better than that, yo. I can't just call to say hello?"

"Sure, you can, Vito. Hello. Now, what do you want?"

"A'ight yo, you got me. I can respect that. I need a lick, Kay. Bad."

Sparkle couldn't believe her ears. "You need a lick? I told your ass after that last lick that I wasn't doing that shit anymore. And don't sit here and act like you forgot that shit that damn fast. Is the weed fucking with your brain? Besides nobody has pissed me off in a while."

"True dat, you. You did tell me that was your last time and all that, but yo, I'm fucked up, Kay. I wouldn't even be asking you this if I didn't have to. I just lost a ton of money on that Pacquiao-Marquez fight. I bet with Manny and that bitch ass nigga quit in me. I can't hit these niggas out here cause they hip to me. I need you, Kay. I got major league problems."

"Your problems are not my problems, Vito."

"Not your problem, huh? Yo, you tryna shine on me, huh? Talking about it's not your problem. Well, let me tell you what would be your problem. If that coon Champ Yelverton was to find out who put them masked gunmen in his business. Or what do you think ole Black Junior would say if he knew that his girl

Sparkle was the one that set him up to get robbed and shot? What's that other nigga's name…oh…Derron. Derron from Potomac Gardens…"

"Okay, okay. I get the picture, Blackmail, huh? That's some ho ass shit, Vito. That's shit that bitches do to one another. And you supposed to be a Muthafuckin' gangsta. Picture that."

"Bitch, I got your bitches and hoes, swinging." Vito exploded. "You know how I get down. The gangsta maker ain't never made a nigga more gangsta than me. Bodymore Murderland and don't you ever forget it."

Forget it. How could she? Vito was right, she did know how he got down. He was a ruthless bastard. The only reason that he hadn't killed any dudes she put him on was because she begged him not to. Had she not they would all be dead. Sparkle had qualms about what she wanted to do, but she sold her soul to the devil, anyway. But not in her wildest dream did she think that he'd come back and use her past to extort her. Where is the honor that supposed to exist amongst thieves? Sparkle instantly regretted ever hooking up with the Baltimore thug.

They met at Club love in D.C…She knew that he wasn't from the city because he had gold teeth in his mouth. That always screamed 'out of town nigga'. But she was drawn magnetically to his swagger. He and his men were popping expensive bottles of wine all night. Sparkle couldn't help but notice the iced out Audemars watch on his wrist and the iced-out chain around his neck. The Red Monkey jeans and Prada top that he rocked gave him a certain kind of confidence that she loved. But she was hesitant to approach him. The big wad of cash that he pulled out to pay for the bottles made her decision for her. Sparkle sent Billie to the bar to get him. That night they hooked up, fucked, popped a few pills, and some bottles and fucked some more. The next day, she had to admit that the arrogant, stocky, dark-skinned thug with the shoulder length dreads had given her the shakes and it was hard to give her the shakes.

"Kay?! Kay, you there?"

"Yeah, I'm here. Let me see what I can do and I'll call you back at this number tomorrow."

Vito exhaled loudly. "Kay, don't play no games with me, yo. I'm tryna hear something tomorrow and no later. If I don't hear from you, I'ma be coming to Pomeroy Road to visit. And if I gotta do that..."

"You don't have to threaten me, Vito. I said I'ma call you tomorrow."

"I'll be waiting." He hung up.

Sparkle hung up her phone and threw it across the room. All kinds of curse words came to mind as she stewed over what Vito was doing to her. She had let revenge and greed, two of life's most deadly sins, put her in a situation where now she was caged in like an alley cat. She felt trapped. They say that when you back a cat into a corner that eventually it'll come out scratching. That's what Sparkle planned to do when the time was right. For the moment, she'd just have to play the game by Vito's rules. The game that she had started. By bringing Vito to the streets of D.C. she had gotten everything she wanted. Revenge on Champ for smacking her after he refused to pay for their date. She should feel special because she fucked a world champion, he said. She didn't. Then there was Richard 'Black Junior' Devaughn, who threw a drink on her at the 'Club Furr' for rebuffing his advances. He just wasn't her type. Derron McMillan was a dude that she knew from the neighborhood. He hated on her every chance he got and Sparkle got sick of it. She called Vito and sicced him on each man, one at a time. And even got richer in the process. When the recession hit D.C. and fast money slowed up for a while, it was Vito that put her down with a couple of big money Baltimore cats. Then Vito just sort of disappeared for a while...

Now he was back and blackmailing her. Sparkle couldn't believe how bad her luck was. If Vito took the time to call her with the demands he laid out, there was no doubt in her mind that he'd make good on the threats. The question to be answered now was, what lick to give him? Sparkle sat up on her bed and grabbed her cup of iced tea.

"I need something stronger to drink." Sparkle, glanced at the watch on her wrist...7:56 p.m. As she crossed the room to find her personal bottle of Hennessey, it came to her like an epiphany. At 12 o'clock, she had to meet Whistle. Why not give him up to Vito? Finding the bottle, Sparkle gulped down two generous pulls and her resolve stiffened. That's what she would do. She'd give up Whistle. Nobody would ever know.

Anthony Fields

Anthony Fields

CHAPTER 8

"Quanda, I gotta find a bathroom, girl. That fried Calamari and baked cheese Ziti got my stomach fucked up." Star said and rushed off in search of a restroom. Inside the restrooms, Star found a stall at the end of the wall and went inside. She laid toilet paper around the toilet seat and sat down fully clothed. Reaching inside her purse, Star found her cell phone, pulled it out, and dialed a number.

* * *

"I know exactly what I have to do...Okay, so be it. I just told you I know what to do. You still telling me the same shit after all this time. But I still don't trust him, Mark. I'm telling you, something ain't right with that nigga. Every time I see him all he wants to talk about is me and him fucking. That's your man, though. If that's what you want me to do, I'll do it. Huh? We good. I'ma put the pictures in the mail, Monday. I gotta new bitch I want you to see. Her name is Star..." Quanda caught a blur of movement on her side and saw Star approaching her. "I gotta go. I'ma holla at you when you call me back. Don't put Mike down with shit we talked about. I know, I know. Tomorrow, I got you. I love you, too. Bye..." Quanda disconnected her call and smiled at Star. "Are you okay, now?"

"Ten pounds lighter," Star replied.

"Well come on then, we are going to Saks Fifth Avenue first."

They walked into Saks and Quanda started pulling clothes off the racks by all high-end designers. Dior. Chanel. Dolce and Gabbana. Gucci. Prada.

"Quan, that skirt is a mean muthafucka and that belt with those Medusa jeans...that shit is hot! You rock that one piece Valentino bodysuit with the right shoes, you gon kill 'em..."

"I'm gon kill 'em? Boo, I been killing 'em dead for years. It's your turn. This shit is for you."

"Hello? Houston, I think we have a problem. Quan, I can't afford that shit. Let's go somewhere where they sell the cheap shit I can afford, like...Bebe, Baby Phat, and Apple Bottoms."

Quanda, shot Star a crazy look. "You, don't wear that shit no more. Who the hell do you think you down with? The Simmons sisters? We gon pack up all that bamma ass gear you be rocking and burn that shit. Nobody in our crew wears that shit. This is not B.E. T, this is the N.H.B.C... You gotta dress like you know the difference.

"But, I can't afford..."

Shushing Star with a finger to her lips, Quanda said, "I got you. Since I'm sponsoring you in, I gotta make sure you have everything you need. It's an NHBC tradition. When shit start popping for you and I know it will, you can pay me back then. It's like signing a record deal and getting an advance."

"But how do you know my sizes?" Star asked incredulously.

"Easy. I can look at you and tell. You're a size 4, a 34B, maybe C cup up top. We're the same height, so that'll put you at around 5'4 or 5'5. And you weigh about a hundred and thirty pounds...give or take a few pounds. You wear a..." Quanda glanced at Star's feet. "...Six...six and a half shoe. Am I right?"

Star was impressed. "Damn, Dionne Warwick, what do you see in my future? Will I find love and happiness?"

Quanda laughed. "I wish I knew the answers to all that. I'd really be rich, then. Speaking of shoes let's go and get you some."

They walked into the shoe section and put the clothes down on the counter. Then Quanda took control. It was easy for Star to see that Quanda was completely in her element surrounded by white people and expensive stuff. Quanda picked up a thigh-high boot by Max Azria and a pair of Ferragamo ankle length boots. To the sales associate, she said, "Let me see these in a six and a six and a half." Then walked over to another display section and picked up three other shoes. One loafer and two heels. "And these, too."

In the Blink of an Eye

The white female sales associate became visibly flustered. "Ma'am, these are Christian Louboutins, Jimmy Choos, and Caroline Herreras."

"I know what the fuck they are!" Quanda snapped heatedly. "Just get the damn shoes, please." The white lady hurried away. Quanda turned to Star and said, "I hate when white people automatically assume that blacks can't afford the best shit. Just because we're two young black chicks, we can't read the labels on the fuckin' shoes. Like all black people are stupid and broke. I bet if we were two white girls coming to buy shoes, she wouldn't have said that shit. Them muthafuckas get on my nerves with that shit."

Star nodded her head in agreement because she knew that what Quanda was saying was the gospel truth. She had experienced similar racism first hand herself. "Quan, don't let that bitch get you upset. She ain't shit."

"Yeah, you right. She ain't nothing. Judgmental ass heifer. She just mad because she can't afford this shit on her employee discount. And she fucked up because she gotta work weekends. Destitute ass hooker."

As if on cue, the sales lady returned with the shoes and boots. She sat them down and offered to help them with them.

"No thank you." Quanda snapped. "We don't need no help. Just give us a few minutes and we'll be ready to purchase."

The saleslady skulked away to the counter but kept her eyes glued to them.

"Star hurry up and try the shoes on to see what size fits you best so that we can get up outta here. Before I have to show this racist ass cracker bitch how we Southeast bitches get down."

At the counter, Quanda put her Amex platinum card down and the saleslady stared at it as if it was poisonous. "Ma'am, I'm gonna need to see three pieces of I.D., please.

Having shopped at Tyson's before and in several stores in Virginia, Quanda knew that she was only required to show two pieces of I.D. for charges. She gave Star an ominous look. Star gave her the 'please stay calm look.' Snatching the card back up, Quanda asked, "How much is the total?"

"The total comes to five thousand seven hundred, forty-two dollars and ninety-nine cents."

Reaching into her purse, Quanda pulled out a wad of hundred dollar bills. She counted out fifty-eight big face hundreds and laid them on the counter. "Now hurry up and bag my shit up bitch, before I go to jail for smacking your pale ass up in here."

The sales associate turned beet red as she expertly folded and bagged the clothes. The boots and shoes were next.

"Grab the rest of them bags," Quanda said to Star as she grabbed most the bags and walked away from the counter.

"Ma'am you forgot your change." The lady called out to them.

"Buy yourself a better life, you broke ass redneck," Quanda called out over her shoulder.

They went to a few more stores and made several other purchases. By the time they reached the car, Star was beat. After putting all the bags in the trunk, she climbed into the passenger seat and reclined it. As they headed back to D.C. Quanda put the new Ronald Randolph CD in the changer and pressed play.

"Aye Star?"

Star turned the music down a little so that she could hear what Quanda was saying. "What's up Quan?"

"Have you ever been fucked in your ass?"

At first, she thought that Quanda was joking, but after seeing the serious look on her face, Star ascertained that she wasn't. "I...uh...tried...not really. I tried it before, but it was hurting too much. I made him stop."

"You do know that you have to do that if that's what your date requests, right?" And nine times outta ten, niggas today gon' ask for some ass. It's a sign of the times. You do know, that right?"

"Yeah, I know. I just..."

Quanda cut her off mid-sentence. "Don't even sweat it, boo. I got you." She said and picked up her cell phone.

Star was to hate the way Quanda always said. "I got you."
She heard Quanda telling somebody on her phone that they'd be
there later. Then she hung up the phone and looked at Star.

"Tonight, you go and see Dex."

"Who the fuck is Dex?"

Anthony Fields

CHAPTER 9

"Tell me a little about yourself," Chico said.

Billie looked around the restaurant and thought about what she wanted the man in front of her to know about her. "There's not much to tell."

Chico smiled. "Well tell me that little bit there is."

"Chico, it's almost ten o'clock. We don't have time for this."

"Says who? I don't have to be back at Hope Village until midnight."

"You must be one of those two-minute brothers then, huh?" Billie asked salaciously and licked her lips.

"Sweetheart, the only thing that I can do in two minutes is tie my shoes."

Billie sipped her apple Martini and then forked a bite of pasta into her mouth. "I thought that you'd be geeking to...you know what I mean."

"You thought that I'd be geeking to fuck you since I just came home? Is that what you mean?"

"Yeah."

"I ain't gon' lie to you, boo. I was at first and you look so good in that outfit, that I've been visualizing you naked all evening. But I wanted to see what was on your mind, first."

"On my mind?" Billie repeated, puzzled by the comment. "What does it matter what's on my mind, if I'm only being paid to fuck you."

Chico calmly sipped his drink and then stared into Billie's eyes. "Hear me out. The whole time I was in jail, I beat my dick thinking about different women. Known and unknown. I did that for eighteen years. When I finally got home and fucked one of my baby mother's, I didn't enjoy it at all. And the part that really turned me off about her was the fact that after all these years; she still ain't got shit on her mind. It's like she stuck in the past or she's doomed to be an idiot forever. I have been home for about eight days now and I have fucked a rack of different women and through it all, all I remember is that they were all just like my baby mother...brainless."

"Okay, now I'm confused. You booked a date with me to see what was on my mind?"

"Naw, boo," Chico laughed. "I booked a date with you to fuck you. I heard a lot about your crew and figured I'd see what all the fuss was about. When I saw, you get out the car, I decided to see if you were the savior for all women or just another brainless one. So, far, is see that you are bright and you happen to have the prettiest smile that I've seen since I been home. I just wanna talk to you, tonight; I'll make another appointment to fuck you if you don't mind."

Billie was feeling Chico's spiel. No man had ever said anything like that to her before. "It's your dime. You wanna pay me a grand to talk? So be it. Let's talk."

"Let's go back to my original statement. Tell me a little bit about yourself."

"This is a little unusual, but here goes. My real name is Billina, but everybody calls me Billie. They say that I look just like Billie Holliday. I was born and raised her in D.C..."

***

Quanda checked her messages and her E-mail on her iPhone. She heard that Mark had called her twice. *Hadn't she already...*

"Please...please...please...take it slow...take it slo...w...w...oowww...hold on for a minute...don't move...wait...wait...!"

"...told Mark that she would handle everything.? Quanda heard Star's cries and pleas coming from the other bedroom and smiled. Everything about the initiation of Star was amusing to her. It all reminded her of when she joined the crew. Even though Vita had broken her in anally, she still had to go and experience Dexter. It was a tradition. Quanda thought back to how she had literally cried a river from all the pain. But, after the pain came the euphoria and ecstasy. Dexter was half Jamaican, dark as

54

night, with long silky dreads, muscles everywhere, and he was fine as shit. He reminded Quanda of a walking Hershey bar with nuts. But it was the dick that brought every new member of the crew to Dexter's house. The man had a dick that wouldn't quit. It had to be at least eleven inches semi-hard and it had a deep curve in it. It was Dexter's job to fuck every hole on the new member's body…well. And for hours non-stop. Since sex would now be their occupation, every new member would have to be able to go the distance. It wasn't a good look to misrepresent the baddest bitches in the city. Vita was the innovator and they swore on oath to carry on the tradition.

Quanda listened to Star's pain and empathized with what she was going through. But rules were rules. Thinking back to the night she experienced Dexter with Vita waiting in the living room for her. Quanda wondered if Vita had felt sorry for her. Probably not, Vita was unsympathetic to a lot of stuff. All Quanda could do was hope that Dex used plenty of lube on Star's ass. Her cell phone vibrating on the table got her attention. It was her brother's partner B.F…

"What's up B.F.?"

"Quan, did you holla at Mark?"

"Um huh."

"What did he say? Is he gonna…"

"Everything is a go for tomorrow. I'ma pick it up and then hit you when I have it." Quanda laid back down on the big comfortable couch.

"That's good news. Hit me tomorrow when you ready. Gone." B.F. hung up.

How deep is a sister's love? Hers had to be deep. Quanda loved both of her brothers a great deal. They were all that she had left in the world. After losing both of their parents in a car accident when they were young, Quanda vowed to always protect and stand by both of her younger brothers.

Her brother Mark had always been the precocious one. He rebelled early against their grandmother's authority and hit the streets, eyes open, palms closed. By the time, Mark was thirteen years old he had a car, money, and harem of older women on his team. He was also a notorious hot head who was rumored to be responsible for several bodies that popped up in Savannah Ridge. Mark staked his claim as the leader in the family and everybody deferred to him.

Her brother Mike was a different story, he was the exact opposite of Mark. Mike was more of a Momma's boy. He attached himself to their grandmother's bosom and never let go. Quanda had had to go outside on numerous occasions and fight boys and girls over Mike. In the projects, ghetto kids exploited any signs of weakness, so Mike got exploited a lot. But weaknesses or none, he was Michael Jasper, her brother and she was his protector.

Quanda understood her younger brother. He wasn't a fighter, he was more of a lover. He loved the ladies and they loved him back. It didn't take long before Mike had a bunch of children running around by a rack of different women. His women and his children became his life and everybody respected that.

Quanda and Mark were more compatible because they both gravitated more to the street life and its codes. Mark became the man to see in the streets and she held him down in every way possible. But, all good things must come to an end. The whole time they were living the good life, the Feds were building a case against Mark. They came in and knocked him off his high horse with a ten-count indictment.

They froze all his bank accounts, seized his property, cars, clothes, jewelry, and safety deposit boxes. Everybody who knew or associated with her brother ran for the hills. He was back to square one with nobody to depend on but Quanda. Stepping straight to the plate, she pawned all her jewelry and sold both of her cars to get up enough cash for Mark's lawyer to put on a decent defense. But it was all in vain. After a one month trial, Mark was convicted of Conspiracy and Racketeering and sentenced to thirty years in federal prison.

In the Blink of an Eye

Despondent and stressed out, needing to pick her life back up and find a way to free Mark, Quanda turned to Vita and confided in her. The next thing she knew she was a part of the NHBC. The money that she made went towards Mark's appeal, Mike and his kids and their grandmother. When a few years had passed and the D.C. Court of Appeals was ready to hear her brother's case, Mark contacted Quanda and told her that the money she had saved wasn't enough. It would take serious money, he said. Just when she thought that she'd have to rob and kill somebody for that money, Mark called her and told her to come and see him.

Their visit took place at the Federal Correctional Institution at Petersburg that weekend. Mark told Quanda that he had a Columbian connect that would front him work on the outside. All he had to do was get somebody to distribute the work to people of his choosing and then pick up the money. Once the money was collected it had to be taken to another spot and dropped off. Mark wanted that person to be her. He couldn't trust anybody else.

How could she say no? Visiting her brother in jail crushed her spirit every time she left him. Quanda agreed to the terms her brother set in place. She'd pick up the work, drop it off to four dudes, and then pick up the money. When they had made enough money to pay for his appeal, they would shut the operation down. That's how it had all started and now she was knee-deep in the drug game. Two years after the deadline, their operation was still going strong and prospering. Nobody in the crew knew about her side hustle and that's the way Quanda planned to keep it.

"...down. Please...put my legs down! I can't...take...it...like...that! Dex...please...e...e...e!"

A smile crossed Quanda's face again as she closed her eyes. Then suddenly, sleep overcame her.

Anthony Fields

CHAPTER 10

Billie sat in her Lexus outside of the townhouse and pondered on the time she had just spent with Chico. In all the years of dating, nobody had ever made her feel how she now felt. The grand that she had been paid was great, but for some reason, Billie felt like she should have paid him. Shaking her head from side to side, it was as if she was losing her mind. Billie looked at herself in the rearview mirror and looked for any signs of a different person sitting there, but she saw none. Tomorrow was supposed to be a busy day for her. She had three dates lined up. One was a can't miss with a newly elected Congressman who had just move to the District. The other two dates were baller niggas in the city that paid well. Then there was Chico. He wanted another date Billie decided to push back her time table and accommodate everybody.

What the hell? The more the merrier.

Sitting there in the car riveted to her seat Billie couldn't get Chico off her mind. After leaving the restaurant, she drove him back to his car. They rode the whole distance in silence. They listened to *Raheem Devaughn's* CD and for some reason, she didn't want the night to end. Before he got out of the car, Chico kissed her. Passion took over her body and Billie took charge of the moment. Ignoring Chico's protests, Billie unzipped his pants and freed his dick. She was glad to see that good looks and a deep conversation wasn't all that he had to offer. By the time her lips touched his dick, she was transported to another place. That place where her body went when she was in tune mind, body, and soul with a dick. Billie deep throated Chico until he pulled her head by her hair. She wasn't going to spoil the moment like that; it was time to swallow all evidence of their tryst.

Snapping out of her reverie, Billie got out of her car and went into the house. As she entered the house, the phone rang incessantly.

"Billie?" a female voice asked.

Billie recognized the voice instantly. "Rho, what's good, boo? How was your flight?"

"Everything is good with me. My flight was great. I feel good despite a little jet lag from yesterday. Monday, I'll feel even better."

"Are you nervous, Rho? I mean…you've never been with Rock as a free man. What if he turns out to be somebody other than who you thought her was?"

"I think four years is more than enough time to get to know someone. We've spent hours together. He is who I think he is. Even if he changes a little, I'm still with him. For better or worse. Ain't that how the saying goes?"

"Yeah. For married muthafuckas. That shit ain't true for pimps and hoes."

Rhoda laughed. "Bitch, my baby ain't no pimp."

"Shid. I can't tell, you're a hoe and he bagged you, didn't he?"

"Yeah, whatever girl," Rhoda said as she strained herself trying not to laugh again. "Why haven't you been answering your phone? I have been calling you all evening."

"Oh shit!" Billie said and reached into her purse. She saw that her cell phone was still turned off. She remembered the exact moment that she decided to make herself unreachable. It was the moment she decided to suck Chico's dick. "My bad, Rho. I was working. You know how I do. I forgot to turn the phone back on afterward. What's up though."

"I ain't want shit. You know I worry about Y'all bitches. I talked to everybody but your crazy ass."

Billie then noticed that all the lights in the house were off and it was deathly quiet. "Where is everybody?" Billie asked.

"Quan took Star to see Dexter. Sparkle said she was going to meet the dude named Whistle and damn that's it. Sometimes I forget that Vee and Cinn are gone."

"Don't feel bad, boo, I do it, too." Billie decided to quickly change the subject because she didn't feel like going down that road with Rhoda. "If you would've caught me earlier, Rho, it would've been hard for me to talk anyway."

"Why is that?" Rhoda asked confused.

"Because I had that dick in my mouth."

Laughing again, Rhoda said, "I know what you mean. Rock called me a couple times when my mouth was full. I wanted to talk to him bad as shit every time, but sometimes you get caught up in a good dick moment. Talk is secondary, can I get a witness?"

"Amen sista!" When the truth comes, falsehood must flee!" Billie laughed along with Rhoda. But no matter how much she laughed and joked with Rhoda, her thoughts ended with the man that she had just left. "Rho, do you know Chico?"

"Chico? What Chico? Old man Chico from Uptown getting all the money?"

"Naw, not him."

"Chico from down Paradise?"

"Yeah. The one and only."

"Of course, I know Chico. Who doesn't know Chico or at least heard of him? That nigga was the shit back in the day. I was jive young, but I know that he had all the bitches. He's been in jail for a long ass time. Why? What's up with him?"

"He's home, he was my date for tonight. I just left him."

"Does he still look good?" Rhoda asked sounding like a schoolgirl with a crush. "How was the dick?"

"Damn, you sound like a groupie."

"Bitch, fuck you answer the question."

"Rho, that nigga is fine as shit, and he sexy as hell. He's like a large cup of Brazilian Hazelnut coffee, early on a Monday morning when it's raining."

"Damn! That good, huh?"

"Better. And the dick is succulent. Can I use that word?"

"Sure, if you're comparing the dick to a steak."

It was Billie's turn to crack up laughing. "Well, in that case, the dick was like a filet mignon."

"Did he pay you?"

Anthony Fields

"Did he pay me? Do I look like the Salvation Army? Of course, he laced my palm with them big faces. I don't eat no sausages for free unless your name is Oscar Meyer or Jimmy Dean."

"Girl, you are a mess. Let me get off this phone so I can get some sleep. I'ma call you and the crew back tomorrow. Y'all be safe. I love you, Billie!"

"Love you, too, Rho. Bye."

Billie climbed the stairs slowly and went to her room. She kicked off her heels and fell across the bed. Her last conscious thought before falling asleep was Chico...

62

CHAPTER 11

"Quanda! Quan! Quan, wake up!"

Quanda opened her eyes and saw Star standing over her. "I'm up, I'm up. What's up?"

"Can you please take me home? I don't feel good." Star pleaded.

Quanda sat up and stretched her arms and legs. Dexter's couch was comfortable, she had slept like a baby. Her watch read 6:48 a.m....Quanda heard noise in the kitchen and knew that it was Dexter mixing himself a vegetable and fruit juice. It was his daily morning ritual. Nobody knew what he really put in there, though. Quanda suspected that the drink had to contain something that made his dick the beast that it was. She pulled the wad of bills out of her purse and peeled off several hundred. Then she dropped the bills onto the coffee table. "Dex, we out, boo. The money is on the table. You take it easy and rest that dick of yours."

The sound of the mixer stopped. "My dick don't need no rest," Dex shouted from the kitchen. "You rest that pussy of yours."

"Not until every dollar in the district is mine."

Outside in the car, Star didn't say a word. Quanda glanced in her direction several times as she drove and tried to gauge what she was feeling. She still remembered how she felt the morning after getting fucked by Dexter for half the night. Her insides were sore and her whole body hurt. That's what Star had to be feeling, Quanda decided and wanted to keep quiet, but she couldn't. "Look, I know how you feel. You feel hurt, sore, violated, and some more shit. I know because that's how I felt the morning I left Dexter's house. And I know that you are probably fucked up at me right now. But Star, you had to go through that. Every has experienced the Dex experience. You had to get the tattoos, too. It's all a part of the initiation process. You made it through, that's most important. You're in Star, do you hear me?"

Star nodded her head but never said a word. Quanda decided to just leave her alone. She has to heal on her own. After she dropped Star off, a short nap and a shower were in order. Then she had to go to church…

* * *

Artinis Winston opened his eyes and squinted as the light from the sun came through the window and assaulted his orbs. Adjusting his focus, he looked at the beautiful face of the woman sleeping next to him. Whistle watched her as her chest rose and fell peacefully in tune with her heartbeat. The world was his oyster and he preferred it on a half shell. Life was as good as can be and the streets were his. In the two years that he'd been home, he'd made the whole Southside bow down and respect his hustle. His partner Manny Stone had seen to that, and for that Whistle remained loyal.

Any time the streets get wind of any one person that's clocking major money, the hyenas come out to prey. In the streets of D.C., made niggas knew how to handle those hyenas. It was the women that the hyenas used to lure made niggas, that ensnared too many good men and made them prey. Whistle had women lined up to be with him, they couldn't resist his thugged out swagger, the cars and the money he represented. He knew that game and how it was played. So, like an old timer had told him, *"Never give your heart to no woman."* Those were the words he lived by.

He went out of his way to guard himself from being emotionally attached. Whistle was tired of trying to figure out who was for real and who was fake. He felt like he was on a continuous episode of *"Flavor of Love."* That's why he dug the dark-skinned beauty lying next to him. She was up front with hers, Sparkle never hesitated to remind him that it was all about the Benjamins with her. She was NHBC for life, no emotions, no feelings, just sex for money with no extras. He respected her style to the fullest. She was just like him…a hustler. And just like he was good at what he did, she was good as what she did. He slung drugs and she slung pussy. *How could he hate on her?* Whistle reached under the covers and rubbed between Sparkle's legs. In seconds, she started to stir as her pussy got wet. He kept rubbing.

"S...s...s...t...top it, bo...o...o...oy!" Sparkle moaned.

Ignoring her words, Whistle moved under the covers and put his tongue where his fingers had just been. He knew that he was dead wrong for what he was doing, but what the hell. He was feeling a little risqué. Whistle put his tongue down flat and drove Sparkle up the walls. After bringing her to several orgasms, he licked up her body and entered her before she could stop him.

"Whistle, stop!" Sparkle protested. She tried vigorously to get him off her. But Whistle was determined to be inside her raw dog. Panic set in just as ecstasy took over and caused her to gasp from the orgasm that was building in her feet and heading upward. The familiar stirring in her center became too much for her to bear. Sparkle screamed out Whistle's name and then felt a warm liquid erupt inside of her.

* * *

Star stood beside the window in the tiny room and watched Quanda's BMW disappear down the block. As she moved around the room gingerly, she thought about Quanda's parting words to her...

"...ain't no such thing as making love nowadays. This is the real world, not a fairy tale. Experiencing Dex just forced you to take off those rose-tinted glasses that you viewed the world through. Baby girl, in the 2000's it's all about money, sex, and murder. You signed up for the money and sex side of the game. And you live every day praying that what you do don't get you murdered. What happened to Vita and Cinnamon can happen to any one of us. In this game, there ain't no love involved, no tenderness, no nothing. So, don't look for any. Don't expect a nigga with a horse dick to take it easy on you out of sympathy, because he won't. Your pain and tears would turn him on. By getting that tattoo and experiencing Dexter, you just signed a contract to play forty-eight minutes in a championship basketball game. The winner busts a nut and the loser goes home. You have to condition your mind and body for the pounding that it's gonna take. You might have to schedule three or four dates in one day. That's why Vita sent everybody to see Dex…"

Star opened one of the closet doors in the room. Underneath a pile of clothes, there was a small lockbox. Wincing from the pain, she lifted the lockbox from the floor. She pulled a chain from around her neck that had a key dangling on it. With that key Star opened the box and extracted her wallet and another set of keys.

"…you're in pain now, I know. I went through the same thing."

What Star felt now was more than pain. She also felt humiliation and anger. The thought of what she had just endured for the past twenty-four hours wouldn't leave her mind. There had to be a better way of achieving the goal she was after. The room she was in reeked of stale cigarettes and mildewed clothes. The smell was making her already queasy stomach more nauseated. She had to get out, Star threw open the room door and stumbled out into the hallway. She noticed that all the rooms on the top floor of the rooming house were closed. Star wondered who her neighbors and housemates were. The best thing about the rooming house was that it was inconspicuous and nobody knew what it was.

Outside, the fresh air was a Godsend. Star inhaled deeply many times and tried to clear her head. She walked briskly up the block, periodically checking behind her to make sure that she wasn't being followed. Star walked the five blocks to Orr Elementary School and spotted her car.

The '08' Chevy Malibu was just as she had left it a few days ago. Five minutes later, she was pulling out into the traffic on Minnesota Avenue and headed towards the Baltimore-Washington Parkway. Star flipped the sun visor down and looked in the mirror at the gauze bandage that covered her new tattoo. Her tears started without provocation. *What the hell have I gotten myself into?* Star's tears continued unabated and blurred her vision. She

66

swiped at the tears forcefully and willed herself to pull it together. *Whoever said that life was gonna be easy? But was her pain worth suffering? Would the ends justify the means?*

Out of nowhere, a pain shot through Star's body. It started at the seat of her pants and ended in her stomach. The thought of how she had been ravished anally brought a whole new fresh set of tears. Her pain was mental as well as physical. Star vowed to herself that when all was said and done, she'd go and see Dexter again. But the circumstances and their positions would be different. If it was the last thing that she ever did, Star wanted to make sure he felt the same pain he had inflicted upon her.

Anthony Fields

CHAPTER 12

"This is a prepaid call...you will not be charged for this call. This call is from...*Rock*...to Refuse this call, hang up. To accept this call, dial five now..." Rhoda pushed the five button on her cell phone.

"Hey, baby!"

"What's up, sweetheart? What are you doing?"

"I'm chilling in Indiana waiting for Monday to get here. What's up with you? I have been here since Friday. Why haven't you called me?"

"I couldn't call you, baby. They had me on lockdown. Those D.C. Brotherhood niggas got at somebody and they had everybody from D.C. locked down. Wasn't anything I could do about that. I thought about you the whole time I was in that cage. I wondered if you'd made it to town safe and sound."

Rhoda got out of the bed and picked up her Bluetooth earpiece. Fastening it in her ear, she said, "Boo, can you hear me?"

"Yeah."

"Good. I had to put my earpiece in so that I can use the bathroom with my hands-free. My flight was smooth and so far, I'm just anxious to be with you. I miss you."

"I miss you, too. You know that." Rock replied.

"Is, that right? You gon need some Viagra or Levitra messing with your girl, baby love." Rhoda said playfully.

"One thing about me, baby, I ain't too proud to go and cop some of that shit. It was made specifically with dudes like me in mind. As a matter of fact, what do you have on right now?"

"Just a thong."

"Is, that right?" Rock asked, rubbing himself through his sweatpants. "And what color would that thong be?"

"Red, baby, your favorite color."

"And your toenails?"

Rhoda glanced down at her toes. "They are a deep red color with designs on both big toes. They look good and I'm wearing that platinum toe ring that you like so much."

"Is that pussy wet, right now?"

"Tell me in detail how you gon put that dick on me tomorrow and it will be."

As Rock described to her how he was gonna fuck her, Rhoda moved her thong to the side and exposed her bare shaved pussy lips. Her fingers came alive with determination as she fingered her clit.

"I want you to get on all fours and..."

Rhoda visualized every move that Rock spoke of. "Baby, you got me playing with myself." She moaned.

"That's right, baby, play with that juicy pussy. I love that pussy, Rho. Make that pussy cum for me, baby. Make me cum."

A soft moan escaped Rhoda's mouth as she stepped up the speed in which she rubbed her clit. "Oooh shit! Ooooooh, Rock! I want your dick so bad!"

"Think about this big dick and cum for me, baby. Imagine yourself eating this dick while I eat that pussy. Can you see it? Can you feel it?"

"Oooooh, Rock, I feel it, boo! I feel...it! I feel you...I see you...I see you...I want you to put your dick in me! I want you to cum in me!"

"Cum for me, Rhoda! I want you to cum for me! Put two fingers in that pussy, baby...you got two fingers in there?"

"Uuuum hmmm!"

"Hit that spot for me, then. Rub that spot and cum for me! I wanna hear you cum for me."

"I'm hitting it! Oooh, baby, I'm hitting it! Baby, it feels so good...damn! My pussy is so...o...o...o wet! My whole hand is wet. Can you hear how wet it is?"

"Let me hear it, baby."

Rhoda took her earpiece out of her ear and put it at the base of her stomach. Then she pushed three fingers in and out of her pussy with her left hand and rubbed her clit with her right. "Oooh, I'ma bout to cum, Rock."

Rock heard Rhoda's moans and wanted to cum with her. But the phone that he was on was in the common area where all the inmates were congregated. He had absolutely no privacy. Rock also heard the slurping sounds of Rhoda's wet pussy. Pre-cum coated his dick and made his boxers stick to his leg.

"Baby I'm...cum...ming! I'm c...c...c...u...u...m...m...m...ing! Shit! Ooh, shit! Ooh! A...a...r...r...g...h...h!" Rhoda struggled to get control of herself. The orgasm was catastrophic. "Damn, that felt good! You got me wet as shit. I gotta call housekeeping to change these sheets messing with your ass. Why you do that?"

Rock laughed at Rhoda. "What the hell did I do?"

"You know what you did. You got me acting all like a heathen early on a Sunday morning. My ass should be in church somewhere. I'm a terrible Christian."

Rock laughed again. He knew that Rhoda didn't have a religious bone in her body. "My bad, Mary Magdalene. I'm sorry for corrupting you. But I'm a cold-blooded heathen. Messing with me you'll never make it to church because I'll fuck that pretty ass every Sunday morning. We can fellowship like that. You can speak in tongues and everything."

"I can't wait. You...*beep*. Was that the phone?" Rhoda asked.

"Yeah, it's about to hang up. I'ma call you back in thirty minutes. I need to go handle some business anyway. My dick is hard as stone right now. I'ma call...*beep*...you in thirty. Be..."

The phone disconnected itself. Rhoda decided to bring herself to one more orgasm before she sent for some breakfast. *All I need is a few minutes...*

* * *

Quanda looked at the run in her stockings and cursed under her breath. She stepped out of the BMW and walked into Our

71

Lady of Perpetual Health Church. As she marched down the aisle to find a seat, Quanda wondered why all the Hispanics that she knew were all so damn religious, for one and two, *why were they all Catholic?*

The church was small compared to a lot of the newer churches that she had seen. Taking a seat in one of the pews, Quanda scanned the many faces in search of the man that she came there to meet. The aisle seat where she sat did not afford her the best view. Although she didn't find his face, Quanda was sure that Alejandro was there. She had seen a beautiful Aston Martin DB-9 in the parking lot and knew that Alejandro owned that car and several like it in all different colors.

Alejandro Rojas was the Columbian intermediary between her brother and the Trinidad Cartel. Their meeting today would be one of many that they had over the last year and change. When the service concluded, Alejandro appeared and walked down the aisle. He glanced at Quanda and nodded his head. That was the signal that all was well and things would go on as scheduled. Quanda knew to wait a while before getting up to leave the church. Outside, she saw that Alejandro had...as she figured...gotten inside the Aston Martin. He was joined by another Hispanic man that she had not seen inside of the church. Alejandro turned in her direction and nodded again.

Never exchanging a word, Quanda knew that their transaction was complete. It was done the same way every time, just at different churches. Without having to check her trunk, she knew that it was now filled with keys of cocaine. The 100 kilos of cocaine would be distributed to the four friends of her brother.

Derrick 'B.F.' Simpson, Dolla Bill Richardson, Maurice Fells, and Randy Shaw would each receive 25 kilos in exchange for a bag full of money. Each bag would total three hundred seventy-five thousand dollars. Quanda knew the routine like the back of her hand. She also knew the risk that came along with her participation. It was well understood amongst all parties that the penitentiary beckoned.

In the Blink of an Eye

To Quanda, the risk was worth the end result if all went well. The Trinidad Cartel fronted Mark 100 kilos a month. In return, she gave the Cartel one million cash the very next day after receiving the kilos. Every transaction was profitable to all sides. Mark made four hundred thousand off each move and she pocketed a hundred grand. At last count, her brother had close to six million dollars put up for his appeal. Financially she was set, Quanda knew that she never had to go on another date in her life, but she had to continue to play the role. She had to be able to justify her income. Plus, she outright enjoyed her job. Quanda admitted to herself a long time ago that she was addicted to sex. Man, or woman, she loved the contact. The date she had set up for later came to mind. It was with one of the Washington Redskins. The quarterback that all the women in D.C. loved. Jayquan Campbell was a pleasure to fuck and Quanda looked forward to it. *"I'ma suck his dick and make him cum back to back to drain him. Them I'ma make him fuck me in the ass until he can't take it no more."*

Reaching for her cell phone, Quanda gave it a command. "Call BF." The call connected as she put the phone to her ear. BF answered on the first ring.

"Quan, what's good, girlfriend?" BF inquired.

"I'll be ready to see you in about two hours," Quanda informed him. "I'll call you back and tell you where to meet me. A'ight?"

"That's a bet. Holla when you ready."

Quanda made three more calls just like the first one as she headed home to get out of the church clothes. The little bit of rest that she had gotten at Dexter's and at home wasn't enough. Fatigue was starting to creep up on her and the day was just beginning.

"I might have to reschedule Jayquan." She thought as she pulled into her parking space on the side of the townhouse.

Walking into the house, Quanda bumped into Sparkle. "Spark what's up?"

"Ain't shit. You look like you had a long night?"

73

"Naw, not really. All I did was take Star to get her tattoo, get something to eat, shop, and then to see Dexter."

"So, it's official, huh? That girl is one of us?"

Quanda detected a hint of facetiousness in Sparkle's voice. "Yeah, she's official now. Why? You wanna tell me something?"

"Naw." Sparkle said. "Why do you ask that?"

"Because I detected a little something in your tone just now, that's why."

"Quan, you trippin. How did she do with Dex?"

"How did she do? Who Star? Oh, she did about as well as we all did against his big dick ass. She hollered and screamed all night. We might've scarred that girl for life. When I dropped her off earlier, she wouldn't even speak to me. Girlfriend is fucked up at me. Hopefully, she'll be a'ight, though. She's a trooper. What you about to do?"

"I'm about to cook me something to eat. You want something?" Sparkle asked as she headed for the kitchen.

Everybody in the house knew that Sparkle couldn't cook. Well everybody, but Sparkle. "I ate already." Quanda lied. "But make sure you cook something for Billie. You know that bitch is greedy as shit. She loves your fried chicken."

"I don't blame her. My chicken do be a smash hit."

Cut the bullshit. Spark. Your chicken is a smash shit, not hit. "You like that, boo."

"That's what I'ma make then. I'ma fry some chicken for everybody just in case you get hungry later."

Quanda giggled all the way to her room. She stepped out of her Dior heels, glad to finally be out of them. Her feet were made for tennis shoes, sandals, and flip-flops and they always reminded her of that when she put on heels. Quanda thought about Sparkle in the kitchen preparing to make fried chicken and smiled. Then she imagined Billie throwing the chicken away when Spark turned her back. Sparkle's chicken tasted like fried whoopee cushions and Billie hated it more than anything in the world.

Slipping out of her dress, Quanda grabbed a pair of 7 For All Mankind jeans out of her closet and a Prada pull over shirt. She put on a pair of Prada tennis shoes, with the matching belt and prepared to drop off the work.

* * *

Sparkle, was in the kitchen cooking when her cell phone vibrated. She knew that it was Vito before she ever picked it up. "Hello?"

"Kay, what's up, you, tell me something good."

"Damn, nigga didn't I...?" Sparkle started but stopped mid-sentence. It was better that he had called her instead of her calling him. She didn't feel as bad. "This is the last time that we do this, Vito. You understand that?"

"I got you, yo," Vito responded.

"I'm not playing, Vito. I don't care how fucked up you become after this. I don't care how many threats you issue out. I'm not gonna let you put me in this position again. Do you hear me?"

"I hear you, Kay. I won't need you again. Hopefully, this lick will put me back where I need to be. I promise, yo, that I never impose on you again."

Sparkle wondered if Vito was a man of his word and kept his promises. Only time would tell she reasoned with herself and then made the biggest mistake of her life. "The dude's name is Artinis, but everybody calls him Whistle..."

75

Anthony Fields

CHAPTER 13

The butterflies in Rhoda's stomach seemed to be as big as pigeons. She struggled to maintain her composure as she easily maneuvered the Benz truck on Highway 65. In the distance, the Federal Correctional Complex at Terre Haute loomed large and in charge on a hill. Rhoda steered the truck up the winding road that leads to the penitentiary's front gate. After waiting for this moment for years, it was hard for her to believe that it was finally here. Rhoda saw three men standing at the bottom of the steps that lead inside the prison. She smiled from ear to ear. One of those men was her baby. Rock was impeccably dressed in the black single breasted John Varvatos suit that she had sent him. A black Yves St. Lauren dress shirt and black YSL loafers rounded out the rest of the fit. He could have easily ripped the runway on B.E.T any day.

Rock spotted the truck she told him that she rented and smiled. His smile melted her heart and comforted her queasy stomach. Just as he had said there would be, the other two men stood on either side of him. They were both white. One was his counselor, Rock had said and the other was his case manager. And just as they had planned, Rhoda knew exactly what she had to do.

Checking to make sure that she had their attention. Rhoda got out of the truck and slowly, sexily walked around to the passenger side of the truck. All eyes were on her. She could feel it. The short, black Donatella Versace skirt that she had on gave her ass that heart shaped effect. Her black Lycra Juicy Couture top had 'Got Dick' emblazoned across her 38DD breasts. The wrap around Versace high heeled open toe sandals complemented her outfit. Her toenail polish matched her lip gloss. *I'm the shit and we all know it.*

"Well, gentlemen, that's my ride," Rock said to the men standing on both sides of him. "Y'all take care."

"You stay in the streets, Blackmon." Mr. Suell said.

"Yeah. Don't ever come back to this place." Paul Gerke added.

"I'd rather die in the streets like a rabid dog." Rock walked up to Rhoda and embraced her. They kissed, then Rock walked to the driver's side of the truck and hopped in.

"You sure you remember how to drive?" Rhoda asked.

"I got this. You ready?"

"I was born ready. Are they still looking at us?"

Rock saw both white men still looking in their direction. He waved and they waved back. "Yeah, they looking."

"Good. Let's give 'em something to thinking about." Rhoda reached across Rock's lap and unzipped his slacks. She pulled his dick out and dropped her head into his lap.

Rock threw his head back and enjoyed what Rhoda was doing to him. He was getting his dick sucked in the parking lot of the prison that held his body captive for more than twenty years. The feelings that he now felt were indescribable. Rock opened his eyes and looked into the faces of the two white men. They both turned a deep shade of pink as they stared at the scene in front of them. Winking his eye, Rock started the truck and carefully pulled out of the parking lot.

"Okay, baby, you can stop now," Rock said when they were out of eyesight. But Rhoda didn't stop. "Rhoda, you can't be doing this out here on these highways in Indiana. These racist ass crackers don't be bullshitting. The town where the head Klu Klux Klan jokers live is right down the road. And the police out here all are with them muthafuckas. The police gon pull us over and lock me up for driving without a license. I ain't tryna go to jail on my first day out of jail."

Rhoda lifted her head from Rock's lap. "My bad, baby. I gotta little carried away."

"Thanks for doing that for me. I wanted to show them crackers that a nigga been locked up for twenty-five years and still ain't washed up. You should've seen the look on their faces."

"You ain't gotta thank me, I loved it. I'm so glad that you are finally home. As a matter of fact, pull over right here."

78

"Why? I can't drive…"

"I ain't worried about you driving. I need to drive because you don't know the way to where we're going, but I do."

"And where's that?" Rock asked.

"There's been a change of plans, baby. There's no way in the world that I can sit here for ten hours waiting to reach D.C…We're going back to the hotel I just left. I need to finish what we started back there. You know me. I hate to leave things done halfway.

Rock looked at Rhoda and smiled. Then he pulled the truck over and switched seats with Rhoda. Minutes later when the truck pulled into the hotel parking lot. Rock finally knew what it felt like to be free…

* * *

"That nigga ugly as shit," Star said from the passenger seat of Quanda's BMW.

"Girl, who gives a fuck. That nigga got that Muthafuckin' paper. Why do you think they call him Dolla Bill? That ugly ass nigga is cake the fuck up. He got that kinda paper that makes lights light up and the whole city knows it. He probably fucks a different bad bitch every day and gets more pussy that all the pretty niggas in the city. He and his man Harold run all this shit uptown. If you think that all the niggas that pay for pussy gon' be good looking, you got another thought coming." Quanda said while thinking about the man that had just given her almost four hundred thousand dollars. Despite what she had just said, she still had to laugh. Star was definitely right about what she said. Dolla Bill Richardson was one ugly muthafucka. *That nigga looks like a scrawny ass plucked chicken.*

Quanda had one more stop to make and her job would be complete. It took them twenty minutes to get back to S.E… Pulling the car off Minnesota Avenue, she turned on B Street and kept riding until she came to Anacostia Road. At the Stone Ridge housing complex. Quanda made a left turn into the first parking lot. In front of the second building sat a smoke gray Bentley GT convertible sitting on twenty-four inch rims. She knew the Bentley belonged to Maurice 'Moe Styles' Fells, the man she had come to see. Quanda Moe on the phone.

"Quan, what's up, good looking?" Moe said.

"I'm outside. Bring that out here."

"No can do," Moe responded.

"What the fuck do you mean, *no can do*?"

"Calm down good looking. They put up cameras on the buildings. I'm not passing you no big ass bag full of money. We'd both be on candid cameras. You gotta come get it."

Quanda knew that Moe was full of shit. Every time she saw him, he propositioned her for sex. *Moe tryna fuck, he thinks he slick. But I gotta respect what he said about being on camera.* "What apartment are you in, Moe?"

"Third floor. I'll be at the door to meet you."

"Chill out for a few minutes, Star. I'll be right back." Quanda said and exited the car. She was buzzed into the building as if by magic. Quanda jogged up the steps until she reached the third floor. a door to her right opened and Moe was standing there in the doorway.

He had a phone at his ear and was talking to someone. "Let me hit you right back..." he said into the phone. Then to Quanda, he said, "Quanda come on in."

Quanda walked into the lavish apartment and stood in the middle of the floor.

"I finally got your pretty ass by yourself," Moe said and grabbed Quanda in a bear hug. He kissed her neck and face passionately.

"Moe, but it out, boy! I ain't here for this." Quanda pleaded. Moe was a pretty boy and she had a weakness for them. It was the reason that she always avoided Moe. He was a light skinned thug with long dark cornrows and good looks. He was Ginuwine fine. Before she could plead any further, Moe had her jeans down and around her ankles. In seconds, his tongue found her pussy. Quanda attempted to stop him one last time, but her protest came

80

out to feeble. Moe's tongue licked her clit and there was nothing else that could be said other than, *"Damn this nigga's head is the bomb!"*

* * *

By the time, they shut the hotel room door, Rhoda was on her knees with Rock's dick in her mouth. She sucked his dick in every position imaginable and swallowed all the fruits of her hard labor. Rhoda licked Rock's toes, ankles, thighs, nuts, arms, chest, and every other part of his body. Then he returned the favor. It had been a long time coming and Rock could've sworn that he could hear Sam Cooke singing in his ear. He had never eaten pussy in his life until that day. Rhoda showed him the way and led him to the mountain top. Rock ate Rhoda's pussy like a starving refugee from Haiti. Rhoda moved all around the room with Rock's face between her legs. She literally tried to run, but he wasn't having it. The orgasms that she experienced were powerful and like nothing, she had ever felt.

By the time, he put the dick in her, it was a wrap. Rhoda begged for a time out, but Rock wasn't in the time out mood. They fucked on the bed, the floor, on a table, in a chair, on the kitchen counter, in the tub, on the bathroom sink, on the balcony, everywhere.

When they finally tired out each other's bodies, it was after eight that evening and dark outside. Before they went to sleep out of pure exhaustion, Rhoda decided that they wouldn't go straight back D.C. Early the next morning, she called Delta Airlines and reserved two plane tickets to Miami. In Miami, they'd board a cruise ship to the Caribbean. Rhoda called the townhouse and informed the crew of her impromptu vacation plans. They all understood and wished them well.

After everything was reserved and paid for online, Rhoda did what she did best. She sucked Rock's dick some more..."

Anthony Fields

CHAPTER 14

Seeing Vito standing on the other side of the door was a complete shock to Sparkle. *What the fuck is this nigga doing here? And how the hell did he get my address?* As she stared through the peephole, Sparkle remembered the night that she had left her purse in the room with Vito and he had gone through it. *I can't stand this nigga.* Sparkle knew then that Vito was reinforcing his threat by reminding her that he knew where she laid her head to rest at night. Cursing under her breath, Sparkle opened the door.

"Vito, what the hell are you doing here?"

"I been tryna reach you, but you don't seem to be taking any calls suddenly. So, I decided to visit the Nation's Capital. I'm a tourist. You don't look happy to see me, Kay, what's really good, yo?"

The smug look on Vito's face made her stomach tighten. *I wish I was capable of murder. I swear I'd kill his ass.* "Vito please don't ever come her again. What if somebody rode pass and spotted you? You wouldn't be able to blackmail me then because I'd be dead. All the reckless shit you probably into, please don't make my spot hot."

Her words fell on deaf ears, Vito's attention was elsewhere. Sparkle's eyes followed his and stopped at her crotch. It was then that she realized that she was only dressed in a chemise and matching panties. Her instincts kicked in and she tried to cover herself.

"Ain't no need for all that. I done seen the good already and had 'em, so you can stop all the shy and bashful shit. Can I come in?"

"No, Vito!"

"Kay, I just spent the last thirty minutes on the Parkway in anticipation of seeing you and this is the way you treat me? Yo, I'm starting to really believe that you don't fuck with me, for real, yo." Vito said and then opened the bottom of his button-down shirt to reveal the butt of a large handgun. "If that's the case, I don't really give a fuck. But today, you need to be nice to me because I'm having a bad day. So, be a good girl and let me in."

"I have roommates, Vito. You can't stay long. They don't like for me to have men in the house. I have to respect them on that."

"How long I stay depends on you," Vito said as he pushed his way past Sparkle into the living room.

"Depends on me, how?"

"Standing outside for so long looking at you done made me horny and now I'm tryna fuck. Then I'ma need some more details on your boy Whistle. When I get both of those issues taken care of, then I'll leave. If I can't get them, I'll stay a while."

Sparkle opened her mouth to protest but was quickly attacked by Vito. He slapped her so hard that she fell to the ground. "Then again, I changed my mind. You no longer have a choice in the matter. Who else is in here? And don't lie, because I'll search the spot and kill everybody in here. Now, who else is here?"

Tears flowed freely down Sparkle's face. She was terrified. "I'm...m...m...th...th...the only one here."

The next thing she knew, Vito was unzipping his jeans and pulling his dick out. "I don't care what you do, eat it or sit on it, but you gotta get it right. Come and make this right." Vito said as she waved his semi-erect dick at Sparkle.

Sparkle got up off the floor and walked over to where Vito was standing. The side of her face where he had smacked her was still stinging from the pain. She wanted to hurry up and get him out of the house and since he wasn't going to leave until she got it right, Sparkle did just that. She dropped to her knees in front of him and grabbed his dick. Putting it in her mouth, Sparkle closed her eyes. In her mind, she found a comfortable place and stayed there. Her mouth and hands were moving on auto pilot. When Vito pushed her head down further onto his dick, Sparkle felt the head hit the back of her throat. She relaxed her muscles and accepted him into her throat.

"Damn! Shit...yeah, yo! Eat that dick...Kay! Eat that whole dick! Fuck yeah,...oooohhh...weee...yes indeed...I'm about to

In the Blink of an Eye

cum...yo! I'm about to bust, Kay! Don't stop! A...r...r...g...g...h!"

Feeling the dick in her throat twitch, Sparkle tried to pull herself off it. But Vito wasn't having it. He grabbed her head and held it in place like a vice grip. he shook and came deep in her throat. Sparkle felt the cum going down her throat and wanted to hurl.

"Damn, yo'," Vito said as he pulled his flaccid dick out of Sparkle's mouth. "Under pressure, your head is fire like a muthafucka. You drained the shit outta me. I might fall asleep behind the wheel on my way back home."

I hope you crash and die a terrible death, muthafucka. Sparkle wiped the leftover seed from her mouth and then wiped tears from her eyes.

"Now tell me everything you know about Whistle."

* * *

"What do you have so far?" The man sitting on Star's sofa in her living room asked.

Star paced the floor as she thought about how much she should tell the man sitting on her couch. He was dressed in Rock Republic jeans, a Hugo Boss Pullover sweatshirt, and Hugo Boss tennis shoes.

"There's not much to tell. I don't know when she meets him or where. I do know that she hits a few dudes with coke and then pick up the money the next day. That's it, in a little while, I'll know everything there is to know about her."

"Well, don't get too caught up in this, Sams. I don't want another Texas situation on our hands. Do what you gotta do and keep me posted." The man rose to leave, at the door, he stopped turned around and said. "And don't enjoy yourself too much."

"Fuck you!" she spat as the door shut behind him. Star hated when he acted all sanctimonious, but she respected the man all at the same time. Whatever he said do...she knew that she would.

85

Anthony Fields

* * *

"Let me put you up on game, boo," Chico said as he opened the Scrabble game and put it on the table inside of Hope Village's visiting room. "Chess, Spades, Dominoes… all that shit is cool, but ain't nothing like Scrabble. Scrabble, tightens up your spelling and adds words to your vocabulary. For example, if you have the X on your rack and you need to spell a short word, you can spell Xu or Xi. Depending on who you're playing, your opponent might not be hip to them words and challenge it. If they do, they'll lose and you'll get another go."

"Xu or Xi? What the fuck is that? I'd challenge both of them myself." Billie said and picked up the Scrabble dictionary. She flipped the pages and then shook her head in disbelief. "A Greek letter and a Vietnamese coin. Who really knows that crazy ass shit?"

"A scrabble player. The whole art of winning at a game like this is knowing the most words. You have to know what's in the dictionary and what's not. A lot of times people will try and bluff you by putting a bullshit word down. You can't let it go if you're not hip to it. Never be afraid to challenge words. Are you taking all of this in or am I overloading your brain?"

"You got jokes, huh? Everybody I know got jokes, lately. No, you're not overloading my brain. I can comprehend really well."

For the next twenty minutes, Chico explained everything there was to know about Scrabble to Billie. Then they started a game. Fifteen minutes into it, Billie decided that she liked Scrabble. It was a game not only based on word building and knowledge, it was a game of defense and strategy as well. And defense was something that she knew a lot about. All her life, Billie put up defenses to keep people from getting close to her heart. Her heart couldn't take any more abuse. After her favorite uncle was killed and her mother and father, move away. Billie thought that she had experienced enough pain. But then her friends Vita and Cinnamon got killed. It was enough to drive a young girl insane. So, she put up a defense mechanism to shield

86

her heart from pain. But Chico was starting to penetrate that shield. Being a member of a crew like the NHBC didn't allow for boyfriends, fiancés, and emotions. One had to have a heart of stone. But sitting there at that table, playing Chico at Scrabble, Billie knew that she was starting to fall in love with him.

Anthony Fields

CHAPTER 15

One Week Later...

Rhoda flushed the toilet and got up. She felt a little better. At least her stomach had settled some. The clam and lobster Alfredo she had devoured in Miami before boarding the plane had disagreed with her system. *I done lost all my class. I shitted on an airplane.* The turbulence that they encountered as the plane cruised to D.C. had compounded the problem of her queasy stomach. Rhoda washed her hands in the sink and then fixed her clothes. Staring at herself in the mirror, she noticed that her skin had a darker hue than it did before she and Rock had departed for the Caribbean.

As she pulled her toothbrush and toothpaste out of her purse, Rhoda thought about the week she had just spent in the Virgin Islands, Puerto Rico, Cozumel, and Mexico. The vacation itself was much needed, but spending every minute of that vacation with Rock was a dream come true. They snorkeled, jet skied, skinny dipped, swam, shopped, ate well, and made love for hours every day. In Cozumel, they laid on the beach and watched the sunset and eventually the moon rise. It was the most beautiful thing that Rhoda had ever seen. They had snuggled close and promised each other the world. Then they had made love until the sun came up.

Rhoda brushed her teeth, flossed, and washed her face. Then she reapplied her lip gloss. It was time to take her man home, home to the place where he was born and home to the place where they would spend the rest of their lives together.

***

Billie pulled the curtain back and watched the Maserati pull into a parking space behind the townhouse. "They're here!" she announced to the whole house and then stepped away from the window. Rhoda had called from the airport and let them know that she and Rock were back and on their way. "Everybody just acts normal now."

89

Even though she had said it, Billie knew that they were any-thing but normal women at the moment. They were all nervous. After so many years, they were finally about to meet Rock. The man who had single-handedly captured Rhoda's heart and changed the way the No Holes Barred Crew did business. Except for Star, they had all spoken to Rock at some point over the years. But now they were about to meet in person, the man, the myth, the mystery.

Sparkle lounged on the couch and faked like she was reading a novel titled Angel Returns, written by one of her clients named Buck. She glanced over at Quanda, who was sitting on the steps polishing her toenails. Star was sitting on the steps too. Two stairs below Quanda listening to her iPod, nodding her head and snap-ping her fingers to the rhythm of whatever beat she was listening to.

The lock on the door clicked and a second later, the door opened. Rhoda walked into the room like a long lost relative and said, "Ladies, I'm home."

One by one everybody got up and hugged Rhoda. "And this everyone is my baby Rock."

Rock Blackman walked into the house and smiled. "Hello, ladies."

All the women in the room openly stared at the handsome man. Rock looked like a better version of Denzel Washington. Billie was the first to speak.

"Day...y...yum! You fine as shit Rock. I see why Rhoda did that bid with you and hid your pictures from everybody. I would've done that bid too, to have a man as fine as you come home to me."

Everybody laughed at Billie's direct bluntness. It broke the ice as Rock went around the room and hugged every woman pre-sent.

"Let me see..." Rock started as Star released him. "...Rhoda has told me so much about y' all. Let me see if I can pick out who's who." He pointed at Billie and said, "A natural comedi-enne, skin the color of coffee with very little cream, dark wavy

90

In the Blink of an Eye

hair, and resemblance to the great Lady Day. You must be Billie. And you..." He turned to Sparkle. "...Dimples, braces, tall with an athletic build and the swagger of America's next top model...you definitely have to be Sparkle. Rock turned to his right. "And you have to be Quanda... light skinned, curly hair, Chinese eyes, and extremely beautiful. Rhoda described you all perfectly." Lastly, Rock turned to face Star. "And since you are the only one left in the room, I assume you are Star?"

"In the flesh." Star retorted and smiled.

"It's good to finally meet y'all. You are a diverse and lovely group of dime pieces. I can see why y'all are giving the city hell."

To the girls, Rhoda said, "I'm gonna show Rock the rest of the house and then take him to his apartment. I brought you all something back from my trip and I wanna see how y'all like my gifts, but we'll do that when I get back. Cancel whatever dates y'all might have, we have to have a sista circle pow wow."

* * *

The Maserati pulled into a gated parking lot. The sign in front of the high-rise apartment building read, 'Belford Towers'. Once the car came to a complete stop she hit the trunk button. "C'mon baby, I think you're gonna love your new bachelor pad."

Rock laughed as he got out of the car. "Oh, now I'm a bachelor, huh?"

"You will be if I catch any young tramps in your apartment."

"Well, what about old tramps? Are they allowed?"

Rhoda playfully punched Rock in the arm as he grabbed his bag out of the trunk. "You know what I mean. Young tramps, old tramps...I don't want any tramps besides me around you. I can be a very jealous woman when I wanna be, Rock. So, let me know now if you ain't ready for this."

Sitting most his bags on the concrete, Rock looked into Rhoda's eyes and saw that she was serious. "Not ready for what?"

"Don't play coy with me, Rock. You know damn well what I mean. You been in jail for twenty-five years, if you need to go out and fuck a couple hundred bitches before you settle down, let me know that now."

"Rho, but the bullshit out."

"I'm not bullshittin', Rock. I never bullshit when it comes to matters that involves my heart."

"Neither do I and no I'm, not tryna fuck no couple hundred bitches, either." Rock grabbed Rhoda and embraced her. She laid her head on his chest. "Not a couple hundred...who do you think I am? Superman? About fifty or sixty will do."

Rhoda lifted her head quickly and searched Rock's face for a sign that he was joking. Just as her heart dropped, he smiled.

"I'm bullshittin', Rho, I'm bullshittin'. Come on and show me this bachelor pad. I'm tired as hell, I'ma lay down for a while and then go and see my sister and nephew."

"I took the liberty of furnishing the apartment, but you can redo it if you want. I just made it inhabitable. Get you some rest, I'ma go home and chill with the girls. When you get up and you're ready to go and see your family, call my cell, and like a trusted chauffeur, I'll be here to drive you around."

"That'll work. How about a quickie to break the bachelor pad in?" Rock asked as he picked the bags back up and they walked to the front entrance.

"I did that already, me and the dude that showed me the place."

Rock stopped dead in his tracks and turned to face Rhoda.

A broad smile crossed her face. "I'm bullshittin', boo. Right back at ya."

* * *

Rock stepped out of the shower and grabbed a large terry cloth towel off the rail in the bathroom. He dried himself off and wrapped the towel around his waist. After making the short trek from the bathroom to the bedroom, Rock laid across the bed and exhaled. His body was tired. Everything that Rhoda did to him literally took a lot out of him. Stamina wise he was no match for the twenty-eight-year-old beauty. He knew it and so did she. They just never verbalized it. Laying there in that king-sized bed, Rock truly felt free. He couldn't remember exactly when the feeling had come over him, but it had. But what he did know was that the feelings he now felt were like nothing else in the world.

The thought of it brought a smile to his face and then just as quickly the smile faded. The fact that his comrades Beanie, Fox, and so many others didn't know the feelings he felt, made him sad.

One day, God willing you all will know what it feels like to be free. Rock's thoughts then turned to Roscoe. His youngster that would never know what it feels like to be free or happy again. He would never see another sunrise or sunset. As always, tears threatened to fall down his cheeks. Rock wiped his eyes and willed himself to not get emotional. He reached over to the stand beside the bed and grabbed the cordless phone. There was one person left that he had to thank. It was the person truly responsible for his freedom. Roscoe had done the footwork and then paid the lawyers for his appeal, but that wouldn't have been possible without the help of the one man that he now called.

Dialing a number that he would never forget, Rock waited to hear his friend's voice. After a series of beeps and a person putting him on hold, he did...

"Hello?" The voice on the other end said.

"Hello, old friend," Rock said into the phone.

"Rock?" His friend Khan asked. "Is that you?"

"It's me, buddy," Rock answered. Then he and Khan talked for hours.

Anthony Fields

CHAPTER 16

"In Cozumel, they have a mall that would put Tyson's 1 and 2 to shame. I damn near fainted at the sight of all them stores." Rhoda said as she dug into bag after bag. "Here this is for you, Billie." She handed Billie a box with a handbag inside. "I know your geeking ass love purses, so I copped you one. That right there is the new signature edition Louis Vuitton bag. It's a patchwork bag, made with pieces of every Louis bag that's been made in the last twenty years. They only made one hundred of these bags and I found you one."

"Thank you, Rho, I love it," Billie responded as she fondled the bag. "Bitches gon really hate me now."

Rhoda handed a bag with a shoe box in it to Quanda. "Check them joints out, girlfriend."

Quanda reached into the bag and extracted the shoe box. She lifted the lid off the box and smiled. Pulling one of the shoes out of the box and inspecting it, she said, "Limited Edition Hermes tennis shoes."

"Not Her-mees, Quan It's pronounced Er-mays. The H is silent and you elongate the E until it sounds like an A. At least that's what the lady who sold 'em to me said. Them joints cost five grand, girl. I hope you like 'em."

"Rho' I love 'em. Thank you." Quanda hugged Rhoda and kissed her cheek.

Rhoda playfully wiped her cheek. "Don't be kissing me and all that shit, girl. I'm on dicks, not clits."

Everybody laughed at Rhoda.

"Now what do you give a woman who had everything?" Rhoda asked looking Sparkle dead in the eyes.

Sparkle shrugged her shoulders and said, "I don't know."

"Neither do I. So, Spark, I just went into every high-end shop they had and bought you a scarf to tie your hair up with. You can wrap those precious braids up in Chanel, Versace, Gucci, Fendi, etcetera..." She handed Sparkle the bag.

"Thanks, Rho, I needed these." Sparkle said as she pulled each scarf out of its box and examined it.

"Last, but not least. The new girl Star, I didn't know what you'd probably like, so I bought what every woman likes... a watch." Rhoda handed the watch to Star. "It's a Cartier Deluxe. Go ahead and put it on."

Star put the platinum watch on her wrist and stared at it. "It's beautiful." Small diamonds encased the bezel. "This is the best gift that I have ever received. I feel like I'm one of the girls on 'Flavor of Love.'"

Rhoda enjoyed seeing the smile on Star's face. "So, you know what time it is, then. And you always have to know what time it is in more ways than one. There are a lot of things that you have to learn. When you do learn them, you'll have so many beautiful gifts coming that you'll run out of places to put them all."

To everybody, Rhoda said, "Okay, ladies, gather around. It's time for our sista circle hug."

All the women in the room came to the middle of the room and formed a circle. They drew each other in close and hugged one another tight.

"We are all we got," Rhoda said. "May God protect us from those that wanna destroy what we have. NHBC for life, ladies. Repeat after me... *We Are All We Got!*

"We Are All We Got!" The rest of the ladies said in unison.

* * *

Later Rhoda decided to pull Star aside and talk to her. She found Star laying across Quanda's bed playing a video game on the X-Box.

"Star, let me talk to you for a minute." Rhoda led Star to her bedroom and closed the door. "Sit down, baby."

Star did as she was told. Her look of bewilderment etched itself deep into her face. "What's wrong, Rhoda?"

"Nothing's wrong, Star. I just wanted to have a little heart to heart with you. Look at this as a post interview of sorts."

"Okay."

"Why did you join the NHBC?" Rhoda asked and then sat down on the bed next to Star.

"Uh...I...uh!" Star stammered.

"Talk woman. What's wrong with you? You do know why you joined the No Holes Barred Crew, right?"

Star wanted to word her response correctly. "I...I heard a lot about the crew...I like the way people cater to y' all. All the girls in the crew seem to be having money a lot. Who wouldn't wanna be a part of a crew of bad girls like the NHBC? To me, it's not just a lifestyle, it's a movement. With the crew, I feel empowered."

"I understand all that but never answer a question with a question. It seems like you tryna avoid something. Again, I ask you, why did you join the NHBC?"

"Uh...the lifestyle, the mon..."

"You do know what we do for a living, right?"

"Ye...eah, I know."

"We fuck strangers and suck dick for a living. Sometimes, depending on the situation and the client, we suck and fuck several strangers at one time. For hours. Is that what you joined the crew for? To fuck and suck niggas every day, go on trips and get paid for it?"

"I...think so...yeah, I wanna get paid. I'm fuckin' niggas for free, anyway."

"You wanna get paid, huh? Why not get a real job? A regular nine to five."

"Real jobs don't pay the type of..."

"Okay. Now we're getting somewhere. You like the big money, huh?"

"Of course, who doesn't."

"And you don't mind fucking strange niggas?"

"I guess not."

"Ain't no you guess not. You must be sure. Do you like to suck dick?"

"Yeah...sometimes...depending on..."

"Ain't no sometimes. Every nigga out here wants his dick sucked all the time. And you just signed up to suck 'em. You said depending on...Depending on what?"

"The...uh...circumstances."

"Ain't no more of that. The person can be anybody and the circumstances maybe anything. Whatever the date wants, they get. Anyway, anyhow, you have to accommodate. Do you understand that?"

"Yeah."

"And you do know that every hole on your body is up for sale, right? Meaning that ass, too, you do know, that right?"

That made Star think of Dexter and what he did to her that night. "I know all that. I understand everything."

"That's good. With all that said, welcome to the family and go give them niggas hell, girlfriend. Now, let me look at that tattoo."

CHAPTER 17

Rock sat in the Maserati with Rhoda and stared at the cluster of tenement buildings called Mayfair. It was the neighborhood that he had grown up in.

"See all these cast iron gates?" Rock asked.

"Yeah."

"They weren't that back then. They make the place look like a concentration camp. The buildings looked smaller than I remember." He turned in his seat. "There used to be a 7-11 right there where the Circle K is. And right there where that long building is on Kenilworth Avenue...that use to be a vacant lot. The carnival came to town every year and set up right there. And over there..." he pointed down a lone street now replace with townhouses...it was only one house on that whole block. That house was a free clinic for the residents of this neighborhood. The next street over, the elementary school that I went to was there. Neval Thomas. I read in the papers years ago that they closed it."

Rock sat riveted in his seat and turned in all directions. He was mesmerized by the filth, squalor, and abject poverty that was his old neighborhood. *Things really have changed in the last twenty years.* He observed the thugs and hustlers congregated in every courtyard and every corner. "I don't know why my nephew hasn't moved his mother out of this hellhole. Come on, Rho, let's go in."

They walked through a gate and found the building with 3730 on it. Up two flights of stairs, they stopped in front of apartment 301. Rock knocked on the door.

A female voice shouted. "Who is it?"

"It's your brother," Rock said with a smile.

The apartment door swung open. Rosetta Blackman grabbed at her chest. "Oh, my God!"

Rock rushed into the living room and grabbed his sister. He lifted her into the air and spent her around.

"Oh, my God! Rock, it's really you!"

Rock put his sister down but still held her close. He saw that she was crying and wiped her tears away. "What are you crying for, woman? You're supposed to be happy."

"I am happy, I just can't believe it's really you...that you're really here. In front of me. God...you're so fine... you look just like Daddy... I can't believe it. Thank you, Lord, thank you, thank you, thank you."

"Rosey, this is my woman. Her name is Rhoda." Rock said as he pulled Rhoda around him and put her at center stage.

Rosetta embraced Rhoda. "Hi ya doing, baby. It's good to finally meet you. Rock spoke about you all the time over the phone."

"He told me a lot about you, too," Rhoda responded.

"Why didn't you tell me you were coming...so that I could have done something...cook a meal...threw a party...something."

"That's why I didn't tell you. I didn't want you to do anything for me. You work hard enough as it is and I didn't want you to be making a big deal about me. You need to get as much rest as you can. Besides, I wanted to surprise you."

"Well, I'm definitely surprised. I thought them devils were gonna hold onto you for life. I thought you had a life sentence?"

"I did, but my lawyers found a loophole and it freed me."

"What about Beanie? Where is he?"

"He'll be home in a year or two. He had another sentence to finish. Where's my nephew?"

"Where are my manners? Sit down, please. Can I get you two something? Anything?"

Rhoda sat on the couch, Rock continued to stand.

"I can't believe that you're home. My big brother is finally home. Oh, my God! I can't believe it." Rosetta rushed into Rock's arms again and hugged him. "I'm so happy, I don't know what to do."

"Rosey, calm down. I'm here and I'm not going anywhere ever again."

100

In the Blink of an Eye

"I wish that Ma was still alive. She died with a broken heart. Her only wish was to see her only son free before she died. I'm glad that I lived to see the day that you came home. Thank you, Jesus!"

"I miss Ma and I wish that she could've been here, too. But, she's not and there ain't nothing that either one of us can do about that. The man upstairs does things on his own time and I accept that. He gave me a second chance at life and I plan to make the best of it. Where's George?"

"George is in Atlanta. He has a friend named David Battle that is in the music industry. They're shooting a video and he wanted George to be in it. When he hears that you're home, he's gonna go crazy. He really loves you. As a matter of fact, I'ma call him right now." Rosetta picked up her phone and dialed a number. George's voicemail picked up. "I can never reach that boy when I really need to. His answering machine came on. I'll call him back later. Right now, Rock, you and Rhoda have to eat something with me. We haven't shared a meal in decades. You both eat chicken, right?"

"Yeah, Rosey, we both eat chicken."

* * *

Later that night, while lying in the bed with Rhoda, Rock was finally able to catch his nephew on the phone.

"What's up nephew?"

"Uncle Rock?"

"It's me. How you doing, young boy?"

"Hold on for a minute. It's after eleven here in Atlanta. That means it's after twelve there in Indiana. How the hell are you still on the phone? You up in that joint making power moves, huh?"

Rock laughed. "Naw, young boy. I ain't making no power moves. I'm home."

"Go head with that bullshit, Unc. You ain't home. I wish you were though. Anyway, what's good? I see you got the new number from Moms."

101

"Gee, you think I'm bullshittin', huh? I'm home. I tell you what. Hang up the phone right now and call me right back at the number on your phone. You see the 301-area code, right?"

"That don't mean shit. You on somebody's three-way."

"Well hang up, call back, and see who answers that phone." Rock disconnected the call. A few seconds later, his phone run. It was George. "Yeah?"

"Uncle Rock you be bullshittin' too much. You got a cell phone in your cell, huh? That's right big boy, do that mutha-fucka."

"You still don't believe I'm on the bricks, huh?"

"Naw, Unc."

"A'ight. Hold on. I'ma let you holla at my baby." Rock passed the phone to Rhoda. "Tell him where I'm at."

"He's home, George. Believe it." Rhoda handed the phone back to Rock.

"Believe me, now?"

"You got a celly that sounds like a bitch. You ain't trickin' me, Unc. I know you ain't celling with no punk. That ain't a good look, Unc."

Rock laughed heartily. "You's a wild young nigga. Just call your mother and ask her and then call me back." He disconnected the call again.

A few minutes later, his phone rang again. It was George and when he answered the phone he could hear the excitement in his nephew's voice.

"Unc, it's on now. We about to do the muthafucka. When did you get released?"

"About eight days ago."

"And you're just calling me."

"I spent a week out of the country. I just got back today. When are you coming back to town?"

"The video should be a wrap in a day or so. I'll be back no later than Thursday. If this shit wasn't so important to my man Dave, I'd bounce right now. But I gotta see everything through. I got money invested in this nigga. I can't wait to see you though big boy."

"Same here, youngin. I got a few moves to make myself over the next few days. So, Thursday is perfect. I should be back from New York by then."

"New York? What's in New York, Unc?"

"An old friend."

"We gon' do it big, Unc. I'ma holla at my man Foo right now, and tell him to put something together for us. I gotta welcome you home the right way. It's only right that I do. We gonna pop some bottles and toast to your freedom. You down with that, Unc?"

"Sure, young boy. You put it together and I'll be there."

"That's love, Unc. You go ahead and get some rest. I'ma call you tomorrow after the video shoot. This your cell phone?"

"Yeah."

"A'ight. You take care, Unc, and tell the young girl that I said to be easy with the old man."

"I will, youngin'. I love you, nephew."

"I love you too, Unc. One love!"

Anthony Fields

In the Blink of an Eye

CHAPTER 18

"To Lil' Kim and nem/you know the women friends/ who carry the weight across state/ for gentlemen, yeah thanks to all the hustlers/ but most importantly, you the customer/ The Roc boys are in the building tonight/ Oh what a feeling, I'm feeling life/ You ain't gotta bring your paper out/ we the dope boys of the year, drinks is on the house/ The Roc boys are in the building tonight..."

"The Roc boys are in the muthafuckin building tonight...look at how I'm chillin', I'm killing this ice...you ain't even gotta bring your purses out, we the dope boys...drinks is on the house...Aye, Foo? Get that waiter over here, nigga." George said and then stood up. "Y'all hear the song...we the dope boys of the year...drinks are on the house. Free drinks for everybody in this bitch...it's on me." He shouted across the VIP room. George turned to the man seated at his right and said, "Welcome home, Uncle Rock. This shit been a long time coming. Things done came full circle, right here. We sitting in this muthafucka, fly as hell, sipping on thousand dollar bottles of champagne like we own this bitch. The last time we had drinks together, I was a kid sipping on baby apple juice or some shit. Hold on, Unc..."

George stood up again. "I wanna propose a toast...yeah. Let's toast to freedom. My uncle got popped in the 80's, gave them crackers twenty-five years and he still standing. Still looking good as a muthafucka and now he's free. So, let's toast to his freedom."

Everybody in the VIP room stood up and toasted his freedom.

Rhoda sat back down and kept her eyes on her man. Rock had, had two drinks already and was starting to look like he was done. It was her job to save him from himself. That was their deal. Looking at her watch, Rhoda saw that it was only a little after 1 a.m. The night was still young. She decided to let Rock enjoy himself for another hour or so. Sitting on Rock's left side, Rhoda half listened to what George was saying to Rock and half admiring him. Rock was dressed in a black single-breasted Georgio Armani Prive' suit, a black Armani silk shirt, and Armani shoes. The platinum Audemars watch was a gift from George that cost over a hundred thousand dollars and didn't have a stone in it. The watch accented the platinum and diamond cuff links that bore Rock's initials. They were a gift from her. Rock's low cut taper was lined up to precision and his waves looked like they had been sculpted into his head. The man was breathtaking and Rhoda was glad that he belonged to her.

Taking her eyes off Rock for a second, Rhoda glanced around the room. She was happy to see all her girls in the club as well. She locked eyes with Quanda and raised her glass. Quanda returned the gesture and nodded at her companion. Rhoda couldn't help but smile. The complete makeover that Quanda had put on Star was worthy of TV. She had to admit to herself that the girl was a beauty. Star reminded Rhoda of the girl who played Rudy on the *Cosby Show Keshia Knight Pulliam*. Star's hair was cut and layered and permed to perfection. Her dress was one that Rhoda recognized instantly. It was an Alfred Fiandaca. She had one just like it in her closet, only in a different color. When she spotted Star's tattoo on her chest from across the room, Rhoda felt a strange sense of pride. The No Holes Barred Crew had come a long way and now they were definitely in the building, representing to the fullest.

At a table, across from Quanda, in the back, sat Billie and her date. It was the first time that Rhoda had seen Chico since the late 80's and he hadn't really changed a bit. He was still sexy. She could see that from across the room. That made her stare at Rock again. A shiver ran up her spine. Rhoda crossed her legs in an attempt to calm her nerves. Her pussy was getting, soaking wet and she wanted Rock to know it.

As George held Rock's attention with his 'We can rule the world speech'. Rhoda grabbed Rock's hand and put it under the table. She guided him to her wet center and let his fingers do the rest. Try as she might, it was hard disguising the pleasure she felt building inside her as Rock's finger expertly danced over her clit and inside her pussy. Rhoda bit down on her bottom lip to keep from moaning. She glanced helplessly around the room to see if anybody was onto her and Rock's clandestine act. That's when she locked eyes with Sparkle. Sitting diagonally away from her, at a table by herself, Sparkle gave her a knowing smile. Rhoda held Sparkle's stare, squeezed her legs together tightly and came.

Sparkle laughed to herself. *"Nasty bitch."* She mumbled and took her eyes off Rhoda. She was ready to bounce. And as soon as her, date a baseball player for the Washington Nationals, came out of the restroom, she'd tell him that. Sparkle glanced at the banner hanging from the ceiling and read it. 'Welcome Home Rock!'. She was genuinely happy for Rock and Rhoda and wished them the best. Downing her fourth drink of the night, she was in a good mood despite the events of the last couple of weeks. Sparkle was still fucked up about Whistle getting killed. When she had first heard the news, she cried like a baby. She knew that she was responsible for his death.

No matter how much Vito lied and said that it was an accident, she knew that it wasn't and she was the person to blame. The whole time that she had sat in that church and attended his funeral, Sparkle wore her guilt on her face like a scarlet letter for the whole world to see. The word on the street was that Whistle's crew was killing people all over the city on a whim to whet their appetites for revenge.

"Foo? Where the rest of them bottles at?"

Sparkle glanced in the direction of the voice she heard and saw that it belonged to the host...George Foreman. George was shouting orders to his people. It wasn't hard to figure out that while Rock was the man of the hour being honored at the club, his nephew, George was the man-period. He had damn near the whole city on smash with drugs and his entourage was just as impressive. Sparkle looked at each face and smiled. She knew them all. She had also slept with most of them. Sitting around the table with George, Rock, and Rhoda was Walter 'Money' Henry,

Antone White, Woozie Fields, Kenny Garmagacoo, Titus Webster, Andy Daniels, Trey Manning, Henry Allen, and Bowlegged Dion Graham. There were several million dollars seated at the table and the whole club knew it. Just as her date sat down, Sparkle, looked over her shoulder and saw Vito sitting at the bar across from the VIP section. Anger and disgust washed over her in seconds, souring her mood instantly. "C'mon, Alex, I'm ready to bounce. I brought that thing with me that you like. Let's go and see if it still works."

Vito Miller watched the tall sexy woman and the muscular dude walk through throngs of people and head for the exit. The dude looked familiar but he couldn't place him. But knowing Sparkle like he did, the dude had to be a celebrity of some kind. He hadn't even known that she was inside the club until she walked right by him leaving the club. Even in a club full of bad bitches, it was hard not to notice Sparkle. If she wasn't so much of a whore, she would have made good wifey material. Just thinking about her made his dick hard, if it was any other time, Vito knew that he would have made a scene and forced Sparkle to leave with him, but tonight was different. He was stuck on his barstool as he watched the scene inside the VIP room.

Turning to his man Keith, Vito said, "It's a lot of loot in that room, yo."

"I'm hip, yo, I'm hip," Keith responded eyes glued to the same thing as Vito's. "Them niggas in there doing the muthafucka, yo. They act like they shooting a Muthafuckin' Jay-Z video or something."

"One of them niggas need to get me, yo," Vito said to his two partners as he sipped on his Remy mixed with a little lemonade.

Vito continued to stare at the tables in the VIP room. He had come to D.C. party and had stumbled up on the gathering of the year. The D.C. boys in the room were literally begging to be robbed by him and his men. "Yo, Vick, I tell you what, yo. Pick one of them niggas out and we gon' get him."

Vick carefully scanned the tables. He knew not to pick one of the obvious Big Willies. They rode with entourages that toted heat and a full-scale shootout in D.C. was what they didn't need. They needed an easy victim. In the back of the room was a lone table that sat away from all the others. At that table sat a dude draped in jewels sitting with a pretty brown skinned bitch. "I choose you, yo."

Outside the H2O nightclub, a crowd of men gathered and talked. After exchanging hugs and shaking hands, they all separated and walked to different vehicles. Rock and Rhoda climbed into his brand-new Mercedes Benz CL 64. George hopped into a mint green Range Rover accompanied by two women. When he pulled out of the parking lot, several SUV's pulled out behind him.

Chico hugged Billie and kissed her passionately as they leaned on Billie's Lexus. "I had a great time, boo, but I gotta go. Them halfway house people gon mess around and send me back to prison messing with your pretty ass."

"Boy, please," Billie said seductively. "You ain't seen this pretty ass yet, but when you do see it and get some of it, you gon wish you was back in prison."

"Damn! It's like that?" Chico asked as he got into the passenger seat of the Lexus.

In the car, they flirted, laughed and joked. They were so caught up in the moment, that neither of them noticed the black Dodge Charger that pulled into the street behind them and followed them.

Anthony Fields

CHAPTER 19

Quanda locked eyes with George as she slowly pulled both of her open toe Jimmy Choo sandals off. Next, she lifted her hips and pulled her thong down her legs. Quanda leaned back on the bed just enough to allow her date a clear shot at her shaved pussy. Then she stood and pulled the Valentino slip dress over her head. Without saying a word, she turned and motioned for Star to stand up. Quanda grabbed Star's hand and pulled her into her embrace. Then she kissed her full on the lips.

Tipsy and horny, Star didn't resist. Even as Quanda pulled her dress over her head, leaving her with only a thong on and her Gucci heels. Quanda glanced over her shoulder and saw George still standing, leaning on the wall by the door. He slowly sipped on a drink in his hand and nodded his head as if to say, *'Please continue'.*

In her heels, Star stood face to face with Quanda. Quanda methodically rubbed both of Star's bare breasts as if she was exploring and seeing them for the first time. Caught up in the moment, Star's nipples hardened under Quanda's touch and her heartbeat started to race. Quanda expertly licked, teased, and sucked on each nipple until soft purrs escaped Star's mouth. Knowing that Star was ready to be seduced, Quanda reached one hand into her thong and felt Star's pussy throbbing. Star gyrated her hips into Quanda's fingers and placed one hand on top of Quanda's head to push her down low.

Quanda caught the hint. She pulled at Star's thong and pulled it all the way down to her ankles. Star subserviently stepped each foot out of her thong. She was in a whole new world and was oblivious to the man leaning on the wall. For the moment, the only two people alive were her and Quanda. Quanda gently pushed Star backward until her body lay sprawled across the bed. Then Quanda unfastened the straps on both of Star's sandals and pulled them off. She wanted to start her sexual seduction from the bottom up. She kissed each of Star's toes and then moved up to her ankles. Quanda gently kissed her way up Star's legs.

She could smell the scent of Star's pussy nearby and it was like an aphrodisiac. Quanda wasted no more time. She found the core to Star's being and exploited it. Star's soft purrs became a full-grown roar as Quanda's tongue found her spot.

"Ooooohhhh, Quan...n...n. I'm a...a...about to cum...m...m in your mouth!"

Quanda stepped up her oral assault on Star's pussy. Just as she could've sworn that Star was speaking a foreign language, Quanda felt Star's body tense up, shiver, and then release itself. Star's body unleashed a stream of wetness that rivaled the levees breaking in New Orleans. Satisfied that her job was done, Quanda kept sucking on Star's clit just because she liked it. She brought Star to another body shaking orgasm and then climbed her body until they were face to face again. Star greedily latched onto Quanda's lips and tongue and kissed her passionately.

Stopping the kiss abruptly, Quanda stood up on the bed and walked over Star's body until she stood directly over her face. While staring directly at George, Quanda lowered herself onto Star's face. She grinded her pussy all over Star's face and in her mouth. Throwing her head back, Quanda rode Star's tongue as if it was a dick. Then she slowed down and winded her body like a snake. Quanda and George's eyes became locked in a mental embrace and neither one turned away. George watched as Quanda's face became distorted. He had fucked her enough to know when she was coming. To watch LaQuanda Jasper in action with a man or woman was well worth the price of admission for every show. Knowing Quanda well, he knew what else was next. After reaching an orgasm, Quanda like something in her mouth to snack on and it wasn't food. So, it was no surprise to him to see Quanda dip low and eat Star again.

Now engaged in an all-out 69, George watched the two women do them. He pulled at his zipper and freed his dick. Slowly, he stroked himself. As if she smelled his dick or at least sensed that one was in the room, Quanda looked up and saw him.

112

In the Blink of an Eye

She licked her lips and wiggled out of Star's embraced. He watched, waited, and stroked himself as Quanda slowly walked over to him and dropped down to her knees. She looked up into his eyes and held his gaze. Then without taking her eyes off him, she put his dick in her mouth and sucked it.

George closed his eyes and threw his head back. Quanda's head game was sick. She always made him moan like a bitch when she ate him. It was at that point when he was most vulnerable and his eyes told the story, so he closed them to hide that from Quanda. Just as he felt that he was getting ready to burst, she stopped sucking him. Before he could open his eyes and see what the problem was, she started again. The feeling was so intense that he had to grab the door knob and squeeze it.

George grabbed the back of Quanda's head and forced more of his dick into her mouth. The gagging sounds she made egged him on further. He felt the familiar stirring starting in his feet and knew that he was getting ready to cum in Quanda's mouth. A couple of deep pulls later, he did just that. Quanda's mouth felt like a vacuum siphoning all the cum out of him. George opened his eyes and looked down to see Quanda's pretty face as she swallowed his seed. But to his surprise, Quanda's face wasn't there. The eyes he now stared into belonged to Quanda's beautiful companion, Star.

Star couldn't remember exactly when it was that she had fallen asleep, but she knew that she hadn't been asleep that long. Her mind drifted back and captured images of the things that she and Quanda had done to George. And at that moment Star didn't know whether to be satisfied that she had played her part well or be repulsed at the fact that she had swallowed George's semen not once but twice. It was the first time that she had ever done such a thing. Star didn't know whether to laugh or cry. Her life was now a never-ending movie reel. Stirring in the bed, she expected to open her eyes and find Quanda or George or both in bed with her, but they weren't there. Star quietly slipped out of bed and tiptoed to the bedroom door which was slightly ajar. She could hear voices but she couldn't see faces. Star focused her ears on the conversation in the next room...

"...Trinidad. He left town but his organization is still in place. What if I told you that I know some people and that they'd guarantee you a better price than what you're paying now?"

"Would I? Hell yeah, I would. What do I look like? An idiot? If you know a muthafucka that's willing to give me a hundred bricks at less than twelve a key, holla at your boy."

"I'll make a few phone calls and then let you know something in a few days, how's that?"

"That's a bet. But right now, I'm focused on what we can do today. You know what my dick does early in the morning, right?"

"Of course, he gets up before you do."

"Well, I need you to make him lay back down."

"What would you like me to do to him?"

"Go get something to lubricate that ass and I'ma let him tell you where he wanna be."

Star ran back to the bed and jumped under the covers. She heard Quanda enter the room but pretended to be asleep. A minute or so later, she heard the door to the bedroom shut. She lay in the bed and thought about the situation that she was in. Eventually, sleep overtook her. Then Star was awakened by Quanda's guttural screams that came from the next room. She had heard those screams before and knew exactly what was going on in the next room.

"Fuck this ass, nigga! Fuck it harder!"

What she had just heard confirmed what she already knew. Star smiled and forced herself to go back to sleep.

CHAPTER 20

Sparkle pulled her Infiniti behind Billie's Lexus. *I ain't never going on another date with that nigga again.* Alex Montoya, the star shortstop for the Nationals had taken the meaning of freak and redefined it. It was one thing for her to have to strap on a dildo and him doggy style, but when he turned around and started sucking on the dildo afterward, that was too much. The lyrics of the old Lil' Kim songs came to mind…

"…9 out of 10 niggas ain't shit/ and 3 out of 5 niggas sucking dick…"

Ain't that the gospel truth? Sparkle thought as she walked up the stairs to the townhouse. *Homo thug ass niggas.*

In the living room, she ran into Billie lying on the couch with a rag over her eyes. "Billie, what's up, boo? Rough night, huh?"

Billie lifted the rag on her eyes and saw Sparkle standing over her. She recovered her eyes and said, "I drunk too much of that Ace of Spade shit. Fuck what the people who make Cristal said about black rappers or whatever, I'm about to be the only bitch popping bottles of Cris, again. The Cris was easier on a bitch head after the fact. My head is pounding right now."

"You gon' be a'ight. You need me to cook you somethin'…"

Billie quickly interjected. "I just told you my head id killing me. You want my stomach to be fucked up too?"

"Fuck you, then." Sparkle said offended.

"Face, it, boo. You can't cook, Spark. We love you and all that shit, but you gotta stop tryna force that shit on us. No bullshit Spark, that shit ain't cool."

Sparkle sat on the couch across from Billie. "Bitch, like I just said, fuck you. I like my cooking. Besides, it beats that fake ass cuisine that the H2O served us."

"I didn't eat that shit, either. That's why my head is probably killing me. I didn't have anything on my stomach. I should've eaten something."

"Besides dick, you mean?"

"Ha, ha, ha. You got a rack of jokes, huh? You gon make me warm your Amy Winehouse looking ass up in here. You got the nerve to talk. With your champion dick eating ass."

"Recognize the real when you see it, then. That's why I get paid the big bucks and you what's left." Sparkle gloated.

"Yeah right. And then you woke up. But anyway, speaking of big bucks, somebody robbed Chico after I dropped him off at the halfway house."

"What?! Somebody robbed Chico?"

"Yeah, they got my baby. He called me about three hours ago and told me. He said three niggas ambushed him right in front of Hope Village. They hit him for his watch, his chain, and all the money he had on him.

"Thirsty ass niggas. Ain't nobody do that but them dusty ass, thirty ass Langston Lane niggas. They always robbing somebody. If all them bamma ass niggas wasn't popping pills, wearing them tight ass clothes, claiming Bloods and tryna be Lil' Wayne, maybe their money would be right. That nigga Gary Freeman need to stop sweating me and help his lil' homies get some money. I know Chick fucked up about that shit, huh?"

"To be honest with you, he didn't sound all that pissed off. He sounded more annoyed that anything. If them niggas knew who he was, they wouldn't have tried that shit."

"Shid. Them niggas up the Lane don't give a fuck. Them niggas would rob Jesus for his cloak and sandals. I'm about to take me a hot bath and then get some sleep. I'll see you when I get up." Sparkle said, got up, and walked up the stairs. She walked into the bathroom and ran hot water into the tub. A thought crossed her mind as she took off her clothes.

"Three niggas ambushed him..."

She thought about seeing Vito in the club sitting at the bar. He was with two other dudes. *Did Vito and his men rob Chico? Naw, it's just a coincidence, that's all.*

Sparkle shook those thoughts from her mind and stepped into the tub.

116

In the Blink of an Eye

* * *

Fleming 'Chico' Carey laid awake in his bunk at the Hope Village halfway house. He had a lot on his mind and none it involved the robbery he was a victim of that early morning. The things that he had lost in the robbery were insignificant to him. The platinum chain with the iced-out cross was one that Block had given him when he first got home. The Bulgari watch was one that Keith Holmes took off his wrist and put on the first time they saw each other. And the 2700 dollars was pocket change that he planned on spending at the club, but everything ended up being on George Foreman. It could all be replaced. Chico knew that if he was on the streets that niggas was going to take care of him. They had to or feel his wrath. To them, he was the Tony Fortune of the 2000's. Everybody in D.C. knew what his gun game was like. And they didn't want to unleash the newly freed beast.

Although he'd been gone for eighteen years, his reputation was still large and lurking over niggas shoulders like the bogeyman. Chico thought about all the blood, sweat, and tears he had lost in the last eighteen years. He visually remembered every beef, every stabbing, and every time he got stabbed or went knife to knife with other gladiators. He thought about his dream deferred or better yet destroyed. His boyhood ambitions of becoming a world champion prizefighter had long since been shattered. He was thirty-six years old and not as quick and as sharp as he used to be.

Prison had taken its toll on his body and his life. And that's what fueled the fire burning inside of him. That fire is one that slowly kindled over the course of eighteen years. Chico thought all the years he was away from his family and how his father had passed away years ago and he couldn't even attend the funeral. His daughter was now nineteen years old and their bond wasn't what it was supposed to be. His eighteen-year-old son didn't even know who he was. Every time he laid back and thought about the last eighteen years, he got angry.

117

That anger had turned into hate many years ago. Chico then thought about the person that was the blame for it all. Everything that he had missed, lost, or barely held onto was because of her. The women that single-handedly ruined his life. The thought of that fateful night over eighteen years ago came rushing back to him like a horror movie...

He had been inside of Betsy's house when they heard the gunshots. Gunshots were so prevalent in the city back then that he didn't even pay them any mind. He kissed Betsy and his daughter Brittany goodbye and the left the apartment. Heading back to Paradise projects, his stomping grounds, he needed to check on his money. As he exited the building, he saw a woman bent over the body of a man. She was crying hysterically. As he approached the woman, she looked up and locked eyes with him. Chico detected movement in his peripheral view. He turned quickly to see a man dart from the bushes and run up 58th street.

Growing up in the streets had taught him when to mind his own business, so he kept walking to his car. He looked back once and saw the woman was still looking at him. Chico quickly left the scene. One hour later, while sitting on the hood of his car in the projects, unmarked and marked police cars came from every direction. They surround his car.

"Keep your hands where we can see them, Chico!" They shouted as they leaped from their vehicles with guns drawn. He was handcuffed and read his rights. Then eventually charged with second-degree murder. As he sat over D.C. jail awaiting trial, the irony of his situation didn't escape him. Out of all the people that he had killed and got away with, he was now locked up for a murder that he didn't commit...

Chico sat up in his bunk and thought about the woman at the scene of the murder. She had come to court and told the jury that he was the person responsible for the death of her brother. He was found guilty based on her testimony alone and sentenced to fifteen years to life in prison. He did eighteen years before the parole board decided that, that was enough.

118

In the Blink of an Eye

Eighteen years of his life wasted, for a crime that he didn't commit. Chico stood up and lifted his mattress. He grabbed an envelope that contained personal papers. From that envelope, he extracted a tattered photo. The face of the woman that had taken the last eighteen years of his life stared back at him. The photo was seventeen years old, but it was as good as any. His eyes focused on the young girl that stood with her mother. In the photo, she had to be seven or eight years old.

The woman in the photo had taken eighteen years of his life for no reason at all and soon he would have his revenge. He promised himself all those years ago, that he would survive whatever prison threw his way just to make sure that he would have his day. He wanted to know why the woman lied on him. He wanted to take the rest of her life away from her, too. After all, it was only fair.

Anthony Fields

In the Blink of an Eye

CHAPTER 21

The traffic light turned green. Rock drove through the light and made a left turn into the new shopping center on Alabama Avenue. He then made a sharp left turn in the parking lot and headed towards the end of a long row of stores as he had been instructed. He spotted the sign that read Sanders and Ross Home Improvement Inc. and pulled into an empty parking space.

When he walked into the store, Rock saw a pretty young woman at the counter. "Excuse me, sweetheart, I'm here to see Tommy Ross."

"Mr. Ross is in the back. He told me you were coming. Go straight through aisle two and you'll see the door that leads to his office."

Rock followed the girl's instructions and found Tommy's office. Tommy Ross looked up from his computer and recognized him instantly. He stood up and came from behind the desk.

"Rock Muthafuckin' Blackman. It's good to see you, slim." Tommy said as he grabbed Rock up into a bear hug.

"Same here, Tommy," Rock responded as he broke the embrace. "I see that time has been kind to you, old timer."

"Me? You, the one walking in here looking like you ain't aged in years. The penitentiary will preserve a muthafucka, though. How is Bean and Fox doing? Have a seat, slim." Tommy sat on the front of his desk while Rock took a seat in the chair that faced it.

"You know how it is in there. They're doing as good as can be. You know that Fox is still the man in there. He sixty-four years old and in tip top shape, daring a muthafucka to jump out there. He sees the board soon; hopefully, they'll let him go. And Beanie will be home in about eighteen months."

"It's been how many years since we last seen each other, Rock?" Tommy asked.

"About twenty-two years or so. We were on the Hill down Lorton. I think you had a Jheri curl back then."

121

Tommy laughed. "Sure did. That and a vicious dope habit. When I came home and got custody of Roscoe. I had to give that shit up. I had a responsibility. That boy meant more..." Tommy got a little choked up. "Roscoe meant a lot to me."

Rock felt Tommy's pain. "I know how you felt about the kid and he felt the same way about you. He spoke highly of you all the time. Roscoe meant a lot to a lot of people, Tommy. His death fucked everybody up. Between you and me, Tom, we got a cake baked for Carlos Trinidad's ass. His day is coming and that's on my dead mother."

"Carlos Trinidad. That's a name I haven't heard in a few years. After Roscoe died, word on the streets was that he took off with Roscoe's girlfriend Angel."

"We gon find him and make shit right, trust and believe that. Other than that, what's up with you, Tommy?"

"I been busy. Baby boy left me everything he owned. Including the nightclub that he was killed in. that club was his dream and the matriculation of it was a journey within itself. Other than wanting to give you the money that Roscoe left you, I asked you to come over here for another reason. I always wanted to do something that I knew that Roscoe would have wanted. The time just never materialized since I was doing so much other stuff. But now that you're home, I believe that now is the perfect time. And that you are the perfect person to do it."

"Stop, beating around the bush and tell me what it is," Rock said impatiently.

"Okay. I think that you should re-open the nightclub that Roscoe built and loved. He put his heart and soul into that place." He paused to let his proposal sink into Rock's head. "I want you to have it, Rock. You'll be the owner. The building is paid for. All you have to do is gut it out and start over. Destroy and rebuild. Roscoe had a lot of money when he died, Rock. He left you 2.5 million dollars. You and Beanie. That's more than enough to get started. And whatever else you need, I'll supply it. You can use my contractors and employees. There's a thousand miegos in the city that'll work dirt cheap. I have faith in you, Rock. If you decide to do it, I know you can pull it off. It's a moneymaker, Rock, do it for you. Do it for Roscoe."

Can I pull it off? Rock sat and contemplated everything that Tommy had just said to him. He did want to go into legitimate business, he just never thought that would be the nightclub business. *Would rebuilding the club really honor his slain comrade by resurrecting his dream? Was he destined to be sitting here having this conversation with Roscoe's father? Didn't he believe that everything happened for a reason?* The more Rock sat and thought about Tommy's offer, the more he warmed to the idea. "Give me a few days to think everything through and I'll be come back here to see you and give you an answer. Is that okay with you?"

"Definitely." Tommy Ross replied. "Take as long as you need."

***

Rock repeatedly tapped his keys lightly on the table as he sat in a booth at the Hard Rock Café in downtown D.C. He turned Tommy's proposal over and over in his head and weighed the pros and cons. The pros outweighed the cons and he was seriously considering accepting the offer. Besides, it was more about honoring Roscoe than anything. How could he decline? Just as he made up his mind, Rock looked out the window and saw Rhoda's new candy apple red convertible Bentley pull up out front. She stepped out of the car wearing Chanel sunglasses and an aura that was hard to match. The skirt she wore fitted her ass like a latex glove. As he watched her sashay into the restaurant, Rock thought briefly about how Rhoda made her money. Most people would think that he was crazy for wifing her, but he didn't see Rhoda as a whore. He saw her as a woman who did what she had to do to survive. Her choices were not ones that he would have wanted his sister, mother, or daughter to make, but that was neither here nor there. She had told him when they first got serious about one another. *"Take me as I am or have nothing at all."* He chose to accept her for who she was. Their life started now and she was no longer taking dates. What she did in the past was just that... her past.

Rock stood up and hugged Rhoda. They kissed. Then he pulled her seat out for her and waited for her to sit before he sat.

"What's up baby?" Rock asked. "How your day been?"

"It's been a little hectic, but I'm good. I had to go to the bank and go off on them crackers up in there. The heifer that manages the NHBC account gon tell me that I can no longer transact business over the phone and that I had to come down to the bank until further notice. I calmly drove down there and acted a cold-blooded ass in there. Needless to say, after I went off on the bitch, her boss got some act right in her and there was peace in the land again."

Rock smiled. He loved the way Rhoda went from savvy businesswoman to ghetto hood rat in seconds. He had the best of both worlds in her. "Okay then, Rocky. Go Rocko, go."

Rhoda's tension evaporated as she laughed at Rock. "Sparkle has been all over me with conspiracy theories; Billie has slowed her hustle because she believes that Chico is her knight in shining armor that has come to take her away from here. As we speak Quanda is moving Star into the townhouse with us, so I spent all morning moving my stuff out of the spare bedroom and moving it to the basement. So, like I said, my day had been a little hectic. What about? What did Roscoe's father want?"

"He gave me a lot of money that Roscoe left me and I decided to get into the nightclub business," Rock said and waved over a waitress.

"The nightclub business? Why, the nightclub business?"

"I didn't choose it, it chose me. Roscoe's father wants me to rebuild, own, and operate Club Immorality."

"What?"

In the Blink of an Eye

* * *

"Is this all the stuff that you have?" Quanda asked as she stuffed the last of Star's bags into the trunk of her BMW. "This looks like just the shit you gained since you been down with us."

"It is everything I got since I been down with y'all. I did what you said and burned all that other shit." Star replied, proud that she could think fast on her feet.

Suddenly the door to the rooming house opened and Star almost panicked. She watched horrified as the old man that slept beneath her exited the house. He didn't say a word as he walked through the gate and headed up the block.

"Who was that?" Quanda asked.

"Uh…that's my…grandfather. Yeah, my grandfather."

"Well, why didn't he speak to us?"

Star took her index finger and circled it around her ear. "He's a little messed up in the head. Vietnam really fucked him up. C'mon, let's get out of here." *Before somebody else come out that damn door.*

Quanda got in the car and pulled out into the street. As they made their way down Good Hope Road, Quanda's cell phone rung. "Hello."

"Quan, what's good, girlfriend?" From the sound of the voice, she knew it was George.

"What's up with you handsome?"

"Did you holla at your folks for me?"

"I was gonna call you later and tell you that everything is everything."

"Oh yeah? 10th Street with Perry Riley or Tyler Polumbus?"

Quanda was a big Redskins fan and so was George, so his code words hit directly home Perry Riley's jersey number was 50 and Tyler Polumbus was 75. "Polumbus on game day."

"Good looking out, boo. I got something for you when I see you."

"I'll look forward to that when I see you. I'll be in touch." Quanda disconnected that call and then made one. Scrolling through her phone, she found the number for B.F. and then pressed the talk button on her phone. A few seconds later, B.F.'s baritone voice bellowed. "What's up?"

"B.F., this Quanda."

"My fault, sis. This cranker bitch been blowing my phone up all day and she got me mad as shit. You ready to scoop that?"

"You know what I like."

"True dat. I'm out here right now, come on through." B.F. said and hung up.

Quanda hit her blinker and then made the left turn onto MLK Avenue and headed to Barry Farms.

***

Derrick 'B.F.' Simpson stood on the basketball court at the top of Steven's Road, but himself, shooting jump shots into a metal bike rim mounted on the pole. He knew that Quanda was going to call him at some point today so he made sure he brought the money out for her. B.F. thought about the 95 eight balls in a Ziploc bag in his boxer briefs and screamed out, "Fuck the police!" He was clocking more money now than he ever had in his life. Then suddenly, his thoughts switched to his man Whistle. Whistle was supposed to still be there getting money with him. But that wasn't the case because somebody had killed him. After he had received word of Whistle's death, he hooked up with a few good men and ripped shit up for his fallen comrade. B.F. wasn't exactly sure how many bodies fell, but the local news was calling the last few weeks the bloodiest month of the year. Anybody that they thought might've killed Whistle got it. Their wrath spared no one. The sounds of a horn blowing snapped him out of his reverie. Looking at the metallic blue BMW, he knew it was Quanda.

"Sit right here, I'll be right back. When we leave here we going out Arlington to the American Service Center. It's time to cop you a ride. You can't keep riding shotgun with me. And don't worry about money because this one is on George.

126

In the Blink of an Eye

Star laid back in her seat and watched Quanda walk across the street. She thought about what Quanda had just said. Being from the area, she knew that the American Service Center sold nothing but Benzes. Quanda was about to buy her a Mercedes. On George, she said. The mere thought of it gave her the chills. Star remembered what she had done to George Foreman that night. And for that she as being rewarded a Benz. *I'm in the wrong line of work, for real.*

Anthony Fields

CHAPTER 22

George ran his hand down the length of the hood of the Benz. "Unc, this a bad muthafucka right here. The CL65, huh? I never heard of it. You been home three weeks and you got a whip that puts my whole fleet to shame. That's crazy."

"It's not what you know all the time, youngin', it's who you know. This joint ain't even available on the American market, yet."

"What's so special about this joint, though?"

"This baby here has 612 horses under the hood. A 6.0-liter engine and 738 pounds of foot/bi-turbo. It's a V12 and it goes from zero to sixty in four seconds flat. It also has all the amenities of the Maybach, for less money."

"How much is this joint running?"

"It was a gift, youngin, but the tag on it is like one seventy-five. Like I said, it ain't always what you know, but who you know. Ride with me for a while, I got something I need to run by you."

"Aye, Tay, you and L go head and bounce. I'ma jump in the Benz with Unc. When I'm ready for y'all to scoop me, I'll call you."

"You got your hammer on you?" Tay asked.

"No doubt," George replied.

"A'ight, holla back."

"C'mon, Unc, let me see what this joint can do."

"...I'm in my cool whip/inside Jell-O/ hopped up out that pretty muthafucka/ like hello.../Hello/ Hello, ladies how Y'all doing/ That nigga crazy girl...don't say nothing to him/ Dey know, dey know/got white, lo-lo/take what/Rob who? (Bloc)hello..."

Rock hit a button on the steering wheel and turned the music in the car down, "Nephew, do you remember a young cat named Roscoe?"

"The one that got killed out Big Sandy in the pen?"

"Naw. That was Vincent Smith. I'm talking about the other Roscoe."

"Oh, yeah, of course. Who don't remember slim? His whole life was the shit that books get written about. Small time stick boy who had half the city shook some years back. Him and his man Moe. He went on a lick and killed everybody in the house. His man snitched, he went in, did a bid and came back out. He got on like a muthafucka and him and his cousin moved more weight in the city than Playful Edwards and nem. They had record labels, rap groups, a nightclub, and all kinds of shit. Why? What about him?"

"The dude that Roscoe killed on that lick he went on was the same nigga that ratted on me and Beanie and got us all that time. So, naturally, when Roscoe came to Terre Haute, we looked out for him. I was the one that went over his court transcripts and found all the loopholes in his shit. That's how he got home. When he got to the streets, I hooked him up with a friend of mine in New York. That's how he got all the work to flood the city with. In return, he had to pay mine and Beanie's lawyers for our appeals. He kept it real and did what he was supposed to do. That's how I got home."

"Damn, that's wild, Unc."

"I know, huh? We were supposed to be out here together. That was the plan. It just didn't work out like that."

"What happened with slim."

"Who, Roscoe?"

"Yeah."

"Carlos Trinidad happened. He…"

"Wait a minute." George interrupted. "What does Carlos Trinidad have to do with Roscoe?"

"Everything. He was the one who had Roscoe and his whole team killed."

George reclined his seat and digested what his uncle had just said. The first thing that came to mind was Quanda. Quanda had brokered a deal for him with Trinidad's people. He was suddenly very confused. *Where does his loyalties lie?*

130

"And." Rock continued. "We gonna kill his ass the first chance we get."

The seventy-five keys that he was gonna get a week at ten a key was too much of a good deal to renege on based on a personal vendetta of his uncle's. *Hell. I didn't even know Roscoe.* George decided to keep his cards close to his chest and reveal nothing. He would see how things played out before making a hard decision.

"That brings me to what I want to talk to you about. Roscoe was killed when his nightclub exploded. His father Tommy, whom I know from back in the day, inherited everything that Roscoe owned. He just offered me a deal that I can't refuse. He gave me full ownership of the club with no strings attached. He wants me to rebuild it in memory of Roscoe. He believes and I agree that Roscoe would want the club to go on."

"And"

"And, I'ma do it. I got the money to do it and Roscoe's father is offering the use of his companies and employees. The reason I'm telling you all this is because I want you to be a part of this."

"I don't know, Unc. Me, in the club business...I don't know about that."

"What the fuck you mean, you don't know? This is the opportunity of a lifetime. You can legitimize your drug money. Remember the other day when we were up in the H2O?"

"Yeah."

"Remember how animated you became when that 'Roc Boys' came on? You don't even have to bring your paper out...we the dope boys of the year...drinks are on the house...remember that?"

"How could I forget?"

"Remember how you felt at that moment? Remember when you said, "We sippin' thousand dollar bottles of champagne in here like we own this bitch? Well, youngin, your words were prophetic because now we can own the bitch."

"What would be my role in all this?" George asked.

"Your name will be included in all the paperwork, thereby making instantly legitimate. You got a team of young soldiers. We give them security jobs and legitimize them. But, the club will be completely off limits to shady dealings. No drugs or drug deals brokered in the club. I find out that you cross me on that, you're out. Non-negotiable."

"I feel that. And what's all that gonna cost me?"

"A million cash. That is if you can raise a million cash."

"*Raise a million*? Unc, you got your nephew fucked up. I ain't out here on no nickel and dime shit. I can give you that right now. The more I think on it, the more I'm feeling that. Once I hit you with the scratch, when does everything go into effect?"

"I can have the paperwork drawn up whenever you ready. I already got a team of lawyers on standby. The gutting and all that should take about six months and then we start rebuilding. We gonna make Club Immorality bigger and better than it was the first time. If all goes well, we expand. New York, L.A. So, what's up, do we have a deal?"

A bright smile lit up George's face. He reached his hand out and shook his uncle's hand. "I knew we were about to do something big, but this I never imagined. You got yourself a deal, Unc. Now, hit the beltway and open this bitch up. I wanna see what them 600 horses can do."

132

Six months later...

Anthony Fields

CHAPTER 23

"Most women these days are a little shy about their bodies. Even if you have a top-notch dime piece, in bed she's gonna worry about whether you like her body. Tell her whatever you need to tell her, you gotta get her to trust you enough to allow you to get between her legs. Beautiful ain't it? Nothing makes a woman more unique than her pussy. Pussies come in all different shapes, sizes, and colors. Some are tucked inside the flesh and some have big pretty lips that come out to greet you. You have to learn to appreciate your woman's unique qualities. Women are more verbal than men, especially during sex, at least I think so. We respond better to verbal love. Meaning, the more we talk nasty to each other, the easier it'll be to make us cum. So, every time you rub, pet, or stroke her pussy, talk to her about it."

"Man, I already know all this shit." Smoke Mahdi said in an exasperated tone.

Rhoda laughed. "Evidently, you must don't. Since it was your wife who paid me to teach you and your men how to properly eat a pussy. Maybe she's just getting you back? I don't know. All I know is, I was paid good money to give this class and that's what I'm gonna do. Do you have any other comments, Smokey?"

"Naw. Go ahead, Rho. Do you."

"Thank you. When you guys get face to face with your woman's pussy, you can't just shake your head and let your tongue go wild. You have to gently pull the pussy lips apart and look at her inner lips. Then lick them a little. You spread the lips open until you find her clit. Women have clits of all different sizes, just like men have different sized dicks. The size of the clit doesn't mean a thing as far as her capacity to have orgasms. All it means is that more of her is hidden under the foreskin.

"This is important, guys. Whenever you touch your woman's clit, make sure that your finger is wet. Lick it or moisten it with juices from her. The clit doesn't have juices of its own it's extremely sensitive. Your finger will hurt her if it's dry. Women love to be teased. The inside of her thigh is her most tender spot. Kiss and lick her there with the tip of your tongue. Make her anticipate you eating her. Lick the crease where her leg joins her pussy. Let me stop right here and bring my ladies into the room."

Rhoda walked to a door that leads to an adjoining suite and knocked on the door. The door opened and in walked Quanda, Sparkle, Billie, and Star.

"Ladies, grab you a man and find you a comfortable place to sit," Rhoda announced, and then watched as Billie grabbed Nehemiah Hampton, Sparkle paired off with Jayvan Allen, Quanda picked Eric Hicks and Star walked over to Smoke. "Star you go with Mr. Keith Dublin over there, Smokey Mahdi belongs to me. Everybody ready? Okay ladies, put those pussies on display. Fellas, this is called on the job training...hands on. We gon put them tongues to the test. Especially yours Smokey..." Rhoda said as she slipped off her thong panties. "...since you say..." she stepped out of her heels "...you already know..." Rhoda sat down on a lazy boy chair and lifted her skirt. She put one foot on each armrest. "...how to eat pussy. I'll be the judge of that. Y' all ready?"

After a chorus of yeahs and let's go, the lesson continued.

"Okay, guys, use your tongue to separate the pussy lips. When they open, run your tongue up and down the layers of the pussy flesh. Gently spread her legs apart with your hands...Everything must be...done gently...unless she asks for it rough. Now stick your tongue...in her pussy...hole...yeah...like that. Tongue-fuck her...Damn! This feels too damn good...this will tease the hell...out of her...and by now she wants you to pay attention to the clit. Look at the clit...see if it's hard and sticking out. If it is...lick it. If you don't see it...it's still waiting for you underneath...bring your tongue up to the top of the slits and feel around her clit...oooh yes...lick the skin that covers it and it'll come out...Pull the pussy lips apart and flick your tongue against the clit.

"...yeah...like that. When you sense that she's about to cum...make your...lips...into an O and put her clit...in your...mouth. Suck on it...gently... and wait for a reaction. If she doesn't react...suck harder...if she does react...still suck her harder. When she lifts her pelvis into the air with the tension of her rising orgasm, move with her...her...every move and...ride with her. Hol...l...d...d...o...o ti...ti...tight and keep...p...p your mouth o...o...on her cl...i...i...it! Ooooh shit! I'm coming! I'm coming!" Rhoda wrapped her legs around Smoke's face and locked her ankle behind his head. Then she came.

"Yes...indeed." She said as she unlocked her legs. "What are you tryna get up for? Class is still in session, keep licking, boy. Take two fingers, fellas, and slide them inside her. One is too skinny and three is too wide. Slide your fingers inside her...slow...now a little faster, fuck her with your fingers...find a rhythm...listen to her breathing...she'll let you know if you're on to something or not...By sucking her clit and finger-fucking her at the same time, you're stimulating her more than you would by just giving her dick alone. Move your tongue in and out of her pussy...alternate...your fingers with your tongue...I'm coming again! Ooooohhh...boy...I'm cumming...fuck...fuck:..yeah...yeah...shit! Smoke...e...e...e...y! Damn!" It took her a minute to recover but when she did, Rhoda said, "I lost myself for a minute there, Where were we?" she opened her eyes and looked around the room. Nobody was paying her any attention. The oral sex session had turned into a full fledged fuck fest. Quanda was on the coffee table, on her back, with Eric pounding away inside her. Star was on the couch with her legs pressed all the way back and Keith long stroked her. Billie had Nehemiah standing up while she deep throated him and Sparkle was on all fours with Jayvan behind her.

"Let your men know that they gotta pay for all this," Rhoda said to smoke as she fixed her clothes. Smoke laughed, then went into his pocket and produced a wad of cash. He counted out five thousand dollars and handed it to Rhoda. "Consider the bill paid in full."

* * *

Pushing the Bently Coupe around the Capital Beltway, Rhoda glanced at the dashboard and saw that she was fastly approaching 140. The Continental GT maxed out at 200rpm, so she was good. After leaving the suite at the Raddison, she felt the for speed to clear her mind. That was the reason that she had dropped over a hundred grand on the luxury sports car in the first place. Somewhere lurking in the cut, Rhoda knew that Maryland State Troopers were lying in waiting to catch people speeding. To counter that, she made sure to take her thong panties back off when got in the car. The thong was in her Prada bag, right by her wallet, waiting to be seen. If she was stopped, Rhoda knew how to avoid a speeding ticket. As her shoeless, pedicured toes pressed down on the gas pedal, she allowed her skirt to rise higher and higher until her shaved pussy was semi-exposed. The cool air that rushed into the car found her center and gave it goose bumps. The goose bumps caused her to get wet down there. Then just as suddenly as it started, it dissipated. Slowing the Bentley, Rhoda saw that up ahead was traffic. Checking her watch, she realized that she had driven herself right in the middle of rush hour traffic.

"Shit!" Rhoda shouted and smacked the steering wheel. Sitting idle in the car would only make her mind wander and that was what she was trying to avoid. As the minutes crept by and the cars in front of her, moved along at a snail's pace, Rhoda thought back to what had just happened at the hotel. Although she hadn't let Smoke put his dick in her, he did finger fuck her and eat her pussy. So, technically she had broken her promise to Rock, or had she?

In the Caribbean, she promised him that she would still lead the NHBC, but she wouldn't take any dates and that, that part of her life was over. For the past six months, she'd kept that promise with no problems until now. Rhoda wasn't exactly sure if she had cheated or not. The question was did oral sex constitute sex? Did there have to be vaginal, oral, or anal penetration to be guilty of infidelity? Did a finger penetrating count as real penetration? Rhoda had no clue but she still felt kind of bad. When she had agreed to teach Smoke and his friends to eat pussy, she hadn't originally planned to become one of the demonstration props. But in the heat of the moment, she had become just that. Although she vowed to never keep anything from Rock, Rhoda decided that the afternoon episode would stay between her and those in room 2012. What happened at the Raddison would stay at the Raddison.

The silence in the car was getting too loud, so she turned on the radio. On WPGC 95.5, *Jennifer Hudson's 'Spotlight'* was on. She sang along to the record until it went off. When T. Pain's latest cut came on, she changed the station. *I'm tired of his funny looking, big bamma hat wearing ass. Him and Lil' Wayne troll looking asses are on every other song on the radio. They need to fall back.* Rhoda switched the music to the *K. Michelle* CD. The first cut on the CD made her think about her girls.

She loved all the girls with all her heart, but maybe it was time to start a separate, different life. She wanted a normal life with a few kids and a dog. She had been trying to figure out a way to talk to Rock about her feelings. But whenever she got her nerves up he would always mention something about the club he was rebuilding to honor Roscoe. The thought alone always made him smile and that smile would cut off the words in her throat. How could she be so selfish? Didn't Rock have a right to dream, live his life, and honor his dead friend, if that's what he wanted to do? It wouldn't be fair to him to steal his joy. So, Rhoda had decided to just sit back and take the ride. It was the only thing to do. Nobody in the crew knew what her feelings were either. *Would they even care?* In the last six months, they had all blown up even more and prospered. Life couldn't be better financially for the No Holes Barred Crew.

Star, the newest member of the crew had surpassed everybody's expectations and emerged as the new 'star' of the crew. She booked the most dates and stacked the most money. And word was she was the nastiest bitch in the crew, hands down. Her burgundy Mercedes-Benz SL 550 with the peanut butter leather was known all around town. And Billie, God Bless her soul, still did her thing but girlfriend was in love. Her heart and mind were always on Chico. Quanda was still Quanda but something was different about her, but Rhoda couldn't tell what it was. Sparkle had overheard Quanda on the phone with her brother one day speaking in code and it sounded to her like Quanda was setting up a drug deal. But she wasn't sure so Rhoda never said a word.

Sparkle, who always seemed to be jealous of Star, was still a bad bitch and her skills were still in high demand everywhere, but Rhoda noticed that Sparkle had become very withdrawn. It was strange because everybody was so used to Sparkle's extroverted talkative nature. She was always in somebody's business and talking about people, but not anymore. Her mood swings were unpredictable and her drinking was borderline alcoholic status. Rhoda wanted to talk to her but Sparkle was so hard to catch up with nowadays.

The time was never right when she did see her. As bad as Rhoda wanted to lead a different life, she knew that the girls needed her so she had to stay. But that didn't mean that she had to live with them. She had moved out of the townhouse and into a four bedroom, six and a half bathroom, three level Colonial style red brick house that sat on over 1.6 acres of land in Montgomery County, Maryland. The house was still sparsely furnished but her and Rock loved it.

Rhoda thought about Rock riding around in his smoke gray Rolls Royce Phantom and smiled. In a lot of ways, Rock was like a kid in a candy store. All the minor things that people took for granted every day meant a lot to him. Rhoda attributed that to his twenty-five years spent in his prison. It was impossible for him to get all those years back so Rock was determined to live the years he had left to the fullest. And no matter where that took him, she planned to be there forever by his side.

CHAPTER 24

She had become his sex slave. How and when she had become ensnared in his web, was beyond her. Sparkle felt like a trapped insect inside a spider's web. Vito had her shook to the bone and it was starting to show. She was so deep in his bullshit that her 900 Giuseppe heels were covered in it and starting to smell. The crazy part about it all was that he now had her driving to Baltimore to be abused. She laughed to herself, but deep down inside she knew that there was nothing funny about her situation. Being victimized never was. Her only solace was that believed in karma and one day Vito was going to get his.

Since she was only doing 50 in the lane designated for 60 or more, she had to get over into another lane. Sparkle glanced over to her right and almost lost control of her car. Driving right beside her with her face glued to a cell phone was Star. Focusing her eyes to make sure that they weren't playing tricks on her, Sparkle was sure that it was Star. *Why is she driving a Chevy Malibu? Whose is it and where is she going? Who was she talking to on the phone and why was there a sticker on her bumper that promoted police organization? What the hell was the Fraternal Order of Police? And what was Star's connection to them?* Curiosity got the better of Sparkle and she decided to follow Star. At the Cherry Road exit in Laurel, Star turned off. Careful to stay at least two cars back, Sparkle followed. The next thing she knew they were on Terrydale Road pulling into an apartment complex called **'Laurel Lakes Condominiums'** Star pulled into a parking space designated for residents and pulled something from the glove box that she hung from the rearview mirror. Sparkle pulled into a space across the lot and watched Star enter building 1330. The outside façade of the building was all glass, so she could see Star walk up two flights of stairs and enter an apartment with a key. *What the fuck? Who lives here? Why hadn't Star ever mentioned Laurel?* After about five minutes, Sparkle left her car and went to the building. In the lobby were a bevy of mailboxes. She walked down the hall until she reached the apartment that Star went in two floors above. The ground apartment was T-104. So that meant that one Star went in was #304. Sparkle went back to the mailboxes and read the name on the mailbox. C. Sams. She took a picture of the mailboxes with her cell phone, walked out of the building and did the same to the Chevy Star was driving. *Maybe somebody will believe me now.*

"What the fuck, yo? I thought I told your ass to be here in an hour?" Vito bellowed as soon as she entered his apartment.

Instead of responding, Sparkle quietly got undressed.

"You don't hear me talking to you?"

"Look, Vito, I ain't tryna argue with you." Sparkle snapped. "Shit, I got stuck in traffic, that's why I'm late."

"Why you ain't answer your cell phone when I called you?"

"My phone was on 'roam', I need a better service provider."

"You better switch to Verizon then. You see that commercial where people who use Verizon got a rack of people walking around with them."

"Yeah, I saw it. I wish they were here now." Sparkle said and then instantly regretted it.

"What did you just say, yo?"

"Nothing."

"Nothing, huh? You still think I'm a lame, huh? I got a trick for your smart mouth ass."

Awe shit! Here we go with this crazy shit again. I should've just kept my mouth closed. Sparkle watched Vito leave the room and then come back a few minutes later.

"Bend over that couch right there, yo."

Sparkle complied. She felt something wet on her ass and then the head of Vito's dick knocking on her back door. Then with one painful push, he entered her. Her ass was on fire it took everything inside her not to scream out or cry. *Don't let him hear you scream. Don't cry. It will only egg him on.*

Sparkle never thought about killing anybody in her life until she met Vito. She hated him with every ounce of her being. As quickly as the assault on her body started, it ended. With a shudder and a few shakes, Vito came in her. The sick part about it all was that just as he came, she did too.

"Look yo' I'm sorry. Kay, I been drinking and smoking too much lately and that's because I been depressed. My money fucked up. On the life of my mother, I promise to leave you alone if you help me out one more time. One more time, Kay, that's it, that's all. I won't bother you again. Are you tryna hear what I gotta say?"

"Say what you gotta say." Sparkle replied, still bent over the couch. She had to give herself a few minutes before she could stand up erect. She was still trying to hide her tears from Vito.

"The word on the streets is that the dude Rock is back on and doing a muthafucka. He used to fuck with my old head Melvin back in the 70's. The word is that the dude Rock is sitting on some millions. And I want me some of 'em. One day I drove by y'all crib and saw a gray Phantom parked outside. My peoples tell me that old head Rock pushes a phantom and fucks with a bad bitch named Rhoda now either there's a rack of bad bitches in D.C. named Rhoda or that Rhoda and your Rhoda have to be one and the same. Does your girl Rhoda fuck with the old head nigga Rock with the gray Rolls Royce?

Sparkle thought about telling a lie but then decided against it. If she did and Vito found out about it, things would only get worse. "Yeah. Rho fuck with Rock."

"Our arrangement ends as soon as you do something for me. One last thing and I'll be gone forever. If you refuse, we'll keep playing these games until one of us gets tired and believe me, it won't be me. So, what's up, yo? You tryna end this shit between us or what?"

Tired, defeated, stressed out, and hurting, Sparkle replied. "Whatever it is, just promise me that Rhoda stays out of it."

"On my mother's life, I promise."

* * *

143

The new doors on the club were already installed by the time George and Scoop pulled up. George hopped out of the Range Rover Sport and asked one of the workers what kind of doors they were.

"These are custom made mahogany wood doors. They were handcrafted by a renowned woodsman named San Sebastian. These are the best doors in the country."

"That nigga got stock in the company," George said to Scoop as they walked into the club. On the first floor of the club, things were starting to come to life. He spotted his uncle across the room talking to one of the contractors. Rock looked up and saw them approaching and came to meet them.

"Nephew, what's up?"

"Ain't shit, Unc. I just wanted to stop by and see how the club was coming along."

"It's coming along. Walk with me." When they go to where several men were working in a corner. Rock said, "I spared no expense on this one, youngin'. I brought in my man from New York and his money is as long as Georgia Avenue. This joint gon be the best club on both coasts. It's gonna have five floors. Three floors to party on and two floors for other things. You have to be a member with an access key to get anywhere above the third floor. the staircase that these dudes are working on is gonna have gold paint on the walls. On the ceiling is gonna be fiber optic lighting that gives you an outside feel. The steps are gonna be made of highly polished black granite with backlit alabaster stone risers.

The elevators will be made of laser cut brass and inlaid wood. Sculpted to match the doors on the club, there's gonna be theaters, suites, a separate strip club, a gym, a clothing outlet, everything immoral you can think of, we gon have it. Sex, a casino, ATM machines, everything."

"I'm feeling that, Unc. This shit gon' be big and I'm glad you made me a part of it."

"You ain't seen nothing yet, youngin. When my man Beanie gets here, we really gon ball out. I feel like I'm living a movie. I just wish that all my fallen comrades and all the dudes that I love that are still behind the wall could be here to live it with me."

"I hear that."

"Young boy, I heard a song the other day that I can't get out of my mind."

"A song by who?"

"That young nigga, Jigga. He said…I'm a bully with them bucks, but don't let the patent leather shoes fool you, youngin. I got the fully in the tux…"

"I'm hip to that joint. Let me find out you on your nigga shit out here. Listening to rap music and all that."

"You're only as old as you feel, youngin. And I feel like I'm nineteen."

George laughed at his uncle. "That's right, Unc. Stay forever young. That's the key to life. May we both live forever."

"Go find us some champagne. That's some shit I'd like to toast to, right there."

Anthony Fields

CHAPTER 25

Keith pulled out the black Dodge Magnum station wagon onto Groverton Street and parked behind a green Jeep Cherokee. "I think this might be the best vantage point right here, yo'. We can see the side of the house, that's enough ain't it."

Vito took the blunt he had been smoking and stomped it out in the ashtray. "Yeah, this good. It don't make no difference anyway. We know he in there and we know that the bitch is with him. We gotta key, all we gotta do is walk in there like we live there. Quiet, though. We wanna surprise them. It wouldn't look good if we end up on a Sean Taylor type beef. Feel me?"

Both of his men nodded their heads. They remembered how the home invasion on Redskin's safety Sean Taylor ended up.

"Yo', this is the game plan. We get in, get the money and get out. That nigga got that ink up in there; we just gotta persuade him to give it to us."

"By any means necessary?" Vick asked.

"*Any means necessary*. But you let me worry about that. I'll take the dude, you and Keith handle the bitch."

"It don't take two niggas to handle no bitch, yo'...," Keith started.

"Shut the fuck up, yo." Vito exploded. "I'll put your ass the fuck out, right now and you can find your way back up the highway on your own. How bout, that, smart ass nigga?"

Keith sucked his teeth but kept quiet.

"Like I was saying, I'ma grab the nigga and y' all hold the bitch down. The ultimate goal is to get that money. We ain't leaving empty handed under no circumstances. If there's any surprises, y'all know what to do, right?"

"If the situation ain't improving, kill everything moving...it's a hard knock life." Vick sang.

"Exactly, let's go."

When he heard the voice in his ear he thought it was Rhoda playing games or that he was dreaming. So, he paid it no mind.

147

But then came the hard crack across the back of his head. Rock opened his eyes immediately. "What the fu…?!"

Then he felt himself being pushed to the floor.

The voice that was just in his ear, said, "Lay flat on your stomach and stretch both your arms like you're flying."

Vito waited until Rock complied before he continued. "You know what this is, yo." He heard a stifled scream and looked over to see Keith with his hand over Rhoda's mouth. "I want the money and whatever else you got in here, yo'. I know you got it in here somewhere. Gimme that shit and then we out, no bullshit. Bullshit me and I'ma blow your head through this floor. Now, talk to me."

"In that drawer over there on the tall dresser, there's a little less than a hundred gr…"

"*A hundred grand*? Cut the bullshit, yo'. Your car cost more than that. I know you got a safe in here somewhere."

"I don't…have no…safe. All the money is tried up in the club. The money in the dre…"

"Where the drugs at then, yo?"

"I don't sell drugs no more."

"Oh yeah? So, you want to me believe that you still spending money from the 70's, huh?"

"I haven't sold drugs…"

Vito smacked Rock again with the gun. He was in no mood for games. "So, you tell me that I came all the way here for some small shit?"

"That's all I have…take it."

"You ain't gotta tell me that, yo. I'ma do that anyway and since you wanna play games, I'ma take your life with it."

"N…o…o…!"

Bloc…Bloc…Bloc…

Rhoda heard the gunshots but couldn't see anything because Rock had been put on the floor. she tried to scream out his name, but the hand still over her mouth, muffled her screams and her cries. She prayed to God that he was okay.

148

"Kill that bitch." She heard a voice say. Rhoda struggled against her captor and tried to get loose. Then she heard a loud sound and then nothing.

* * *

Emily Ann Weiss was having trouble sleeping, so she figured that a cup of warm milk would do her some good. Standing at her kitchen counter, she was just about to pour the milk when she heard the unmistakable sounds of gunfire. She dropped the carton of milk from her hand and raced to the window. She saw three black-clad figures emerge out of the darkness and run to a nearby car. Emily walked briskly to the phone on the wall and dialed 911.

"Montgomery County Police Department. What is your emergency?"

"Across the way…gunshots…I heard gunshots. Three people just ran from over there…"

"Ma'am…are you okay? Ma'am?"

Emily Weiss had fainted.

* * *

"Girl, did you see that bitch Trina Boo at the Love the other day?" Billie asked Quanda.

"Naw…I ain't see her."

"She had on a sheer, no…make that see through body suit with nothing but a thong on. That shit was not cute. Girlfriend needs to sit her ass down somewhere. She like forty years old still tryna party with Essence. With her gecko frog looking ass."

Quanda cracked up laughing at Billie. Billie stayed on some bullshit, joning on people. What made it so funny was that there was no such thing as a gecko frog, it was a gecko lizard.

The phone ringing in the living room broke her train of thought. Quanda went to answer it. "Hello?"

"Who dis?" the male caller asked.

149

"Nigga, you called here…"

"Quanda…Rhoda…my uncle…" That was as far as he got before she screamed. "Quan? Quanda?"

Billie saw the scene unfold and rushed to Quanda's side. She held Quanda and tried to get her to speak but she wouldn't. She was crying hysterically and everybody in the living room was mystified.

Sparkle came running down the stairs. "What the fuck happened? What's wrong with, Quanda?"

"I don't know…she answered the phone and then she just went off."

"Who was on the phone?" Sparkle asked as she went and retrieved the phone. She picked it up and said, "Hello?"

George told Sparkle what happened. All she could say was, "Oh my God."

Star sat in the lobby of the Emergency Room at Montgomery General, squeezing her hands together, crying. She had never experienced losing somebody close to her before. She cried because she was scared, she cried because she was angry, because she was helpless, and she just didn't know what else to do. So, she cried and she prayed. She remembered when the doctor had just come out of the room and told them that Rhoda was in bad shape. She had been shot in the face and had little chance of making it.

"…her chances of surviving are not good. I'm sorry."

Quanda had completely lost it at that point and it took everybody present to try and calm her down. She was kicking and screaming and crying. The scene was too much for Star to handle so she went and sat in the lobby. She could still hear Quanda's cries reverberating in her ears like a drum. Nothing she could do would drown them out.

"Noooooo! Get off of meeee! Nooooo! Rhooooooo! Rhoooodaaaa! Don't dooo this to meeee! Rhooooo! Oh God, pleeeeeeaaaase don't take her! Nooooo! Rhooodaaaa! Don't touch meeeee!"

No matter how much she swiped at the tears in her eyes, others came to replace the ones she wiped. Star looked around the lobby. She spotted a man she recognized, sitting by himself, in a seat all the way in the back. His face was covered in tears as well. The man with the tear stained face was Rock's nephew George.

There was no need to look up because he knew where all the wails and cries were coming from. The hospital's emergency room was packed with people, including his own family. George was inconsolable. His phone vibrated every two minutes, but he refused to answer. The last call that he answered was his mother calling to tell him that his uncle was dead. A home invasion, the police said. A fucking home invasion. Why hadn't his uncle installed the alarm system like he told him to? George kept asking himself but he already knew the answer. Rock was too fucking hard headed. He wasn't in the life anymore so he thought he wasn't a target.

George wept in his hands and thought about what could've been. He never idolized any man in his life until he grew close to his uncle. Rock was one of the throwback gangsters and he wanted to be just like him. George felt like a kid that had just been told that there would be no more Christmas again...ever.

The pain in his body started in his heart and moved all over. Once his tears started they never stopped. To George, everything that was pure and good about the game died with his uncle. All honor amongst thieves went straight out the window. Because whoever robbed and killed his uncle didn't have to kill him. Rock was a lot of things, but a fool wasn't one of them. George was sure that his uncle had complied with his killer's demands. That's just the way Rock was. With the club opening in a few months, his desire to honor his slain comrade Roscoe, his intense love for Rhoda, Beanie and his family, his uncle would have weighed all that automatically and decided that it was senseless to be macho over some small money. So, whoever killed his uncle killed him just because he could and that's what angered George so. Rhoda was probably shot to eliminate all witnesses. *That was the law of the streets.*

George thought about his uncle's smile. And if nobody had seen Rock's eyes truly light up, he had. The fact that some faceless person had extinguished that light forever made him angrier. With his uncle gone and a better understanding of just how truly fragile life was. George made a promise to himself. That everybody involved in his uncle's death would die. George pulled his cell phone from his hip and dialed a number. "Tay, it's me. Get everybody together and meet me on Hanna Place, in the circle. It's time to go to work."

George wiped his eyes once more and quietly left the hospital.

Once Rhoda's mother showed up at the hospital, Sparkle knew that it was time for her to go. It was too much for her to try and comfort the mother of the woman that she was responsible for putting there. Sitting inside her car, still in the parking lot, Sparkle watched George Foreman leave the hospital and walk over to his Range Rover. He was in pain and that was visible even in the still of the early morning. Something inside her wanted to run over to him and tell him everything. But that would only implicate her. There was no way that she could weave the story to fit a better mold. One that would leave her hands without blood on them. Tears continuously fell down her face as the thought of Rhoda dying loomed over her. *Hadn't he promised her that Rhoda wouldn't get hurt? Why would Vito kill Rock and shoot Rhoda? Why?* Ask it as she may, Sparkle knew that it was a rhetorical question. The truth was that Vito's word didn't mean shit and he did whatever he wanted to do. He had done the same thing to Whistle.

There was no person alive that she hated more than Vito. Now more so than ever. Her stomach rumbling reminded Sparkle that she hadn't eaten all day and she needed to. Sparkle thought about the news she found out at her doctor appointment a few days ago. She was without a doubt, six weeks pregnant. She had argued with Dr. Absalom to no avail. There was no mistake. He gave her some multivitamins and told her to eat more.

In the Blink of an Eye

Six weeks. Her child had been conceived six weeks ago. The realization of what that meant wasn't lost on Sparkle. Right there in the parking lot, crying for Rhoda and praying for them all, Sparkle came to grips with her situation. A little over six weeks ago, she went to Baltimore to see Vito. They had argued and fought. Then Vito called three of his friends over and all four men repeatedly raped her. They ran a train on her for hours. One of them, she didn't know which one, was the father of her unborn child.

Anthony Fields

CHAPTER 26

By the time, he pulled up on Hanna Place, there were exotic cars and SUVs everywhere. Tucking his .45 ACP in his waistband. George walked over to where his team had assembled. When they looked up and saw the look on his face and the condition he was in all conversation ceased.

"Check this out. Somebody went out my uncle's house and robbed him. Then they killed him and tried to kill his woman. They shot her in the head, but somehow, she survived it. T-Roc, I want you and Doe to go to Montgomery General Hospital and protect her and everybody that she loves. Y'all gon be there as long as she's alive in there. We need her to tell us what happened to my uncle. Her name is Rhoda Buchanan and you're her personal security. If anybody asked, go do that now." George waited until both men left before continuing. "Hasan, I want you, Lips, Lucky, and T-Mac to hit the streets and find out what the streets are saying about this. Put a few crackheads and dope fiends on the move to ask questions all over and see what they come up with. I want y'all to twist arms, break legs, whatever it takes to get the 411 on whoever did this. I need to kill me a few muthafuckas. Y'all got me?"

"No doubt, moe," Hasan stated and nodded his head at Lips. They left. Then T-Mack and Lucky did the same.

When the circle was down to just three people left, George looked into the eyes of his two thoroughest young niggas—Tay and L.B. "I want y'all to go out Glassmanor and get Scoop. Then drive out Palmer Park and get Cain. I want the four of y'all to rob every Muthafuckin' strip in the city. Kill one muthafucka on each one so they feel the heat. In the next forty-eight hours, I want the pavement in every hood to be vibrating. I want niggas to know that ain't no money gon' be made in their hood until I find out what happened to my uncle. I'll be in touch when I need to. Y'all be careful and be safe. I'm out." George turned to leave.

"Aye, Gee?" Tay called out.

George turned around.

"I'm sorry to hear about your uncle, moe. Rock was cool as a muthafucka. When you hurt, I hurt and when I hurt, I make niggas feel my pain. Kill my mother, I'ma find out who hit him and when I do, I'ma flat line them and their mother and her mother."

"I feel that, young boy. Take care of that business. I'm gone." George walked away feeling a genuine love for the two young dudes he had just left. And although L.B. hadn't said a word, the look on his face spoke volumes. George was one of the only people who knew that while Eliot 'L.B.' Johnson was quiet, he was the most dangerous person on the streets.

* * *

Since she wasn't allowed to use her cell phone inside the hospital, Billie walked outside and called Chico. Glancing at her watch, she saw that it was fifteen minutes after 5 a.m. *Chico, please answer the phone!* After a few rings, she heard him say, "Hello."

Thank you, Jesus. "Chico, baby, I need you right now."

"Billie, what's wrong?" Chico asked sounding half asleep.

"Somebody killed Rock Blackman and shot Rhoda…" That was as far as Billie got before her dam broke, her voice gave out and she dissolved into tears.

"Where are you? I'm coming right now."

Billie struggled to regain her composure. "I'm…m…m at Montgomery General…"

"I know where it is. I'm on my way, baby. Okay?"

"Okay…okay," Billie said and turned off her phone. To her, Chico was the man in the fairy tale books. The one Anita Baker sang about and the one that Fantasia sung to Aretha Franklin about.

Everybody here for Rhoda Buchanan, please gather around me now, so as I don't have to repeat myself. Thank you." The tall blond haired Caucasian surgeon announced. "As you know we

156

have one of the best teams of young surgeons in the nation. That team, myself included, has been working for the last fourteen hours to save Ms. Buchanan. There's good news and bad news. I'll start with the good news first. We were able to remove a single bullet from the right side of Ms. Buchanan's head. Thank God that whoever fired that shot was standing over her at a specific angle. Had he or she not fired the gun from that angle, the bullet entry wound itself would have killed Ms. Buchanan. The bullet just sort of went in at the side of her right eye socket and stopped. That was a blessing. Had it continued, it would have destroyed brain tissue that would have caused instantaneous death. That's the good news. There are no signs of any brain damage. Now the bad news. The bullet did manage to sever several aortic valves and tendons around the eye. We tried like hell to save that right eye, but we failed. There was too much extensive damage to the orb and eye socket. So, Ms. Buchanan's progress is that she'll live, but her life will be a little different minus that right eye. She lost a lot of blood, but we replaced it with transfusions. She's stable and responding well to medicines. She's resting right now and should be doing so for the next week or so. She should be able to receive visitors in the next three to four days. Thank you all for being so patient and please take care of yourselves."

The collective sighs of relief were palpable inside the hospital. After hugging everyone and saying her goodbyes, Billie grabbed Chico's hand and led him out of the hospital. "Can I go home with you and spend the day with you?"

"You know I charge by the hour, right?" Chico joked.

"I don't care. I can afford it. I'll follow you. Let's bounce."

***

Quanda rode with Star back to the townhouse. Reclining in the big body Benz's spacious passenger seat, she said a prayer to God silently and thanked him for sparing Rhoda. There were so many questions in her mind that her brain threatened to shut down. Who the fuck wanted to kill Rock? The man hadn't even been home eight months. Why try and kill Rhoda?"

Suddenly, Sparkle's conspiracy theories came to mind...

"...what if Ping wasn't the intended target? What if Cinnamon and Vita were?"

That would explain why the killer tried to kill Rhoda, too. But that still didn't make sense because Rhoda was a target for far too long. Why wait until Rock had been home seven months to kill Rhoda? Then Quanda thought about the fact that Rock was connected to Roscoe. What if his death was connected to Roscoe's past crimes?

Star's hand rubbing her leg, broke Quanda's thought pattern. She looked over at Star and decided that it was time for her to bed her young protegee again. She was long overdue. Star seemed to enjoy their lesbian sex too much, but if that's what she wanted that's what she'd get. After hearing that Rhoda was gonna live, Quanda felt she needed a release anyway. That release might as well be sexual and with Star.

Tomorrow, I'll get the girls together so that we can all talk about what's on our minds.

***

"I don't care what the fuck you do, nigga. It's over today!" Sparkle screamed into her cell phone at Vito.

"Kay, you need to calm your ass down before I..."

"I ain't calming down shit. Before you do what, Vito? Kill me, too?"

"Bitch, don't you know that these signals can be intercepted and listened to?" Vito exploded. "Ain't a damn thing over until I say it's over. Now watch your mouth on the phone and tell me what's wrong."

"Why did you kill them? You promised..."

"Didn't I just...hold on...what the fuck? You wired or some shit, yo'?" *...Click...*

In the Blink of an Eye

"Hello? Hello? Vito? Vito?" Sparkle shouted into the phone and couldn't believe that he had hung up on her. *Bitch nigga. I hope you die a terrible death.*

Anthony Fields

.

CHAPTER 27

Sparkle laid back in the recliner and listened to all the stories that were weaved together about what had happened to Rock and Rhoda. The whole NHBC was in the living room of the townhouse discussing any and everything...

"...he got found guilty of two murders. Coo Wop's lil ass is through." Billie was saying.

"That's sad...what about Antwan, Jo-Jo, and Boy-Boy? What happened with them?" Quanda asked.

"Moochie told me that they got found guilty on some light shit and they are about to come home. She said Don—Cookie and nem brother, beat all that Congress Park shit..."

She listened to the rest of the conversation but her mind was elsewhere. If Rhoda would have died, she would never have forgiven herself. Sparkle wanted desperately to tell somebody about everything, but who could she tell? She looked around the room and felt like an outcast, a pariah, the enemy. The only person that would listen to her and keep her secret was Billie. Star, she wouldn't tell shit and Quanda would probably beat the shit out of her. Billie was definitely the one. Sparkle made up her mind to confide in Billie later.

"...and them muthafuckas talking about the little boy had a gun. Them police killed that little boy and now they tryna cover it up. They did all that shit about a Muthafuckin' moped. That's crazy. Them muthafuckas up Condon Terrace should be still tearing shit up..."

* * *

Sparkle cornered Billie at the top of the stairs, in the hallway. "Billie, I need to talk to you."

"Can it wait until tomorrow, Spark? I swear to God I'm tired." Billie responded a little agitated.

"No, Billie it can't wait. I have to say this now while I still have the nerve to say it. Tomorrow might be too late."

Billie looked at her watch. "Come on, Spark." Billie relented and led Sparkle into her bedroom. "I ain't in the mood for none of your conspiracy shi…"

"Do you remember the Baltimore nigga I told you about a while back? The one I met at the club that night we were together."

"Together when? How am I gonna remember one nigga, Spark?" Billie asked.

"Okay, listen. I met Vito…that's the Baltimore niggas name, Vito…at the club. I was feeling his swagger, so I got with him. He had that bread back then. One day he hit a rough spot and fucked up a rack of money. He asked me to direct his path to a nigga I knew that had money…"

"You mean like…set a nigga up for him?"

"For a lack of a better term…yeah. I agreed to do it because I had a few niggas that got on my bad side…like Champ. You know Lil Reggie Yelverton, right?"

"The boxer?"

"Yeah."

"I don't know him personally, but I know who he is, yeah?"

"Do you remember when I had the black eye and I told y'all that some bitches jumped me?"

"Of course."

"Well, I lied. Champ…that's what they call Lil' Reggie…punched me in my face. He tried to tell me that he wasn't gonna pay me after I spent the night with him. I cussed him out and he beat me up. So, when Vito came to me, I gave him Champ, because I was mad. Vito came to DC and robbed Champ. I ended up putting Vito on about three or four niggas. That was it. I didn't hear from him in a while. Then about nine months ago, he calls me…"

"Vito?"

"Yeah, Vito. He calls me and tells me that he's fucked up again and needs me to put him on some more niggas. I refused.

His bamma ass told me that he was gonna come to DC and let all the dudes that I set up, know that it was me who set them up. Unless I help him out."

"He blackmailed you?"

"Yeah." Sparkle said and sat down next to Billie, defeated. She put her hand on her head and broke down crying.

Billie reached out to console Sparkle, but Sparkle rebuffed her and stood up. "I felt like I was backed into a corner, you know? I couldn't let Champ, Gary, and Derron know that I set them up. They would've killed me...so I agreed to set somebody else up. I gave him Whistle."

"Whistle? Whistle from the Valley that got killed about eight months ago."

Sparkle nodded.

"Sparkle, what the fuck are you telling me? Didn't Whistle get killed while somebody was robbing him?"

"It was Vito. Vito robbed him and killed him. He was supposed to just rob him, not kill him."

"Spark, why are you telling me all this shit?"

"Wait. There's more."

"More?"

"Yes. After he killed Whistle, Vito held that over my head, too. *"If I go down, you go down."* He said. With Vito, everything is about control. He wanted to control me. He lured me to Baltimore one day, Billie. He raped me and let three of his friends fuck me. They took turns...they all went at once. I cried and cried and begged them to stop..." Sparkle searched Billie's face for some empathy. "My spirits were broken. I was in pain...I just wanted the pain to stop. Eventually, it did, but he still held my past over my head. So, like a dutiful and obedient whore, whenever he called for me...I went to him. About two weeks ago, he promised me that everything would stop and he'd let me go if I helped him one last time. One last big score."

"And you gave him Rock?" Billie whispered. She had just put two and two together. "You gave Rock up to Vito, didn't you?"

"Yes, Billie, don't look at me like that. Please, I need you to understand."

Billie's tears started about then. "Understand what, Spark? That you're the reason that Rho is in the hospital? Understand that you got Rock killed..."

"I was being abused! I was mentally unstable...it was him or me. Rhoda wasn't supposed to get hurt. Please believe me! He promised me that he wouldn't hurt Rhoda. When I gave him the key, he said that all he wanted was the money..."

"*The key*? You gave him a key to Rock's house?"

"I took the key offa Rhoda's ring one day, duplicated it and replaced it. She never knew about it. He wasn't supposed to hurt anybody..."

Sparkle and Billie both cried and then sat in complete silence. Finally, Sparkle broke the silence. "I know you probably hate me, but you can't hate me more than I have myself. When Rhoda is well enough to listen to me, I'm gonna tell her everything. I pray that one day she can forgive me. After I've made my peace with Rhoda, I'm outta here. I'ma go back home for a while and get my life together. Get in the church or something."

"What about Vito?" Billie asked.

"God don't like ugly, Billie. That's why he's pushing me. Vito is gonna get his one day, karma always comes back around. I called him and tried to ask him why he did it and he hung up on me. I need to make this right my way, Billie. Please don't let what I've told you get outta this room. Okay?"

"Okay."

"You promise?"

"I promise."

Sparkle opened Billie's door up. "Oh...two more things and I'm gone. Star is not who she says is. Nobody believes me but it's true. She drives a blue Chevy Malibu and lives in a complex out Laurel. Her real name is not Saquina Samuels...it's C. Sams. Do you remember the date that I went on and on about her?"

"Yeah."

"I did that because I remembered her from somewhere, but I couldn't remember where. Well after I followed her to Laurel that day, it came to me. The night I met Vito at the club, I also met another dude. His name was Anthony Manley. Anthony was a DC police officer. One day he took me to Blue Plains to a training facility where they train new cops. He had to teach a class that day. The class was for thirty minutes, he was paying for my time, so I waited outside in his Navigator until it was over. When he came out of the facility, so did all the others. I remember counting that there were twenty-six men and one woman that came out of that class. The one woman stood out because I remembered thinking that she looked awfully young to be a police officer. That woman that I saw that day is in our living room, Billie. I watched her walk to a blue Chevy Malibu. Star is the police. Use that info how you will, she might be moonlighting as a hooker. And I'm pregnant." With that said, Sparkle opened the door and left the room.

Billie laid in her bed and thought about all the stuff Sparkle had just told her. It was all a heavy pill to swallow. *Star a cop? The Baltimore nigga, Vito being behind Rock's death and Rhoda's shooting? Sparkle being responsible for it all?* And she had just promised Sparkle that she wouldn't tell a soul. Billie thought about the one person that she had grown to love and trust more than anyone...Chico. Chico completed her and made her existence worth it. He was everything that she loved about love and about life. Billie had long since admitted to herself that she was head over heels in love with Chico. And when they went to her parent's house for Thanksgiving, she planned to tell him so.

Billie made the decision to tell Chico her dilemma right before she drifted off to sleep.

Anthony Fields

In the Blink of an Eye

CHAPTER 28

The next day, Billie met Chico for lunch at a sports bar on Capitol Boulevard. They ate and talked about everything on Billie's mind. Then they went to the hospital and checked on Rhoda. She still couldn't receive any visitors, but the nurse told them that Rhoda was doing fine. They ended up at Chico's apartment where they made love over and over again. They were destined to be together, he whispered to her over and over as they made love. Nobody had ever made Billie feel so special. So, during pillow talk, Billie confided in the only person that she knew she could trust.

Chico looked over his shoulder to make sure that Billie was still asleep. Satisfied that she was, he closed the bathroom door behind him. He took a much-needed piss and then washed his hands. After washing his hands, Chico pulled Billie's cell phone out of his pajama pants pockets. He purposely left the sink water running and locked the door. Then he placed a call. A male voice answered on the second ring.

"Hello?"

"Gee?"

"Yeah, this me. Billie?"

"Naw, slim, this Chico."

"What's up, slim? Where you been hiding at?"

"I been chillin'. I got some good news for you, though, slim." Chico said.

"Oh yeah? What's up?"

"I just found out who killed your uncle."

"Who?"

"It was a Baltimore nigga named Vito."

"Vito? A Baltimore nigga?"

"Listen to me, slim. I promised Billie that I wouldn't say nothing, but fuck that, Rock Blackman was a legend and a stand-up nigga. All these niggas out here catering to these rats, but slim wasn't with that shit. I respected that. I don't have all the details…all I know is that your uncle got robbed and killed by a Baltimore nigga named Vito and that the bitch Sparkle set it up."

"Sparkle?"

"Yeah. That No Holes Barred Bitch Sparkle. Billie and Rhoda's girl Sparkle. She duplicated one of Rhoda's keys and gave it to the nigga. That's how he got in the spot. Grab that scandalous ass bitch and get your answers to the questions you seek. I'm gone, slim, but you gon owe a favor. And one day, I plan on collecting."

"I got you, slim. On my mother, good looking out."

"I'll be in touch. Grab that bitch and remember…we never had this conversation. I'm out."

Chico disconnected the call and then deleted it from the outgoing call log. Putting the phone back in his pocket, Chico ran his wet hand over his face. He thought about George getting his revenge and smiled. One day soon, he would have his.

* * *

A Muthafuckin' out of town nigga had killed his uncle. George couldn't believe what he had just heard. And Rhoda's buddy Sparkle had set it up. George thought back to the last time that he had seen his uncle. It was the day that he had taken him and Scoop on tour of the renovated club. He thought about all the big plans they had made. And most of all he remembered his uncle's parting words to him.

"It's time for you to get outta the game, youngin. The odds are stack against you. There are too many police agencies, now. It seems like they coming up with new ones every day. The females you deal with are the police. The dudes you buy all them expensive cars from on them dummy lots are the police. Them muthafuckas that own Solbiato and Hugo Boss are the police. Everybody around you is the police. That's how you gotta think to stay ahead. Ain't no such thing as a long run in the game no more. Wash your money up and get out…before it's too late."

In the Blink of an Eye

As the tears formed in his eyes, George realized that although his uncle was no longer in the game, he met the fate of a nigga still in the game. He had gotten out...but it was still too late. George picked up his Bluetooth earpiece and put it in his ear. It was time for answers. "Hello, Tay? You, Scoop, L.B., and Cain come out Riverdale to my spot...Naw, fuck that...I know what I said. Y'all drop everything and come out here now. I'll tell y'all when y'all get here."

Anthony Fields

CHAPTER 29

Star stared at herself in the mirror over the sink. She opened her Dior blouse and stared at the tattoo over her left breast. The naked woman sitting on the stack of cash stared back at her with mesmerizing eyes. Reminding herself for future notice, Star wanted to ask Quanda who the image of the woman was. Then she prepared herself mentally for the job at hand.

In the bedroom waiting for her was Joshua Sawyer, a powerful lobbyist for the National Rifle Association. It was her first date with him and Star didn't know what to expect. She pulled her blouse off and then her bra. Wiggling out of her Dior skirt, Star noticed that the hair on her legs needed to be shaved again. She silently cursed the fact that she was so hairy. Checking to make sure she was ready, Star decided that she was and went into the bedroom of the expensive suite. Star was awestruck at the sight she witnessed once she got in the bedroom. Not at the fact that Joshua Sawyer was beating his dick, but at the sheer size of it. Her mind quickly did the math. The middle-aged white man stood about five feet nine or ten and weighed about two hundred pounds. And twenty of them had to be in his dick. Joshua Sawyer was hung like a baby gorilla. Star stood transfixed to her spot.

"Come on baby! Come to Poppa." The white man said.

All-Star could do was stare. Eventually, she spoke. "Oh...my...God!"

* * *

The rain started coming down harder as she walked to her car. Sparkle put her umbrella up and prayed that the rain wouldn't mess with the glue that kept her tracks in place in her hair. Upon approach, the Infiniti's door unlocked automatically. Sparkle slid into the driver's seat and threw her umbrella into the back seat. She shook the dampness out of her clothes and turned the heat on in the car. Kicking her Dolce & Gabbana heels off, she elected to

171

work the pedals barefoot. It was a habit that was hard to break. The sounds of *Musiq Soulchild's 'Teach Me'* filled the car.

Singing along to the music, Sparkle never saw the Range Rover that fell into traffic behind her. She was feeling good as she left the happy hour at the Zanzibar on the Waterfront. That couple of hours of music and several drinks were just what the doctor ordered at a time like this. Sparkle didn't see herself as an alcoholic. Drinking just helped her drown her problems. Knowing that she could have stayed home and hit the bottle, Sparkle told herself that she was tired of being cooped in the house.

Sparkle sang along to Tank's 'Heartbreaker', as she turned off Suitland Parkway onto Sheridan Road. Just as she turned left, the impact of the collision sent her head forward into the steering wheel. Then her airbags deployed snapping her head back the other way.

"What the fuck?" Sparkle said as she turned around to see a truck right on her bumper. The next thing she knew, the driver was at her window knocking on it. She rolled her window down. "What happened?" She asked the man standing there.

"My brakes gave out on the truck and I ran into the back of you. Are you okay?"

"I'm okay…I think. Is my car damaged badly in the back?"

"It's not bad but you should check it out, I'm sorry ma'am."

Sparkle cursed under her breath. This was all she needed. If the cops came, they would be able to smell liquor on her breath and know that she was a little inebriated. That wouldn't be a good look. "No cops." Sparkle mumbled as she got out of the car. The rain had stopped for a while and for that she was grateful. Walking to the back of her car, Sparkle tried to focus on the bumper. *It's not that bad.* That's what her conscious thought before something crashed into the back of her and the lights went out.

* * *

"Wake her ass up," George told Tay.

In the Blink of an Eye

Tay grabbed the ammonia rag and put it under Sparkle's nose. She coughed twice and mumbled something that they couldn't understand. Slob ran down both corners of her mouth.

"How hard did you hit her?" Tay turned and asked L.B.

"I just swung the tire jack, slim. I don't know how I swung it." L.B. replied shrugging his shoulders. Tay kept putting the ammonia under her nose until eventually, Sparkle came around.

Sparkle opened her eyes and a sharp pain started in her eyes and ran directly to her brain. She grimaced and tried to grab her head, but she discovered that her hands were tied to the back of a chair. The gravity of her situation set in as she stared into the bloodshot red eyes of George Foreman. *Somebody gave me up? Was it Billie or Vito?*

"Sparkle, what's up, boo?" George said to her.

"What's going on? Why am I tied to a chair?"

"Let me make something clear to you, boo. I'm fucked up about my uncle's death, but I'm still a sane man. I'm reasonable and rational. I don't necessarily believe that it was your fault that the Baltimore nigga killed my uncle."

At the mention of the word Baltimore, Sparkle became very afraid. George knew something, but what exactly did he know?

"The Baltimore nigga must've acted alone. But I need you to make me believe that. I need you to tell me everything that went down so that I can convince these two young niggas that you didn't do anything wrong. I don't have time for games, Sparkle. If I think that you're playing games or lying to me, I'm gonna kill you. Point blank, as simple as that. Do you understand me?"

Tears fell down Sparkle's face as she nodded.

"Okay." George grabbed a chair and sat in down right in front of Sparkle. They were face to face and not three feet apart. "Start at the beginning and tell me everything that happened. And I promise you that I won't kill you.

Sparkle ran the whole spiel down to George about how she met Vito and how he started blackmailing her. She told him about her setting up the dudes for her and how he kept threatening her.

173

She told him about the abuse she suffered, the rapes, gang bangs, and how afraid she was…"

"…where he got Rock's name from, but he said that his peoples knew him from back in the day. He said something about Rock sitting on millions of dollars and that he wanted some of 'em. He asked me was Rhoda's Rock and the one that he had heard about, the same person. I was scared of him…I told him they were the same person. He said he just wanted to rob Rock and that he wasn't gonna hurt anybody else. He promised. He forced me to get Rhoda's keys duplicated so that he could get into the house. He wasn't supposed to kill Rock, George, I swear to God…you gotta believe me…"

"Calm down, Sparkle. I believe you. But I still need your help. I need you tell me everything you know about Vito. I'ma make sure that Vito never hurts you or anybody else again. Tay, get something to write with. Tell me everything you know about Vito."

For the next thirty minutes, Sparkle did just that.

"Did you get all that, Tay?" George asked.

"I got it, moe," Tay replied.

When Sparkle saw, George stand up and put the chair back up against the wall, she thought that he was about to untie her. When nobody made a move to free her, Sparkle spoke up. "George, please let me go. You promised that you wouldn't kill me."

George stopped where he was and turned to face Sparkle. "Let you go? I'm sorry, boo. I can't do that. You are the direct reason that my uncle is dead. You facilitated the whole move. Whether it was coercion or collusion. I can't let you get away with that. You are just as much to blame as Vito."

Sparkle knew that her life was over. Her tears fell harder than they had ever before. "Please don't do this!" She cried. "I can help you find him…I can call him and set him up…I can…you promised me that you wouldn't kill me! You promised!"

"I know what I promised you and I'm a man of my word. I'm not gonna kill you."

174

In the Blink of an Eye

Sparkle breathed a deep sigh of relief.

"L.B., kill that bitch for me."

"With pleasure," L.B. said as he pulled a chrome .357 from his waistband.

"N...o...o...o...o...o...o!" Sparkle screamed as L.B. approached her.

L.B. put the barrel of the gun to her head and fired two times. By the time, he pulled the gun back, Sparkle was no longer recognizable.

"Get rid of that body and then y'all get ready to go to Baltimore. Take Cain and Scoop with y'all."

Tay laid a piece of industrial plastic down on the floor. "Bodymore Murderland, huh?"

"I'ma body more of them niggas than anybody has ever seen. Watch my work. I'ma paint the town red with blood." L.B. hissed then he helped Tay with the disposal of Sparkle's body.

* * *

Star grabbed the comforter on the bed and put her face down in it. She had to bite down on the comforter to keep from crying. Whimpers still escaped her mouth through clenched teeth. The man behind her ramming his dick into her small frame was possessed. Nobody had hurt her so much during sex since Dexter.

After seeing how big his dick was, Star had wanted to decline Joshua's offer to have sex. But she knew that if she did, he would tell Quanda, who he regularly dated, and that would arouse some suspicion. As the man's behemoth, sized penis jack hammered into her from the back. Star repeatedly cursed under her breath. There had to be a better way to make a living. All the punishment that her body had endured over the last eight or nine months was enough to last her a lifetime. Glancing over her shoulder, Star saw that the white man was sweating profusely and his face was contorted. *I hope he's about to cum.* Joshua Sawyer grabbed her waist and thrust himself deeper and deeper into her.

"O...o...o...w...w! Oooowww! Oooow!" Star screamed into the comforter. After a few more thrusts, grunts, and a roar,

175

the man inside her came so hard in his condom that she felt it blow up like it was about to explode. Then he pulled himself out of her.

With her insides inflamed and hurting. Star decided that she had had enough. Her days as a part of the No Holes Barred Crew was almost over.

CHAPTER 30

Billie, Quanda, and Star stood around Rhoda's bed and stared at their fallen sister. The bandages that covered part of her head and all of her right eye were what drew most of the attention to her face. Quanda noticed how thin Rhoda looked. *We gonna have to get Sparkle to cook you something to eat.* Quanda smiled through her tears and said another silent prayer for her friend. She looked around the room at Star and Billie, who both were misty-eyed as well.

"Look at us," Quanda said, laughed and wiped her eyes. "We standing here crying like a bunch of weak bitches. That's our girl laying right there and I know that she's gonna be okay. One eye and all. She may look a little different, but hey she's still here. So, let's dry our eyes and reminisce on the good times."

Everybody, even Star told a Rhoda story and they all laughed about the fun they shared. "She gon need us when she gets outta here. Y'all know how in love she was with Rock." The girls said a prayer each aloud and then they left the hospital. Outside in the parking lot, Quanda asked Billie, "Have you seen or talked to Sparkle?"

"The last time I saw Sparkle, she was leaving the house on the way to the Zanzibar on the Waterfront. She said she needed to unwind and get a few drinks. What about you, Star?"

"I last saw her about two days ago. Has anybody called her phone?" Star replied.

"Yeah," Quanda said as she pulled her cell phone out of her purse. "I have been calling her since yesterday. She hasn't been answering her phone." Quanda dialed Sparkle's number and got her voicemail again. "Now her phone just goes straight to voicemail. Where the hell could she be and why hasn't she called one of us?"

Billie knew that she had promised Sparkle that she wouldn't tell anybody her secret, but Billie felt that she had to clear, for everybody's sake. "Look y'all, Spark made me promise I wouldn't tell y'all this, but this may explain her absence. I think the guilt of what she did may have overwhelmed her and she's left town for a while or something."

"The guilt of what she did overwhelmed her? What the fuck did she do?" Quanda asked vexed.

"The long and the short of it is this. A nigga that Sparkle got tangled up with, he talked her into setting up some dudes for him to rob. Then he blackmailed Sparkle with that information and made her keep doing it. He beat her and raped her and made his boys rape her...he did all kinds of shit to her. She was the one that gave Rock up to the dudes who killed him and shot Rhoda."

"What!" Quanda shouted. "Sparkle knows who killed Rock and shot Rhoda?"

Billie nodded her head.

"I can't fuckin' believe this shit! She was with that shit? And you knew about it?"

"Hold on one fuckin' minute! I knew as of about four days ago when Sparkle came to my room and told me. Like I said, I promised her I wouldn't say anything. She wanted to make things right on her own. According to Sparkle, the dude who did all of this is a Baltimore dude named Vito. And she never meant for anyone to get hurt. She said the dude promised her that he would only rob Rock."

"Who is the dude again?" Star asked.

Billie remembered what Sparkle had said about Star. Was she really the police? "Some dude named Vito. She said he looked like T-Pain, the singer. That ain't all of it, either."

Both women looked at Billie at the same time. "The dude Vito killed Whistle from down the Valley, too."

Quanda's head began to hurt instantly. "I need to talk to Sparkle's ass and then I'ma fuck her up."

"But...the dude...beat her and raped her, Quan..."

"I don't give a fuck. Fuck all that. Rhoda is lying in that hospital because of her. We are her girls, she could've come to one of us and told us what the hell was going on with her. She didn't so fuck it. I'ma beat that ass when I catch her." Quanda dialed Sparkle's number again.

"…This is Sparkle…please leave a message…"

Quanda hung up the phone. "She's gonna come back one day and I'ma be waiting for her ass."

* * *

"Hey, baby!" Chico said as Billie rushed into his arms as soon as he opened his apartment door. "What's wrong?"

"Just hold me," Billie said and squeezed the love of her life.

After several minutes, Billie broke the embrace and walked into Chico's apartment. She went straight to the kitchen and poured herself a cup of apple juice. After draining over half the cup, she said. "Everything is spinning out of control."

"Tell me about it, baby," Chico replied and sat down on his couch.

"Rock is dead. Rhoda was almost killed. She in the hospital fighting for her life with one eye gone and now Sparkle is missing. Nobody has seen or heard from her in two days, Quanda is threatening to kill her on sight and I'm scared for everybody."

"That's deep. But Sparkle is probably just getting away from it all. She'll turn up."

"We just went to see Rhoda, you know?"

"Oh yeah? How is she doing?"

"She's still unresponsive, but she's stable. They downgraded her condition from critical to serious. I miss her so…" Billie started crying.

Chico went to her and wrapped her in his arms. "You need to let me take you away from here."

"I'd like that," Billie said. "Where would we go?"

"Are you gonna be my wife one day?"

Billie stared into Chico's hazel eyes and let her tears fall again. But this time they fell for a different reason. These were tears of joy. "Yes, baby, I am."

"Well, we've been together almost ten months now, don't you think it's time I met your parents?"

Billie responded by grabbing Chico's face and kissing him long and hard on the lips.

* * *

Quanda hit the off button and put the cordless phone back on its base. She walked over to where Star was sitting, laid down, and put her head in Star's lap.

"Who was that on the phone?" Star asked.

"That was Billie. She said that she's stressed out and in desperate need of a vacation. She's taking Chico to meet her parents in New Jersey. I asked her how long she'd be gone and she told me about a week or two. I don't blame her. I need a vacation, too. I'ma go and see my brother maybe this weekend and then I'ma bounce too."

Star continuously rubbed Quanda's curly locks. "Can I come with you?"

Quanda grabbed Star's diamond link chain and pulled her to her until their faces were inches from one another. "Sure, you can. We can go to Disneyland." Then she kissed Star's lips.

Star lifted Quanda's head from her lap and stood up. Then she grabbed her hand and pulled her upstairs to her room. Star didn't know when exactly she had become a lesbian, or even if she was, but she did know that she enjoyed sex with Quanda more than anything. Without a word between them, Star undressed Quanda and then herself. She stood in the middle of the floor and kissed Quanda passionately. Rubbing her fingers across Quanda's pussy, Star felt the wetness come down quickly. Slowly, gently, she slid each finger into Quanda. Then she extracted them and licked each finger. Star dropped to her knees. Her tongue took on a life of its own as it explored every crease, every crevice, and every orifice on Quanda's body. No feeling that she had ever experienced with any man could rival the one she felt now. Star licked Quanda's clit and pussy with a passion that she never knew was inside her. It was if they'd be melting into each other for the last time. Star crawled around Quanda to the back of her and spread her butt. She pressed her face in the darkest of places and slowly tossed Quanda's salad.

Unable to keep silent any longer, Quanda cried out for more as she struggled to stand. She curled her toes into the rug and gave herself over to the heat that generated between them. Quanda bit down on her bottom lip and gyrated her hips in an attempt to get more of Star's tongue into her anus. In seconds, Quanda knew that she was coming.

When Quanda informed Star she was coming, Star ate her ass with a renewed sense of vigor. She stood up and pushed Quanda forward so that she'd be bent over and latched her lips onto Quanda's pussy. She went wild with passion and sucked Quanda into several breathtaking orgasms. Then Quanda knew that it was her turn to return the favor. But Star refused.

"Tonight is your night, I'll have mine when we get to Disneyland." Those were the only words that would be uttered between them that night. Star's appetite was voracious and she let nothing stand in the way of her quenching thirst.

***

The vibration of her phone and the text message woke Star. She rubbed the sleep from her eyes and squinted from the direct rays of sunlight that accosted her eyes. Star looked at the screen on her phone and got up. It was time for her to leave. Checking to make sure that Quanda was still asleep, she got out of bed and went to her closet. She packed a small bag and pulled a notepad from her dresser. Star grabbed a pen and left a brief not where she knew Quanda would find it. She walked over to Quanda and softly kissed her. Then she dressed and left the townhouse without looking back.

CHAPTER 31

"Man, you got me out here early as shit," Tay said to the man that he had driven across town to meet. Issac 'Zeke' Burgess was the man to see when you needed guns, grenades, etc. They knew that they were gonna need some serious artillery when they made their foray into Baltimore because the dudes out there played the warfare game just as they did…for keeps.

"The early bird catches the worm, young boy," Zeke said as he kept looking up and down the street. "And it helps you beat the police at work. They changing shifts, right about now. So, what can I do for y' all, today?"

"We need some big boy shit. Some 'knock bricks from the building and crush niggas tryna hide' type shit. We tryna put some big holes in niggas. Hit his arm—tear it off, hit his leg—tear it off type shit." L.B. responded.

"I got what y'all need, then. I got shit fresh off the factory floor. I got MP-40s with reversible clips. I got fully auto MP-5s with noise reduction equipment attached. I got MPK-5 submachine guns that fire fifty rounds before you have to reload. I got M-16s, AK-47s, and all the new AR-15s I got a Muthafuckin' AR-15 and an M-16 pistol."

"What the fuck is an AR-15 pistol?" Tay asked.

"They got seven and a half inch barrels equipped with flash hiders. They're regular AR-15s shortened to look more compact like the Heckler and Koch versions. Them joints come with one hundred shot clips."

"That's what we want then. Do them joints come with that noise reduction shit, too?"

"I'ma put something together for y'all. How many of them joints y'all tryna cop?" Zeke asked.

L.B. quickly did the math in his head. "We gon need eight of them joints with extra clips and plenty of ammo."

"I got y'all give me one hour and I'll be ready to fill that order. But don't come back here to Gainesville Street, this joint gets hot as the day grows long. Meet me up the street at Fort Stanton Rec. in one hour."

"We'll be there," L.B. said and turned to leave. Then he stopped and called out to Zeke.

"What's up, young boy?"

"Is it true what they say?"

"Is what true?" Zeke replied.

"What they say about you?"

Zeke smiled. "What do they say about me?"

"That you're a rat, you told on Corey Mouse over the jail in ninety-six."

"Of course not. Niggas be hating a real nigga." Zeke replied.

L.B. upped his guns and pointed it at Zeke. "I don't believe you, slim." He fired the gun three times and watched Zeke body drop.

***

"Tell me about your parents," Chico said.

"My parents left D.C. in nineteen ninety-one when I was eight years old. After my uncle got killed, they just up and moved to New Jersey, but I wanted no parts of it. I loved my school, my neighborhood, and my grandparents too much. I didn't want to be uprooted and taken to a new place, so I cried a thousand tears and acted out. Finally, my parents relented and let me stay with my grandparents in D.C." Billie said as she lay back in her seat in Chico's comfortable Benz.

Chico listened attentively as he drove up the Interstate towards New Jersey.

"My father got a job at a local car dealership and my mother went to nursing school. After she became a certified RPN, they brought their house in a newly gated community called the 'Lion's Gate'. They've been living there ever since. I try to get up there at least twice a year to visit, but it doesn't always work out like that. You know what's funny?"

"What?"

184

In the Blink of an Eye

"My parents think I work for a company called the National Housing and Building Corporation. Get it? NHBC as a different acronym. If my father only knew what I did in the streets, he'd die." Billie read the signs on the side of the road. "We should be in New Jersey in forty minutes. Then it'll take another thirty minutes to get to Lawnside."

Chico nodded his head but never said a word. He couldn't wait to meet Billie's parents. The thought of her mother recognizing him never even crossed his mind. His hair was different, he had grown his facial hair, and the personality glasses he wore worked wonders to hide an identity. Chico knew that he'd be remembered when it was time to reveal himself, that he was sure of. His adrenaline was slowly starting to build. It would reach its peak when they to Lawnside.

* * *

Quanda woke up in a bed that wasn't her own. She looked around the room and remembered that she had spent the night with Star. She wondered where Star was. There was no denying the fact that Star was starting to get to her. Her feelings were starting to get involved and that was rare for Quanda. Never really declaring herself a true lesbian, Quanda was a little shocked she felt for Star. Quanda walked down the hall to the bathroom and answered the call of nature. Afterward, she washed her hands and face. As she reached for her toothbrush, Quanda noticed the piece of paper taped to the shower curtain. She moved in close and snatched it down. She read the brief note and wondered what it meant.

I hope that one day you find happiness and that every day for you is like Disneyland. Love Star.

Quanda smiled as she balled the note up and threw it into the wastebasket. She remembered she told Star that she was going to Disneyland and Star asked her if she could come. She had told her yes, right before Star had pulled her upstairs and made love to her for hours. *Where did Star go?* Quanda sniffed the air to see if she smelled food cooking. Maybe Star was cooking breakfast? But she smelled nothing. Then the loud knocking on the door downstairs startled her. *What now?* Quanda rushed into her room and slipped on a pair of sweatpants and a T-shirt. "I'm coming!" She yelled downstairs. Who the hell would be banging on their door early in the morning like they were the police? Whoever it was going to get cussed out. Quanda slipped her feet into a pair of flip flops and went to answer the door.

"Who the hell is it?" She yelled as she undid the top and bottom locks. When she opened the door, staring back at her was about twenty police officers in plain clothes and windbreakers.

"LaQuanda Jasper?" The white cop in front of the crowd asked.

"Yes."

"Ms. Jasper, you are under arrest..."

Everything moved in slow motion as the cops burst into her home and spread out like flies. The man who had asked her name was placing a pair of handcuffs on her wrists.

"...anything you say, can be used against you in a court of law. You have the right to an attorney..."

Quanda looked around bewildered as she was led outside to an unmarked police car.

"...you cannot afford an attorney. One will be appointed to you..."

When the car door shut and Quanda was in the backseat of the police car alone, it dawned on her. She was going to jail. Then she started to cry.

* * *

Cain and Scoop changed the license plate on both Range Rovers, while L.B. and Tay double checked all the guns and ammo. They divided the artillery up and pronounced themselves ready. It was time to go to Baltimore.

In the Blink of an Eye

***

"When you pull into the gate, turn left. Go down the street some more and you'll see my parent's house on the right-hand side. It's the last house from the corner."

Chico followed her instructions well. As he spotted the red brick two story townhouse, with the perfectly manicured lawn, Billie said "That's it right there. My father's home, but my mother hasn't gotten off work yet."

Spotting the black Ford F150 in the driveway, Chico figured that it must belong to her father. "Do you want me to park behind the truck in the driveway?"

"My mother is gonna need to park her car in the driveway, so go ahead and park right here in front of the house."

As they walked up the stairs to the front door, Chico's stomach was in knots. Billie pulled out a set of keys and opened the door.

"Dad...d...d...dy! Daddy, it's me, Billie! Where are you?"

"I'm in the game room, baby!" her father shouted back. "C'mon back here."

Chico followed Billie through a labyrinth of rooms until they reached a room filled with pinball machines, a pool table, a mini movie theater, and a big screen TV hooked up to a Nintendo Wii. Billie's father's back was to them as they approached. He was playing a video game on the Wii. "Hey, honey." He called out over his shoulder but continued to play the game.

"Daddy, I came to spend some time with you and Mommy for a while."

"That's good precious. We...always...love to see our...precious...hold on for a minute, baby...they tryna kill...me!"

"Daddy, you and your video games. You're worse than a little kid. I just wanted to let you know that I brought my boyfriend with me to meet y'all. His name is Chico."

"Where is he?"

"Behind you. Standing here with me." Billie replied.

"What's up Chico...hold on, I'm being rude." Billie's father put the game on pause and stood up. Melvin Valentine stood up and turned around. He walked over to Chico and shook his hand. "It's nice to meet you, Chico. This is the first time that Billie has brought a man home to meet the folks. You must be special."

"He is." Billie chimed in.

"Well good. I'm happy for you baby." He said and embraced Billie. Then he turned back to Chico. "Don't ever put your hands on my daughter, Chico and you and I will get along fine. You got that?"

Chico was too stunned to respond. He was in a daze. He wasn't in Lawnside, New Jersey. He was on 58th Street North East, nineteen years ago. Chico couldn't believe his eyes. He had aged a lot and had gray hairs sprinkled into the black, but the man in front of him was definitely the same man that had darted from the bushes and ran down the street, the night the murder was committed. And that man was Billie's father. The realization of what that meant hit Chico like a blow to the gut. He finally understood what had happened. "I got that, sir."

Now it all made sense.

CHAPTER 32

The room that they put her in was empty except for a table that was nailed to the floor, two chairs, and a metal bench. Attached to the metal bench was a riveted circular shape of metal. Her left arm was handcuffed to that piece of metal. The room was redolent of disinfectant that tried to mask the other smells of cigarettes, urine, and musky feet. It was nauseating.

Quanda couldn't believe that she had been arrested. It was like a nightmare that she hadn't woken up from. Here she was trying to help Mark get out of jail and now she was in jail herself. But charged with what? Who had given her up? They had taken her watch, but she knew that she had been in the little room for at least an hour, so it was almost noon. Goosebumps formed on her arm as the room got chillier by the minute. Quanda rubbed her arm with her free hand and smiled. Making the room cold was a tactic to make a person confess quicker. She had learned that from her favorite show, *First 48*. To leave a person in a room alone, cold, hungry, and in need of water and a restroom and guessing why they were locked up, usually broke people and made them talk. But not her, Quanda was raised in Southeast D.C, and where she was from; the streets didn't raise any punk bitches. The police would want her to tell on somebody, she knew it. *'Snitches end up in ditches.'* Quanda repeated over and over to herself as she stoically braved her conditions. *Dominique and Michael Jasper didn't birth no rats.* And that's the way it would stay. Quanda had heard about all the notorious rats in the D.C. drug circles and scoffed at their weaknesses. Rayful, Lee Lee, Fat Sean, Steve Graham, Street Frog from Talbert Street, Ratbo, Monyay, Tone Tone Lemons, Quincey 'Que' Walters, Creeko, and many others. Quanda was determined not to be like them.

Just as she was slowly contemplating the rest of the best rats D.C. had to offer, the door to the room opened. A man walked into the room and uncuffed her. She had never seen him before.

Anthony Fields

The black baldheaded man was impeccably dressed in street attire. He had on a black Solbiato sweatsuit and a matching headband. On his feet were the new Prada tennis shoes. If it wasn't for the badge hanging around his neck, he could've been mistaken for a hustler.

"Please have a seat in the chair, LaQuanda."

Quanda got up off the metal bench and sat in the chair at the table. He pulled out chair opposite of hers and sat down. "Do you mind if I call you, Quanda?"

Quanda didn't respond.

"Well, I guess your reticence lets me know that you won't mind. We've been investigating you for about a year now, Quanda. We know all about your whorish activities as a part of the notorious No Holes Barred Crew. But prostitution is not what started this investigation. We were watching one of the dudes that you sell drugs to and sort of stumbled upon you. We know everything there is to know about Quanda Jasper. The colors you love all the way down to your favorite foods.

"But somehow you got away from us. What do I mean by that you ask? Just when we snagged a piece of the puzzle that we thought would lead us to cracking this case wide open, we found out that can't touch you."

Quanda listened to what she was being told and wondered if it was the truth. Or was it a play to make her talk?

"My words about an hour ago, were. *Ain't this a bitch!* After all the resources we put in, man hours and money we spent, the Feds came in and slapped our wrists and told us that we had to go play in another sandbox. Can you believe that? Neither can I. I wish I could tell you that you're free to go, but unfortunately, I can't do that, either. The Feds want you held. They say they'll see you in a few days. So, it looks like you'll be over the jail for a while. The Feds will come and get you when they're ready. But please mark my words, Quanda, you and I will meet again." He stood up to leave but stopped short of the door. "Damn my bad. I didn't even tell you my name. I'm Detective Eric Rawlings.

190

In the Blink of an Eye

You've already met my partner, right? No? let me properly introduce y'all." Eric Rawlings produced a radio and said, "Detective Sams, would you please come in here for a minute?"

A couple minutes later, the door opened and in walked Star.

Quanda was visibly shocked, hurt, and upset. She thought about all the stuff that Sparkle had said about Star and realized that Sparkle was not lunching after all.

"Hi, Quanda," Star said.

Quanda stared at Star with open hate and disgust in her eyes.

"I know that you are messed up at me, right now, but hey, I was doing my job. I understand your anger and your pain. You trusted me and I tricked you, betrayed you. Well, get over it. Everything that we shared or experienced was just a means to an end. It was all for the job. I learned about your meeting with the Colombian every Sunday, the dudes you sold drugs to and how you picked up the money. I recorded all your calls, bugged your phone, your car, and your room. You sell drugs to your own people for your own selfish gain and I loathe you for…"

"Bitch you don't know me. You think you do, but you don't. You don't been recording and bugging my shit for the last ten months but you still don't know me. *You loathe me?* Bitch, eat a dick, like you been doing ad miss me with that shit. When you were sucking all them dicks and swallowing cum, was that a part of the job, too? When you fucked all them drug dealers and let them fuck you in your ass until you cried, did you loathe them, too? Huh? Answer that Ms. Smart Ass Detective. It's Sams, huh? Which one were you when you copped that brand-new Benz, courtesy of the people you loathe? You can say whatever you want, boo, but that tattoo on your chest will always remind you of who you really are. And that's a whore hiding behind a badge. And it's good to see you again because I never got the chance to thank you for the way you ate my ass out last night. That shit was indescribable. If you ever decide to be a whore again, please come and holler at me. I'll be chilling in that part of society that you loathe so much."

Anthony Fields

Star opened her mouth to speak, but nothing came out. She turned and ran out of the room before anybody could see her tears.

Eric Rawlings looked at Quanda and smiled a devilish grin. "You did that on purpose. You knew exactly what buttons to push. I respect that. You're an asshole, Quanda, but I respect you. You might know how to run my partner out of the room, but not me. You'll never run me out of a room. And if the Feds don't keep you; I'ma make you wanna run out of the room. But you won't be able to. You know why, Quanda? Because your cell door will be locked. There will be nowhere for you to run. Until next time. You take care."

Quanda watched as the detective left the room.

* * *

Christina Sams ran water into the sink and then splashed it over her face. The water running down her face did not manage to hide the tears that she cried. The things that Quanda had just said to her had cut into her like a knife. The more she spoke, the more the knife turned in her heart. And the crazy part was that every word Quanda said was true. How could she ever get sanctimonious and judge somebody like Quanda and the people she dealt with. Especially when she had just fucked and sucked them all for months? By sexing them, she had become one of them. In mind, body, and soul. Now she was confused. Hadn't she just been doing her job? Or had she done that job too well?

Just like she had done in Houston, Texas two years ago. When the District of Columbia had sent her to gather information on Mecca Senegal. But she had blown the whole investigation when she had inadvertently fallen in love with her target. During one night of pillow talk, she had let certain things slip out. Certain things that only a cop would know. When she awoke the next morning, Mecca was gone. He disappeared without a trace.

It had taken two years of therapy and a trip back through the academy to get her mind right. Through it all her partner Eric had

192

never let her forget that she needed to redeem herself. But her she was right back in the same position as two years ago. Was she a cop or a member of the No Holes Barred Crew? Christina didn't have an answer for herself. She thought about all the sexual encounters she had for the last ten months and couldn't say that she hadn't enjoyed most of them.

She had willingly given her body to the very people she had sworn to protect society from. She had swallowed their semen and let them into her every orifice. They initiated her and made her part of their world forever. Christina's eyes dropped to her tattoo on her breasts...

"That tattoo on your chest will always remind you of who you really are...a whore hiding behind a badge..."

Those words would haunt her forever. The tattoos on both her breasts had changed her life permanently. Even if she had them removed. Christina Sams dried her face with paper towels and got herself together before leaving the restroom. Outside in the hallway, her partner was waiting.

"Are you okay, Sams?"

"I'm fine, Rawlings. Do me a favor and have somebody call Baltimore PD. See if they have anything on a guy named Vito."

"As in the mobster from the movie?"

"Yes. One of the girls said that a dude named Vito from Baltimore is responsible for the deaths of two people here. Artinis Winston and just recently Rock Blackman. Then have homicide pick up Katia 'Sparkle' Reed. She has vital info on both those cases."

"And what about you, Sams? What are you about to do?"

"What do you mean, Rawlings, what about me? I'm about to take a much-needed vacation. I'm going to file the paperwork right now."

"Whatever you do, just make sure that I can reach you when I need to."

Christina 'Star' Sams ignored the last remark and walked down the hall to her office. She turned on her computer and thought about how to word her resignation.

* * *

Sandra Buchanan held onto her daughter's hand and prayed. The bandages that wrapped her daughter's head brought her to tears every time she saw them. Why had she always put her needs before her daughter's? She knew what Rhoda did for a living but had never said a word. *Why? Because you were chasing coke and some dick yourself.* But while she was more discreet, she had heard all the rumors and even listened to the boys that congregated outside her window as the spoke about Rhoda and her friends. Deep in her heart, she always made herself believe that what everyone said about Rhoda was false. They were just hating. She told herself, but in all reality. Sandra knew that it was all true. Her daughter had lived the lifestyle of the world's oldest profession...prostitution.

And now that life had come back to almost claim her life as it had one to her friends Vita and Cinnamon. It was now up to her to try and save her only daughter from further peril. Sandra rubbed outlines of Rhoda's face and then said another prayer.

CHAPTER 33

At D.C. jail, they were led into three separate cages. The smell that hit Quanda instantly made her eyes water. It was almost unbearable. She didn't know if it was the cage itself or the women in it. Quanda stood on the back wall and eyed every woman in the cage. What she saw was indicative of what the streets of D.C. had to offer. All around her were crackheads, dope fiends, prostitutes, drunks, women who looked homeless, hardcore young dykes, and a few women like her that looked like they didn't belong there. Looking into their faced, Quanda wondered what every one of their stories was. Then she thought her own story. Hers was one made for a movie on the Lifetime channel. Young girl in the ghetto, Parents killed. Young girl forced to raise younger brothers. One brother goes to jail and girl does everything necessary to free him. A young girl turns to prostitution and drugs. Friend betrays girl and turns out to be a cop. Girl goes to jail. End of story.

Quanda thought about Star and how easy it must have been for her to trick her. After seeing Star at a rack of parties, she had never questioned the authenticity of the pretty young girl that wanted to be down with the NHBC. Star had been the one to suggest it. But at the time, that didn't seem strange because all the females in the city wanted to be down with them. They knew the reputation that the NHBC had and all the money they generated. Then she thought about how her tirade had run Star out of the room at the police station. *Fuck her.* Star was a cop and Quanda hated cops. What did the Feds think that they were gonna get from her? Information on the Colombians? Info on the dudes she dealt with in the streets? Something to hang on her brother? Whatever it was, they had another thought coming. She was determined to remain strong in the face of all adversity and keep quiet. She'd never be referred to as *'hot ass Quanda'*.

Quanda thought about the worst-case scenario and what type of time she was facing. Then she said, "Fuck it, bring it on."

Just as the smell of fishy pussy, armpits, stinky feet, bad breath, and rotten flesh threatened to make her gag, their cage door was opened and a female CO stepped in.

"Ladies, welcome to the D.C. jail. I need you all to strip completely naked and line up in front of this black line. Please leave all contraband...for example...dope needles, crack pipes, and stems, vials of crack, bags of dope, cigarettes, weed, weapons, money...in the room that you are now in. We are going to search your pussies, your asshole, and your mouth, so please don't try to be slick or smart. You are not smarter than us. We've seen it all. If you attempt to cross the black line with anything considered a weapon, we will see that as an act of aggression and beat the shit outta you. If you attempt to smuggle anything that I just named and we find it we are going to beat your ass. If you think that you are tough and you're looking for some rec...try us, we won't disappoint you. When your name is called, give me your DCDC number and step into the next room. Thompson...Kimberly..."

"301567." A short brown-skinned woman with long hair and hazel eyes said as she stepped into the next room.

Standing in nothing but her thong, Quanda waited for her number to be called, three minutes later it was.

"...Jasper, LaQuanda..."

"I don't know my DCDC number," Quanda said as she stepped forward.

The female CO looked Quanda up and down admiringly and smiled. "It's your first time here, huh? That's good. I'ma give you this number, remember it. It identifies you now. It will never change. Your DC number is..."

***

As the credits started to roll, Chico never realized that the movie was over. It would've been his first time seeing the Tyler Perry movie, *'Madea Goes to Jail',* but he never got the chance to see it. When the movie came on and Billie dropped her head in his lap and covered it with her jacket, he couldn't help but close his eyes as he surrendered his body to the pleasure that her mouth brought. He had already come once and was about to come again. As he held Billie's head and came in her throat, he noticed that the lights had come on in the theater and that people were exiting the movie.

As Billie, brought her head from under the jacket, she locked eyes with a woman who knew what she was doing. The woman smiled and gave her a conspirator's wink and then hugged the man she was walking with. Billie wiped the excess saliva from her hand and from around her mouth and stood up. "Damn, that was some good shit."

Outside, Billie and Chico walked arm and arm to the Benz.

"Are we spending the night at your parent's joint or are we getting a room?" Chico asked.

"They got a basement with a guest room in it. We can sleep there, but I wouldn't feel comfortable fuckin' in there. Let's spend the night tonight and then we can get a room tomorrow."

"That's cool, but since you don't feel comfortable giving a nigga no pussy under the family roof. I guess I gotta get some before we go in?"

"And how do you plan on doing that?" Billie asked with a smirk.

"Come on." Inside the car, he said, "On the way here, I saw a park not too far from your parent's house."

The park was a small campground with a picnic area and a jiffy john. Chico pulled the Benz to the back of the park and hit the lights. He got out of the car and walked around to the passenger side of the car. He opened Billie's door and told her to step out.

"Boy, somebody's gonna come back here... we gon' get locked up."

"Be quiet. Ain't nobody gon see us. It's getting dark out here." He grabbed Billie and kissed her fiercely. Then he unbuckled her belt and pulled on her jeans until they rested at her ankles. "Turn around and bend over. Grab the car seat or the floor board."

Billie did as she was told. She felt Chico rubbing his dick around her opening as if to tease her. "Stop playing, boy and gimme that dick!"

Chico slid his dick into her. "Got damn, boy!" For some reason, his dick felt like it had grown larger than the day before. Billie gripped the Benz seats as Chico held firmly onto her waist and gave her a pounding. "Fuck yeah! Fuck this pussy! Fuck it!"

* * *

Dontay 'Tay' Kidd looked over at his partner L.B. as he rapped along with the Backyard Band CD. They had been parked at the far corner of Edmondson Avenue all day. He looked at his watch 7:46 p.m. The sun was setting and they still hadn't seen their targets. Tay was starting to get restless. "Aye, L?"

"What's up, slim?"

"That nigga Big G still rap for Backyard?"

"Yeah."

"And that nigga be all in them rap niggas videos and shit. But ain't he supposed to be hot?" Tay asked.

L.B. quickly ejected the CD and tossed it out the window of the truck. "I heard that slim is supposed to be wicked, but I ain't never seen no paperwork or met nobody that he told on."

"Oh yeah? So why did you eject the CD and toss it?"

"Because of something I just thought about," L.B. responded. "When I was down Lorton, this old timer told me that the suspicion of an impropriety is worse than the actual impropriety itself."

Tay sat back in his seat and thought about what L.B. had just said. "So, you saying that having niggas think that you hot is actually worse than being hot?"

"Exactly."

"I can go for that. I never thought about it like, though. Man, where these niggas at?"

L.B. shrugged his shoulders, and then he raised his Nextel flip phone to his mouth and pushed a button. "Scoop?"

198

In the Blink of an Eye

His phone's walkie-talkie chirped twice and then he heard, "What's up moe?"

"Y'all seen anybody, yet?"

"Hell naw! And to tell you the truth, I'm getting tired as shit. We been up since early this morning. I'm hungry and I gotta shit. Run the cars and descriptions down to me one more time."

L.B. grabbed the paper from Tay. "The dude Keith is about six feet, brown-skinned, and skinny. He got a low haircut and he got braces on his teeth. He drives a burgundy Tahoe. Vick is dark skinned, and about five ten. He keeps his hair in cornrows, he's stocky and bowlegged. The paper says that he be pushing a black new model Lincoln...the signature series. The nigga Vito look like T-pain, the singer nigga minus the blond tips on his dreads. He stocky, but jive chubby, and dark skinned. He like five nine or something. He is liable to be in anything. He switches cars a lot. The last dude's name is Apple. He's an ill nigga, about five six and a hundred something pounds. Shorty got a big head; he light skinned and got freckles. He got a red Dodge Charger and a motorcycle. You got all that?"

"I got it, moe. But them niggas ain't out here."

"Well, look y'all go head and hit a spot where you can handle your business. Get something to eat. Me and Tay gon do the same thing. Hit me on the chirp in two hours. A'ight?"

"I heard that. Later."

"How long we gon stay out here in B-More, slim?" Tay asked as he pulled the truck away from the curb.

"However long it takes to find them niggas and kill 'em. I ain't going back home until they dead."

* * *

"Do you have any diseases that we need to know about?"

Quanda looked at the fat black nurse like she was retarded. "Hell naw."

"Well, go piss in this cup and drop this strip in there for me, then come back."

Ignoring all the catcalls and all the niggas tryna holla, Quanda closed herself off in the single person restroom. It smelled like period blood. She didn't want to touch anything in the room, so she took down her jumper and squatted to piss in the cup. She had to pee badly but decided to hold her piss for a cleaner toilet. She looked for the soap to wash her hands but found none. *This some trifling shit right here.*

For the next thirty minutes or so, Quanda was poked, prodded, and blood tested. Finally, she was led to South 2, the lone female housing unit in the jail.

"Jasper...you're in cell twenty-two. That's on the bottom tier left. The second cell from the shower. Gray? You go with her, you're her cellmate."

Inside cell twenty-two, Quanda quickly established order. "Look here, boo, I got the bottom bunk. I don't like to talk much, especially to people I don't know, but I will when I feel like it. My name is Quanda, what's yours?"

"Evelyn Gray. But everybody calls me Lynn."

"A'ight Lynn, it's good to meet you and all that, but I gotta use the bathroom and get some sleep and I can't do either one of them until I clean this cell up. So, get on your bunk and let me do me."

Quanda took her washcloth and a bar of soap and cleaned the whole cell.

CHAPTER 34

"My mother's home!" Billie announced as they pulled up to the house.

Chico noticed the beige Chrysler 300M that sat in the parking lot behind the Ford truck. Billie jumped out of the car like a little girl who hadn't seen her family in years. "Go ahead to the door. I gotta check something on my car." He acted like he was inspecting something under the hood of the Benz, but he wasn't. he surreptitiously hit the automatic trunk release button and waited for the trunk to open. Inside the trunk was a Gucci duffel bag that held his personal things. Chico opened that bag and extracted two things from it. He pocketed what he took from the bag and shut the trunk. Chico jogged up to the front door where Billie was holding it open for him.

"Mommy, where are you?" Billie shouted from the foyer.

Out of nowhere, Belinda Valentine appeared. "Billie…baby! It's good to see you!" Her mother said as they embraced.

"I know I told you I was coming on Thanksgiving, but I decided to come early, plus I wanted you to meet someone." Billie turned to face Chico. "Mom, this…"

"…is Chico." Belinda Valentine said.

Chico was alarmed. Does she recognize me?

"Your father told me his name when I came home," Belinda said and turned to face Chico.

Chico's heartbeat slowed as he realized that she didn't recognize him. "Hello, Mrs. Valentine."

"You look so familiar, Chico."

"I have that effect on everybody," Chico said and laughed.

"Well, it's nice to meet you. We've been waiting for the both of you to return. Dinner is waiting in the dining room. Chico, I hope you like pot roast, baked potatoes, and macaroni and cheese. Because that's what I prepared for dinner."

"That sounds delicious," Chico replied.

"Good. Let's go eat then."

***

I got a cousin that lives in Park Heights out here in B-More, named Delmont. He told me that most of the Edmondson Avenue niggas hang out at a skating rink called the Shake and Bake on Pennsylvania Avenue, not too far from here." Cain told Scoop. "Let's hit that joint."

"A'ight. Get on the horn and tell L and Tay where we going."

Cain hit the chirp button and repeated what he had just said to Scoop. Then he told Scoop. "Drive up the block until you see the Record Store on the corner and then make a right. That's Pennsylvania Avenue. Take that all the way out."

***

After the meal was finished and the table was cleared, Belinda Valentine served everyone a generous helping of banana pudding. As they ate dessert, it happened…

"Chico what part of the city are you from and why do you look so familiar to me?" Belinda asked.

Chico purposely took his time chewing the last of his dessert. He wanted to prolong the moment. Finally, it was time to revisit the past. "I'm from Northeast. I was raised in Paradise Projects, but I used to hang on 58th Street."

At the mention of 58th Street, both Melvin and Belinda looked at each other, then at Chico.

"But I just spent the last eighteen years of my life in prison for a murder that I didn't commit. That's why I look so familiar to you, Mrs. Valentine. I'm the man that you sent to prison for eighteen years."

The room became deathly quiet.

Billie's mind began to race a mile a minute. "Ma, what is he talking about?"

"I…I…" Belinda stammered.

In the Blink of an Eye

"Go ahead Mrs. Valentine, tell Billie how you lied on me to protect your husband. For years, I couldn't understand why you did it. But today, when I met your husband and recognized who he was, I figured it out. Your husband was the man I saw dart out of the bushes and run down the street."

Melvin Valentine shot out of his chair. "Now wait a god damn minute..."

"Melvin sit down!" Belinda said and exhaled. "Billie might as well hear the truth from us. It's been a family secret for way too long."

"Mom, what secret and..."

Belinda Valentine silenced her daughter with a stern look. "What Chico said is true. Nineteen years ago..."

Melvin Valentine dropped his head into his hands. "Why do we have to do this now?"

"Because honey, our dirty little secret happens to be sitting at our dining room table, right now. So, let's deal with it. Please do not interrupt me again. You or Billie. Nineteen years ago, I caught my brother William stealing outta my purse. William was my younger brother and I loved him a great deal. But crack cocaine had him living in a different reality and nobody could reach him. He brutalized and terrorized my whole family.

"Billie, you were around six or seven years old then. The day that I caught William in my purse, he had just taken money that your father had given me for things that you needed. I struggled and fought with my brother to give me the money back. But he wouldn't. Then your father knocked on the door. I let him in and told him what William had done. They began to fight. The fight spilled outside. Nobody knew that William was carrying a gun.

"As they scuffled, William pulled that gun. They continued to wrestle around until finally, the gun went off. I screamed I didn't know who was shot or if anybody was. Then William collapsed and I saw the blood stain spread across the front of his shirt. Your father panicked and ran into the bushes. I bent over William and tried to stop the bleeding...my hand was covered in blood. Then I saw this guy come out of the building. He walked right by me. We locked eyes, but he kept walking. I heard the sirens in the distance. I was distraught but rational.

"I knew that Melvin would be arrested for shooting William. And as a mother and a love, I couldn't let that happen. I saw Melvin come out of the bushes and run down the street. I made my decision quickly. I picked up the gun and ran it in the house. I hid it. Then I ran back outside and sat with William. I watched him take his last breath. I cried and cried. When the police asked me, what happened, I lied. I lied to protect Melvin. I lied to protect you, Billie. You needed your father and I needed him, too. I loved my brother with all my heart, but the person that he had become...was not my brother that I knew and loved. He was gone.

I couldn't lose them both." Belinda stopped momentarily and glanced at her daughter, who was now openly crying. "I lied to the police. I told them that another man did it. A light brown skinned young man, with cat eyes and a gold Acura Legend two door coupe. I gave them a part of his license plate number. What I had memorized. Later that night, they took me a street somewhere and shined a light in a man's face. They asked me if he was the man that killed my brother and I said yes.

"By the time the guilt set in, it was too late. I had to finish what I started. I went to court and testified against an innocent man. I sent an innocent man to prison, away from his family, to protect mine. I did what I thought I had to do. I thought it was right. I have been living with this guilt for nineteen years and I'm glad it's out."

Chico quietly pulled a silenced 9mm out of each pants pocket under the table. He rested them in his lap. "You ruined my life and destroyed my family to protect yours? I have a twenty-year-old daughter named Ashley that blames me for never being there for her. She doesn't speak to me at all. I have a nineteen-year-old son named Quinton, whose mother poisoned him against me and now he calls another man Daddy. My daughter Brittany never knew who I was until she was twelve years old. She was the only person on earth who believed me when I said that I was innocent. My father died while I was in prison and they wouldn't even let me attend his funeral. My mother went through hell for years with an abusive boyfriend and I couldn't help her. I thought that God was just punishing me for something else I had done. I lived every day behind those walls waiting for this day to come. You destroyed my life to protect your family and now look. It was all for nothing."

"How so?" Belinda asked.

"Because you can't protect them now." Chico stood up with a gun in each hand. The first person he shot was Melvin Valentine, his brains were all over the wall behind him.

Billie and her mother screamed at the same time.

Chico turned to face Billie. He put one gun up to his mouth. "S...s...h...h...h! The sins of the parents are sometimes revisited on the children." He then shot Billie twice in the head. The impact of the bullets and the proximity caused her head to snap back and her body to fall back still in her chair. Chico walked slowly around to where Billie lay and pumped two more bullets into her face.

Belinda Valentine could do nothing but mouth a silent prayer. She closed her eyes as Chico approached her.

"Don't you dare close your eyes. Look at me, the man that you sent to jail for eighteen years. Ask yourself this question before you die. Did you really protect your family or merely prolong their lives? The answer is no. You didn't protect them. It was you who killed them." Chico pointed both guns at Belinda Valentine and pulled the triggers.

Chico searched the house until he found a flammable liquid. He doused the whole house with kerosene and made a long wick out of toilet paper. The wick was about twenty-five feet long. Chico knew that once he lit the wick, it would take about twenty minutes for it to burn down to where the kerosene lay. And twenty minutes was all he needed. It was enough time for him to be that much closer to D.C.

He exited the house through the back door and ran to his car. A minute or so later he was headed for I-95 South...

Anthony Fields

CHAPTER 35

In the parking lot of the Shake and Bake Skating Rink, Scoop scanned it for any of the cars they were looking for. He didn't see any, just as he was about to pull out, Cain said, "Wait a minute, slim. Look back there, that looks like another parking area.

Scoop pulled around to the back of the rink. "Bingo, baby!" He said excitedly. "That's a red Dodge Charger right there."

"And the burgundy Tahoe is over there. The black Lincoln parked right next to it. Cain got on the walkie talkie and relayed the good news to his men.

* * *

"A'ight, we on our way. Out." L.B. hit the button for the stash spot. The secret compartment made onto the dash of the Rover revealed itself. L.B. was just about to grab the AR-15 pistols when a thought hit him. He slammed the stash spot back shut.

"What's up, moe, why you do that?" Tay asked.

L.B. grabbed his phone and connected to Scoop and Cain. "Aye, slim, check this out, In our haste to get at these niggas, we lunchin' good. I'm willing to bet that, that skating rink got security and off-duty cops in it. We can't set it off in that parking lot. If we do it's gon' be like we playing Monopoly. Go straight to jail and don't pass go. I'm tryna hit these niggas and get back up the road. So, let's follow 'em and hit them somewhere else."

"I feel that." Scoop said. "But what if they all split up? If they're all in separate cars...meaning Vito, too...then that means there's four of them and two of us. How we gon pull that off? Somebody gonna get away and I don't want that to happen. When we leave, I ain't tryna come back. I'm tryna crush all these niggas now. We might have to do the parking lot thing and say fuck security."

L.B. thought about their dilemma. "I ain't on no cowboy shit, slim. That's why I been around this long, I still say that we split and follow two cars...preferably Vito and whoever...and get them somewhere away from the cops.

Vito is the number one target. All the other niggas is just extra. We came to crush Vito, so let's get that one above all else. Follow the nigga somewhere else and crush' em."

"A'ight, moe. It's your call."

* * *

Vick stood at the concession stand and ate a chili dog. He looked around the rink and noticed all the Baltimore street niggas in the spot. On one side of the rink was the Park Heights niggas deep as hell. Vick eyed Delmont, Detwaun, Antwaun, and Poppa walk around as if they owned the place. They had an entourage of bitches with them that had to total at least thirty. On the other side of the rink, the Murphy Homes niggas popped bottles and their collars, while all the rest of the people in the spot sweated them. Vick's eyes Ache with obvious hate. His partners Itchyman, Doughboy, and Lil Hicks were always by his side. The Baltimore Avenue and Gilmore Street niggas were in the building repping their hood to the fullest.

Markell was the man with the money over there and Vick wanted desperately to catch him somewhere alone and slipping. He'd relieve him of his cash, jewels, and his life. If it wasn't for his right-hand men, Peppy and Black, Markell would've been food for the E.A. boys. Vick then spotted the Sandtown niggas and the CBS boys...Lil Arnold, Lil Troy, and Turner holding it down in the middle of the floor in skates. The double doors at the entrance to the rink slammed open and their arch enemies walked in. Vick tapped Keith on the leg and nodded in the direction of the entrance. Keith followed his gaze and frowned. They hated the niggas from Saratoga and Stricker.

"Look who just walked in, Ap," Keith said to Apple.

Lil Apple saw Goldmouth, Shotgun, D-Nice, and Gee and suddenly didn't like the taste in his mouth. So, he spits on the floor. "Y'all wanna step to 'em, yo?"

In the Blink of an Eye

"Naw," Keith said. "Let them bitch niggas live. For now. We got plenty of time to murk them pussies. But I've suddenly lost my appetite for this spot. Let's hit the block. We can get some dinners from Ms. Puddin and fuck a few of the homegirls.

Vick locked eyes with Goldmouth. He raised his cup of soda and saluted. Goldmouth returned the gesture. "I'ma fuck that coon around something terrible, yo'. Let's bounce before I do it tonight."

Keith, Apple, and Vick made their way to the exit.

* * *

Outside in the parking lot Range Rover, Cain focused his eyes on the three men who had just exited the skating rink. "I think we got 'em, moe."

Scoop opened his eyes and stared at the three men then he came instantly awake and agreed. "It's them. But where's Vito?"

"Good question," Cain replied as they watched the three men walk to their cars.

Without even checking, Scoop knew that the second Range Rover was nearby and seeing the same things that they were. Scoop hit the chirp button. "Vito ain't with them."

"I see that, slim," L.B. responded.

"What we gon do?"

"Follow them like we said and hopefully they lead us to Vito."

"Follow who? Which ones?" Scoop replied agitatedly.

The line went dead for a minute and then he heard the familiar chirp and static. "We gon' get the black Lincoln. Y'all get the Tahoe. Hopefully, all these niggas headed to the same spot. Let's see."

"A'ight I'm out."

L.B.'s heart started beating at a rapid pace and his adrenaline built. He waited until the last car pulled out of the parking lot before starting the truck. All three vehicles pulled out of the lot right behind one another. Slowly he pulled out behind them. L.B.

fingered the bullet in his left hand as he drove. It was his good luck charm.

Lil Apple turned down Myrtle Avenue and hit Freemont. Then he turned right onto Edmondson Avenue and parked the Charger behind a Toyota Camry. He stepped out of his car just as his men were parking theirs. Apple walked up to their homie Rick and asked, "Is it pumping out here, yo?"

"It's slow as shit. Muthafuckas ain't shooting no dope to-night." Rick replied.

"That's how Monday nights is," Apple said and walked over to where a crap game had started down the block. A few minutes later, Keith and Vick joined the crap game, too.

"Do you see what is see?" L.B. asked Scoop on the walkie talkie.

"Do I ever. We got a crap game, with our three in it and four other niggas. Is one of 'em, Vito?"

"I don't see no dreads. I say we go head and fuck the whole block up, and then bounce."

Scoop glanced out the corner of his eye. "What about the young dude sitting on the steps over there?"

"Where? Oh...I see him. He shouldn't be out here this late. Leave nobody to tell the story. On the count of five, let's roll...One..."

"...two...three..." Scoop counted.

"...four...five...let's rock, baby!"

Scoop drove down the block and came to a complete stop in the middle of Edmondson Avenue. Cain leaped out with an AR in each hand. He spit both machine pistols at the crowds gathered on the block. Scoop simultaneously raced around the front of the truck and hit everybody that tried to run up the block

BOK...BOK...BOK...BOK...BOK...BOK...BOK...BOK

L.B. ran up the street from the opposite direction and blasted on anybody who tried to exit the block from that way. Tay was looking for their targets. He spotted Apple trying to hide behind a parked car. As Tay ran up on the car, Apple rose and fired a handgun at him.

"Fuck y'all niggas!" He screamed as he left off round after round.

With no cover, all Tay could do was stand there and go bullet for bullet with the dude. Two of Tay's bullets found their mark and Apple collapsed on the ground. Tay ran up on him and pumped a few more rounds into him and then he surveyed the rest of the block. Cain turned around just in time to see the young boy that had been sitting on the stoop, run out of the house with a gun and fire. The first bullet hit him directly in the shoulder. His left arm drooped as he fired the other pistol with his good arm. Out of nowhere, Scoop appeared and blew the young boy's body up the stairs. It landed awkwardly in front of the house's front door.

Scoop looked down the street and saw L.B. and Tay standing over dudes, firing their weapons. There were bodies everywhere and sirens could be heard. Scoop screamed at Cain, "Let's go!"

Tay saw Cain and Scoop hopping into the Rover and ran towards his with L.B. on his heels. They got in the truck and got ghost. Once they were safely away from the scene, Tay asked, "What now, slim?"

L.B. kept his eyes on the road as he drove. "We gotta stay and get Vito. I told you I ain't leaving without his head."

"So, we staying here?"

"Yeah. We gotta dump the Range and find somewhere to lay low, but we ain't leaving until the job is done."

"Fuck it. I'm with you, slim." Tay replied and looked back to see if any cops were behind them. Seeing none, he relaxed a little.

LB picked up the Nextel and hit the chirp. "Scoop? Cain?"

"What's up, slim?" It was Scoop.

"Y'all good?"

"We good. Cain hit in the shoulder, though. He crying like a bitch…"

"Nigga fuck you!" Cain hollered out.

"Where y'all at?" L.B. asked.

"We hitting the beltway right now. I gotta get Cain to the family doctor. Where y'all at?"

"We staying."

Anthony Fields

"Slim, we just left about nine niggas dead back there, what the fuck you mean, y'all staying." Scoop vented.

"Holla at Gee when y'all back and let him know what happened. Let him know that me and Tay stayed back to get Vito."

"A'ight. Y'all be safe and keep in touch. If y'all need me, holla."

"One love, slim. Tell Cocaine I said he gon' be a'ight. I'm out." L.B. looked over at Tay. "We gotta get outta this truck. You UUV skills still up to par?"

"Nigga I'm the best car thief on the East Coast." Tay retorted.

"We'll see."

CHAPTER 36

Quanda awoke when she heard the cell click and open. She sat up in the bed and stretched. The thin mattress on the steel bunk had done nothing to cushion her body from the hardness. Quanda washed her face and brushed her teeth and still couldn't believe the sudden turn events. The day before at that time she had been in her comfortable...no she was wrong...she had been in Star's bed sleeping off a high brought on by multiple orgasms. And now she was in jail, waking up to the sounds of clinking metal and loud voices.

Pulling on her orange jumpsuit and slipping her feet into her flip flops, Quanda walked out of the cell and looked around. There were four tiers in the block with what she counted at twenty cells per tier. In the middle of the block was a common area with four long white cafeteria styled tables. At those tables sat various women playing board games and cards. There were two TV rooms that sat at the end of the two top tiers. There were four tables in each TV room. Quanda found an empty spot in the back of the room and sat down. The morning news was on the TV...

"...Wilson. This morning's top story comes from Baltimore. We now go live to our affiliate station there, Fox News 7. We have Aniyah Fields standing by...Aniyah?"

"Good morning, Maria."

"Aniyah, can you tell us what's going on out there in Baltimore?"

"Certainly. Maria, I'm standing here in the 4600 block of Edmondson Avenue in West Baltimore, where just up the street here, BPD is still at the scene of several homicides. Maria, the scene here is one that is hard to describe. Two SUVs pulled onto the block from both directions and four gunmen got out of the trucks and opened fire on everybody that was congregated here. Nothing has been confirmed yet, Maria, but our sources close to the scene say that as many as ten people may be dead."

"Aniyah...does anyone there know why this tragedy took place?"

"All we know Maria is that Baltimore authorities are still trying to learn why this happened. Witnesses say that maybe a gang war between the men from this block and another rival block is the reason for this. But, again, nothing has been confirmed yet."

"Aniyah, please keep us updated."

"I will, Maria."

"In other news, this morning...D.C. Police have identified the man that they found in the unit block of Nelson Place, Southeast, as twenty-nine-year-old Stanley Currie. Authorities believe that Stanley Currie's death was the result of his testimony recently against convicted killer Thomas Hager...D.C. Police are looking to determine the identity of a woman whose body was fished out of the Potomac yesterday. The woman was wrapped in several layers of plastic and had been shot to death...Last night as you slept, D.C. Police in conjunction with a federal task force executed warrants and arrested four men that they say are responsible for over fifty percent of the District's cocaine supply. Authorities arrested twenty-nine-year-old Derrick Simpson, thirty-year-old Maurice Fells, thirty-two-year-old Ricky Jones, and forty-one-year-old Billy Richardson. The four men have been linked to the Trinidad Cartel."

Quanda's heart was in the pit of her stomach. All the dudes that she did business with were now in jail. Since she was arrested a day before them, the perception would be that she told on them. Quanda got up and went to the common area. There were eight phones along the wall and two of them were available. Grabbing one, she dialed a number collect. *Please answer the phone.*

A recording went through the motions and then a voice said, "Hello, Quanda."

"Yeah, Mike it's me..."

"Quanda, what the hell did you do? Why..."

"Mike, listen to me. I'll explain everything later. Right now, I need you to..."

In the Blink of an Eye

CHAPTER 37

Vito, vibed off a Scarface CD as he rolled up his 4th blunt of the day. He didn't usually put PCP in his weed, but ever since his block got shot up and all his men got killed, he needed something stronger to ease the pain. Unstrapping his bulletproof vest and taking it off, he thought back on all the stuff he had done in the last five days after their deaths.

Knowing that they all had various beefs all over Baltimore, he started with the most serious one. Coming out only at night, Vito went through each neighborhood in a different car each time and ripped up whoever was outside. The murder rate was up and at an all-time high. His first destination had been Saratoga and Stricker. He caught Goldmouth, D-Nice, and Shotgun slipping badly in a car on their block. He Swiss cheesed the car and killed them all. Then just like that, he walked away. That was the first of many of his journey into niggas hoods.

Vito puffed on the Backwood filled with hydro, dipped in PCP and thought about what crackhead Wanda had just told him minutes ago...

"This shit has got to stop, Vito. I know how you felt about Apple and Keith and nem. Shit, we all loved them, niggas. But killing everybody in West Baltimore ain't gonna bring them, boys, back. And I been tryna find you anyway...the dudes that killed everybody on the block that day wasn't no city niggas. My sister said she was up that night when the shots started. She went to the window and looked outside. She said she saw four niggas get out of two trucks. One was black and the other one was another dark color but she couldn't make it out. She said the trucks were Range Rovers. The..."

At the mention of Ranger Rovers, Vito's antennas had gone up.

"...one them rappers be driving. She said she saw them same trucks out there earlier that day just sitting. She even saw the license plate on one of 'em. She used to work in D.C. at the DMV.

215

She said that the truck had D.C. plates on it. Them were some D.C. niggas that put that work in. Y'all out here killing each other and them D.C. niggas back in D.C. laughing at y'all asses. The cops out here everywhere deep as shit and can't nobody get no money, or sell no dope. And I can't cop no coke. I can't have that shit. I need a blast bad as shit. Gimme some money…"

Vito blew smoke in the air and pondered what Wanda had said. The night that they went to D.C. to party and they ended at the H2O, there was a rack of ballers in that club that night. That was the night they robbed the nigga for the jewelry and cash that got in the Lexus. As they waited for the dude to leave the Club, he remembered seeing about six Range Rovers in the parking lot that night. When the first Range Rover pulled out of the lot, the other pulled behind it. The whole picture began to come together. Sparkle was there that night, too. Being who she was, she had to know the dudes in the club. One of them had to be to Rock Blackman. Vito thought about Sparkle and visualized himself killing her. She must have told the dudes that were down with Rock about him. Sparkle was the only person in D.C. that knew him. She knew where he lived. She knew who his friends were and what kind of cars they drove. Vito cursed himself for underestimating Sparkle. He had been too cocky, too confident. He never thought that Sparkle would give him and his men up. Vito thought that he controlled her mind, body, and spirit. He reminded himself to throw away that *'48 Laws of Pimpin'* book by the dude Pimpin' Ken. That shit didn't work. He thought that he was mackin', but all the time, he was fooling himself. Vito inhaled the acrid smoke again and dialed Sparkle's number on his cell phone.

"…have reached Sparkle…please leave…"

Vito thought about leaving her a threatening message but nixed that idea. He wanted to surprise her. Sparkle was the key to him finding out who hit his block and killed his men. He'd make her tell him everything…then he'd kill her…slowly.

Why put off for tomorrow, what can be done today? Putting his blunt out, Vito put his vest back on and grabbed two handguns and the AK-.5 minutes later he was on the highway. Destination...Washington D.C...

* * *

"22 cell, Jasper! LaQuanda Jasper!" The CO shouted above the din of loud noises and ruckus.

Quanda walked up to her. "I'm LaQuanda Jasper. What's up?"

"You got court, Jasper."

"*Court?*" Quanda repeated confused. She looked at the clock on the wall above the CO station. It read 11:21 a.m. The few days that she had been there, Quanda knew the routine like the back of her hand. She knew that the court load went out at 5 a.m...Not 11 a.m. "Are you sure?"

"LaQuanda Jasper, DCDC 313-999, that's you, right?"

"Yeah."

"You got to court. The Marshals are waiting for you downstairs."

Thirty minutes later, Quanda was handcuffed, shackled, and being led out of D.C. jail. The Marshals said that she was going to District Court on 3rd Street. Quanda sat back in her seat and wondered what was in store for her. Who was she going to see at District Court? *The Feds?*

Anthony Fields

CHAPTER 38

The townhouse on Pomeroy Road was darkened. All the lights were out. That told Vito that nobody was home. He searched the parking lot and the whole block for Sparkle's Infiniti, but couldn't find it. Vito decided to sit, wait, and see who came home first. Whichever girl came home first, he'd force his way into the house and wait for Sparkle there. Maybe he'd have a little fun while he waited. The No Holes Barred Crew was a group of whores anyway. They deserved to be treated like shit.

* * *

She was led into a room that resembled the room at the police station, only that one was cleaner, warmer and smelled better.

"Somebody will be in to you see, shortly." An older U.S. Marshal said and then left the room, closing the door behind him.

Ten minutes or so went by and then the door opened. In walked two men. One white and one black. The tall white man resembled the basketball great Larry Bird. The black man dressed in a very conservative, perfectly tailored navy blue suit, could pass for Idris Elba. The white man spoke first.

"Ms. Jasper, my name is Donovan Glasgow. I am a federal agent with the FBI. This…" he pointed at the black man. "…is my partner Gregory Stallings. We are the agents assigned to this case. Do you know why you're here?"

Quanda remained silent.

"You don't talk much, huh?"

No response.

"I know you can talk, LaQuanda. But it's fine with me if you don't want to speak. You can just listen and hear me out. Then if you'd like to say something, please feel free to do so. We are investigating the Carlos Trinidad Organization. You've heard of him, right? Carlos Trinidad?"

Silence.

"The organization is responsible for almost all of the illegal narcotics distributed in D.C. The man that you work for is a part of that organization. What do you know about your connect, Alejandro Rojas?"

Quanda shifted in her seat but kept quiet.

"Let me give you the history of the Trinidad Organization. The organization that has been your employer for the last few years. It was started by Colombians here in the city. A man by the name of Tomas Trujillo. Tomas Trujillo employed a young firebrand named Carlos Venegas to commit several acts including, but not limited to, murder. At some point, the two men had a difference of opinions and Carlos killed Tomas Trujillo and every living member of his family. Carlos Venegas became Carlos Trinidad and assumed power and the authority to take over the organization by the powerful Medellin family called the Bali Cartel. That Cartel is headed by Don Pablo Blanco Ruiz.

"Over the years' things went smoothly. At some point, Carlos decided to leave the organization that he helped build. But he left people in place to run it. That person is a man named Jesus Vargas. Alejandro Rojas, the man you've been meeting every Sunday, works for him."

Quanda was amazed at how much the Feds knew about everything. If they knew she was meeting Alejandro every Sunday, why hadn't they arrested her sooner?

"Alejandro Rojas is small potatoes compared to the other men I've named. We know everything he does. We've been trying to build a case on Jesus Vargas and Carlos Trinidad for years with no success. But we have an opportunity now to cripple it from the bottom up. We can grab Rojas right now, but what do we really have? He never gave you anything and you never gave him anything. We know that the drugs ended up in your car some kind of way, but we still don't know how he did it."

So, the almighty Feds don't know everything, huh?

"But we have an ace in the hole." Agent Stallings joined in. "We have you and we have your brother."

In the Blink of an Eye

Quanda stared into the face of the black agent. What did he mean by that? He had me and my brother? What did they have on Mark?"

"If we can get you to testify against Rojas, we can get him and eventually break him. But we need you to lie a little." Agent Glasgow continued. "You have to say that he gave you drugs directly and you gave him money. If you do that, it will help Mark go free."

Help Mark go free? What the fuck are talking about? Do they know about her trying to help Mark get out of jail? And why would they even be concerned with Mark coming home? Shouldn't they be threatening him with more time? Confusion was etched all over her face as Quanda tried to figure out what the agents were up to. "What do you mean by you'll help my brother go free?"

Glasgow looked at Stallings and said, "So, she does speak. For a moment, there I thought you were mute." He smiled. Quanda did not. "Mark helped his case for freedom by cooperating with…"

"I don't believe you," Quanda interjected. "Mark wouldn't do that."

"He didn't tell you, huh?" Agent Stallings asked. He looked at his partner. "He didn't tell her, Glas."

Agent Glasgow sat down on the table. "LaQuanda, your brother Mark is a federal informant. He came to us. Apparently, he doesn't want to spend the next thirty years in prison."

"You're fuckin' lying!" Quanda spat venomously. "I don't believe your cracker ass. Y'all been lying to black folks for hundreds of years. And twenty fourteen ain't no different."

"What if you hear it from me?" Stallings added.

"I wouldn't believe your house nigga ass either."

"Listen, whether you believe us or not, Mark Jasper is a federal informant. He sleeps in a dorm style unit at Petersburg Medium FCI, three cubicles away from Manuel Estrada. Mr. Estrada is an associate of Jesus Vargas. Your brother initiated contact with him and brokered a deal to distribute keys of cocaine to people that he knew in D.C. Estrada contacted Vargas and Vargas put Alejandro Rojas with you."

"If y'all have all that what the fuck do y'all need from me and Mark? Or want from us rather?"

"The answer to your question is…what does Mark want from us? Why did he come to us with information? Why did he agree to set up Estrada and testify against him? He wants his freedom. You agreed to help him…yeah, he told us that, too…because you want to get him home. We don't care if Mark goes home. He's nobody to us. We need Rojas, Estrada, and Vargas. He's agreed to do his part from there. We need you to do your part from here."

"What about the other?"

"Who? Richardson, Fells, Simpson, and Shaw?"

"Yeah."

"We could care less about those guys. They were picked up because of you. The other guy George Foreman that you dealt with…whose gonna be apprehended any day now…they are small fish in a gigantic pond. Your cooperation…and I do mean cooperation because we're asking you to lie…would free them, too. If you agree to help us, we'll drop all the charges against them. And you'll be helping your brother."

Quanda couldn't believe what she was hearing. Her brother, the gangsta, her strength, her heart, her hero, had become someone that she hated. After all that he had done, there was no way that he had willingly become a rat. She needed to speak to him, she needed answers. "I hear everything that y'all are saying and I'm open to cooperating, but I have to talk to Mark first."

"No problem." Agent Glasgow said. "We can set up a call to the prison…"

"No way. I need to talk to him face to face. I need to make sure that y'all ain't tryna trick me. Y'all are the Feds, y'all can make shit happen. Have Mark brought here and let me talk to him. Then I'll do whatever y'all want. If y'all can't do that, I keep my trap closed and go to jail. It makes no difference to me."

In the Blink of an Eye

"Let me go and call my supervisor and I'll be right back."
Glasgow said and headed for the door."
"You do that."

* * *

His patience was wearing thin as his high came down. Vito
wished that he had brought more drugs, but in his haste to get to
D.C., he had left his stash behind. Glancing up at the townhouse,
he saw that there was still no sign of movement in the house.
Where was everybody? *"Out fucking. Fuckin' whores."*
Vito started the car up and pulled away from the curb. He
decided to ride around for a while. Maybe he'd come up on somebody that he needed to see. He hit Suitland Parkway and came off
on Alabama Avenue. His stomach rumbled as he passed the New
York Fried Chicken carryout. *"When was the last time I ate something?"* He asked himself as he made a U-turn in the middle of
the street. *"I'm gonna get me some chicken."* So, focused on his
growing hunger, Vito never saw the police car that was parked
on Shipley Terrace. The cop pulled behind Vito and activated his
lights.
Vito acted like he didn't see any flashing lights. He calmly
drove straight through the light and turned down the exit leading
back to Suitland Parkway. Once he hit the parkway, he floored
the Magnum. The Hemi engine roared as it came to life and did
the whole 140 on the dash. Before long, there were four more cars
involved in the chase. Knowing the Parkway, a little, Vito knew
that it ended on the Pennsylvania Avenue extension, which leads
to Upper Marlboro. If he kept going, he'd have not one but two
different police behind him...D.C.'s and PG County's.
And that was a combination that he knew that he couldn't
win against, so at the last possible moment, he turned off Suitland
Parkway onto Silver Hill Road. He could at least race back to
D.C., hit a small street, hop out and maybe get away on foot. The
Magnum fishtailed at she cut sharply into a different lane and
sped down Branch Avenue. Vito looked in his rearview mirror

223

and whistled. There seemed to be about a hundred police cars behind him.

Vito floored the Magnum and it jumped out ahead of all the other cars as Branch Avenue gave way to Minnesota Avenue. A police car came out of nowhere just as he came out of the circle by a park and rammed him. Vito lost control of the car as it spun, jumped a curb and ran into a tree. The airbags deployed and that's all he remembered.

***

"My boss says that can be arranged. Give us a few days and your brother will be writted back to D.C. Just as you suggested, your meeting will take place here at the court building. Any other requests? Usually, people ask for a conjugal visit." Agent Glasgow said and smiled.

"Yeah. Can I got back to jail now?"

"Sure, you can."

CHAPTER 39

"...Breaking news...D.C. Police was involved in a high-speed chase today. A black Dodge Magnum that police attempted to pull over for a traffic violation, failed to stop. The high-speed chase involved police from PG County as well. The car eventually crashed into a tree in Southeast.

"Rescue vehicles arrived on the scene and cut a man out of the badly damaged vehicle. D.C. Police have identified that man as twenty-six-year-old Valentine 'Vito' Miller, a Baltimore native. D.C. Police believe that Vito Miller is responsible for at least two murders in the district. Authorities say that Vito Miller is suspected of killing Artinis Winston in October of last year. He is also believed to be the shooter in the death of Ronald Blackman. Mr. Miller was rushed to D.C. General Hospital, where he is now listed as being seriously injured. More about this breaking news tonight at C.U.S. Fox News at 11..."

George Foreman clicked off the TV once the news bulletin went off. His anger was palpable and could be felt in the room. He had failed his uncle. The dude Vito had gotten away. How did the cops know that Vito killed Rock? What the fuck was Vito doing in D.C. and L.B. and Tay were still in Baltimore?

George picked up the phone and made the call.

"Yeah?" Tay answered.

"Have y'all found the dude, Vito yet?" George asked.

"Naw, moe. This nigga ain't showing his face nowhere."

"You know why?"

"Why?"

"Because he's here in D.C."

"What? How?"

"Just tell L.B. that I said it's time to bring y'all asses home. I'll tell y'all the rest then."

* * *

B.F. watched the news program fade back into an episode of Law and Order SVU. He was already disturbed about being locked up in the dirty ass D.C. jail, but what he had just heard on the news, broke his peace for real. The police had a dude in custody that they say killed Whistle. A Baltimore nigga at that. B.F. was beyond upset. He walked out of the TV room, glancing one last time at the dudes in the room. *Why in the hell do all them niggas wanna watch a show about the police? What is niggas fascination with cops shows while in jail? I can't understand that shit.*

B.F. thought about the visit he had gotten from Mark and Quanda's brother, Mike and the message that Quanda had sent. She was in jail, too and she wasn't the person who gave everybody up. She would never be the weakest link. She just wanted them to know that. B.F. believed every word. But if the culprit wasn't Quanda who was it?

On the top tier, B.F. stopped and hollered at his men, Yukon Ron and Whop. They were in D.C. jail waiting to go to trial on a body. Then he made his way down the tier where his co-defendants were congregated at. B.F. shook hands with Moe Styles and Ricky but just gave Dollar a head nod. He didn't know him like that.

"Let me ask y'all something," B.F. said to the group. "Since all of us gotta visit from Mike and we now know that Quanda's in, too, and she ain't the one that put us here. Who did put is here?"

"I don't know, cuz," Moe said.

Ricky Jones just shrugged his shoulders.

Dollar Bill Richardson rubbed the beard stubble on his face and said, "My lawyer said it's the Feds holding us, but we ain't been charged with nothing, yet. We gon know what's up when they ready to tell us."

"You sure right, dawg, you sure right," B.F. replied. He listened to what everybody had to say but he only half heard them. His mind was elsewhere. *Vito Miller, huh? He gotta come over this jail. I'll see him then.*

CHAPTER 40

The table benches in the housing unit were hard as hell, so Quanda put a towel down before she sat in front of the phone. Then she called her brother's cell phone. "Mike, what's up, baby?"

"Quan, you sound like you been doing push-ups over there. Let me find out that them bitches over there tryna take that lil coochie?"

Quanda laughed. "Boy, I wish, you know me."

"Yeah, you right. I do know your freaked-out ass. I did everything you told me to do. I went to see everybody. They say they feel you and keep your head up. I called the dude George, but his number is disconnected. I called the hospital and they said that they can't release any information about Rhoda's condition over the phone because her case is being investigated by the police. I called her mother, but I never caught her. I called Billie's cell phone and the numbers you gave me for Chico and nobody answers any of them joints..."

That's strange. Quanda thought to herself.

"...and I'm sorry about Sparkle, Quan I "

"Hold it...hold it. Sorry about Sparkle...what?"

Mike got quiet for a minute. "You don't know? You haven't heard? It was all over the news..."

"What the fuck happened with Sparkle, Mike?"

"They found Sparkle dead last week. She was floating in the water down by the wharf when some fishermen found her. The news said she was wrapped in plastic, but she had been shot to death. I'm sorry Quan. I thought you knew."

Quanda's tears started and fell unabated. For all of Sparkle's shortcomings, she didn't deserve to die like that. A sense of hopeless depression gripped Quanda and wouldn't let go.

"I spoke to Mark today. That's good news, right? He's back in D.C."

"What did he say?" She mumbled through her tears.

"He's happy as shit to be back in the city."

"What block is he in over there?" Quanda asked.

He's not over there. He's over CTF, he said. He said it's better than jail and that he getting conjugal visits over there."

Her tears came in bunches now. Quanda cried for Sparkle. She cried for Mark. By coming back to D.C. and going to CTF was admission enough that he had switched sides, but to now hear that Mark was allowed conjugal visit...

"...most people usually want a conjugal visit..."

...that was the nail that sealed the coffin. Mark was no longer a part of the death before dishonor. Everything in her life had changed that fast and it was hard to believe. The rest of the phone call with Mike went by in a blur. As Quanda dried her eyes, her resolve hardened. There would be no more time for tears. Crying wouldn't change nothing. Her tears couldn't bring Vita, Cinnamon, Sparkle, or Rock back. They couldn't give Rhoda her eyes back. And they definitely couldn't change the way she now felt about her brother.

"Let me say this to you, baby boy before this phone hangs up. I always felt responsible for you and Mark. But I showed him favoritism because he was more like our father, to me. I felt that you were more like our mother. I thought that you were the weak one. I criticized you in my head and condemned you in my heart. But now I realize that I was wrong. We were the weak ones and you were strong. You still are. It takes a strong man to be responsible for his children, work every day, and be content with that. You are the strong one, Mike. don't ever forget that. I thought that me and Mark were the smart ones, but you are smarter than both of us. You knew to stay away from gangs, drugs, and the street life. Mark and I are in jail and you're free. That makes you way smarter than the both of us. Keep being smarter than us. You hear me?"

"I hear you, Quan."

"Always remember that no matter what, I love you and I will always love you..."

In the Blink of an Eye

The phone had hung up, Quanda dried her eyes again and got up. Then she walked down the tier to 75 cell. She knocked on the cell door.

"Who's there?"

"It's me, Quanda, Shonell."

"Come in, Quan."

Shonell Reed was in jail for killing her boyfriend. She had come home from work early one day to find him having sex with her teenage daughter. Without saying a word, Shonell went to the kitchen and retrieved a knife. She went back into her daughter's room and stabbed him to death. Quanda had gotten the whole story from Shonell herself.

"Do you still have what I said I might need?" Quanda asked.

"Most definitely." Shonell replied.

"What do you want for it?"

"Give me five tunas and a box of Ritz crackers and it's yours."

Quanda went back to her cell. She grabbed five tunas out of her canteen bag and a box of crackers. Then she went back to Shonell's cell and gave her the food items. Shonell pulled a Bible off her desk and gave it to Quanda.

"What the fuck is this?" Quanda asked. "I don't need Jesus right now, I need what I asked you for."

"Calm down, boo, trust me, it's in there."

Quanda took Shonell at her word and left. Back inside her cell, she put a towel wrapped around a roll of toilet paper in the window of her cell door. Then she flipped the Bible over and over until she saw the crease in the flap and opened the Bible's cover. Quanda reached her hand into the flap and removed what she needed. The fiberglass shank was flat, light and easy to conceal. Having always carried one in her purse, Quanda knew what a good knife looked like. The one she now held was sturdy but a little dull. Quanda got on her hands and knees and scraped the shank up against the brick wall. When it was sharpened to her satisfaction, she made a cover for it out of the cardboard roll in the middle of the toilet paper. She added some tape and then admired her work. She was satisfied that I would do. Instead of going back out of the cell, Quanda laid down in her bunk. She had a lot to think about.

In the Blink of an Eye

CHAPTER 41

It was lunch time when the nurse woke him up. Vito sat up, but it was hard to eat with one hand handcuffed to the bed. He gave up after two more tries. "I can't eat like this, yo. You can't just cuff my leg to the rail?"

"Don't even worry about it, Miller." The officer said. "Because that's your last meal at this hospital. As we speak, a transport vehicle is on the way to take you to your new home. You'll like D.C. jail. It's loud, it's crowded, it's dirty, and it's dangerous just like you like it. One thing though, them boys in there don't like no out of towners. You came to D.C. and killed two people and you from Baltimore...you must be crazy."

"I didn't kill nobody," Vito responded. There was nobody that could prove he did. He had heard about Sparkle on the news. Somebody had killed the bitch and did him a favor. All he had to fight was the gun charges that they hit him with. The AK would carry ten years by itself.

"Tell it to the judge and jury, not me." He said and then looked behind him. "As a matter of fact, your ride is here. Let's go B-More."

Two burly correctional officers came into the room and put their shackles and cuffs on him.

"Good luck over the jail, B-More. You gon need it."

"Fuck you, yo!" Vito spat as he was led out of the hospital room.

***

The Marshals were putting her shackles on when the big door opened. Quanda watched as a man was led into the jail. *That nigga looks like T-pain.* He looked familiar but she couldn't place him. At the sight of her, the dude smiled. Quanda smiled back. He was kind of cute, even if he did have gold teeth in his mouth.

"Let's go, Jasper." The Marshal said.

Twenty minutes later, they were pulling into the court building. The whole floor dropped as the van lowered. Quanda was taken off the van and unshackled. She was made to walk through a metal detector and then taken to the same room as before. When she walked into the room, Quanda observed Agents Glasgow and Stallings engaged in a conversation with Mark. They all laughed. The sound of Mark's laughter steadied her frayed nerves.

Mark stood up when he saw her. He came around the table and hugged her. Quanda hugged him back. "I'm glad that you asked for this meeting because we need to talk." He said.

Quanda looked at both federal agents. "Can I speak to my brother alone, please?"

The agents looked at each other and shrugged. "Sure. We'll be right outside when you need us." Both agents left the room.

The room became deathly quiet. They both sat down.

"I know what you are probably thinking..."

"Tell what you think I'm thinking Mark?"

"You think that I'm a bitch for what I'm doing. You think that I'ma hypocrite for hating on dudes like Rayful, Alpo, and T.I. and now I'm one of them."

"So, it's true, huh? You are a rat?"

"Look, Quan you can call me whatever you want, but you won't call me stupid. Not anymore, I got a rack of time for some bullshit. Because of some other niggas. I was never going to see the streets again. The world might don't be here in thirty years. I don't have no kids, never been married, nothing. I was done, Quan."

"I raised the money for you; you could've done thing the right way."

"The right way? You raised the money? Quan, no amount of money was gonna free me. so, I had to free myself."

"And by freeing yourself, you just said, fuck the code that we lived by? Fuck the death before dishonor?"

"Fuck the street code and the death before dishonor!" Mark exploded. "That shit ain't nothing but some shit a few niggas in prison made up. That shit ain't loyal to nobody. Look at all the

In the Blink of an Eye

muthafuckas that snitched on me and other niggas. Them niggas out here living and don't nobody care, Quan. Don't you get it? Don't you see it? Hot muthafuckas accepted in the hoods now. Ain't no more street code. The street code and the death before dishonor ain't done a damn thing for me...but got me thirty years in prison. That shit don't feed a nigga when he hungry or make a nigga bid easier. Fuck all that shit! I want out. I'm too young to spend the next thirty years of my life in prison."

"Why did you involve me in all of this? If that's the way you feel, cool. But why drag me into this shit when you know how I feel about that hot shit?"

"I didn't want to, Quan. But I figured that your love for me would supersede all the other shit. I knew that you wanted me home just as bad as I wanna be home. So, I figured that the end would justify the means and you'd understand despite the foul moves I made. Plus, I needed somebody that I could trust. And the only person that I trust is you, Quan. This move wasn't to hurt you, B.F. or nobody else. It was about the Colombians. Fuck them muthafuckas, Quan. All they care about is the fuckin' money. They would've done the same thing to me. I knew that you wouldn't get any time. It was a part of the deal. I asked that you be held at the jail for your own protection."

Quanda had heard enough. "I wouldn't need protection if you wouldn't have put me in this position. You used me, Mark. After all, I did for you, you used me. You put my life in danger. You wanna make me a rat. And that's what you call protecting me? I did everything I could to help you. I sold my body to niggas...for you. Why do you think I became part of the NHBC? Huh? Because I wanted to be fucked by strange niggas and paid for it? Naw, baby boy. I did it all for you. And this is how you repay me? What you're doing now shows me that it was always about you. All you care about is you!"

"That's not true." Mark pleaded.

"It's true. You are a selfish, weak nigga and I see that now. I used to admire you, but now I see that you were faking to make

233

it the whole time. All that dope you sold in the hood. All the bodies you caught and now you wanna rat on the Colombians? That's bitch shit. You should be wearing one of my thongs instead of a pair of boxers. Despite all that, I'ma help you. I'll do what the Feds want me to do. If that will get you home, so be it."

Quanda feigned acceptance and compliance as she quietly unbuttoned her jumper under the table.

"Quan, I know you mad at me but in time, you'll understand that what I'm doing is right. I wanna be home with you and Mike. With Grandma and my nieces and nephews. That's not being selfish."

"It don't even matter." Quanda lifted up a little and reached into her jumpsuit. She put her hand inside her panties. "We need to be a family again."

"So, do you feel where I'm coming from?"

Using her vaginal muscles, Quanda pushed the shank downward. When she felt the handle of it she grabbed it and eased it out of her pussy. "Oh...I feel you. I definitely feel you."

Mark became animated. "Everything is gonna be alright, Quan. Watch. We gon move to another state and do the muthafucka."

"We gon move right next door to Sammy the Bull, Rayful Edmonds, and Nicky Barnes." Quanda joked as she unwrapped the plastic off the shank. "They gon make a movie about us and Curtbone gon direct it."

"Go head with that bullshit, Quan. This us, we don't have to answer to nobody but God."

Quanda dropped the plastic on the floor, palmed the shank in her right hand, and cuffed it. "I love you, Mark. I always have and I always will."

"I love you too, Quan!"

"Come and gimme a hug. I need one right now."

Mark came around the table and hugged Quanda. Quanda hugged him back with her left arm, but her right arm, she kept behind her. She kissed her baby brother on his cheek.

234

"You will always be a part of me and live forever in my heart." Suddenly, she tightened her grip on Mark. Quanda brought her right arm around and stabbed Mark in the neck repeatedly. He grabbed at his neck with one hand and tried to get her off him with the other. But Quanda wouldn't let go. They fell to the ground. She repeatedly plunged the shank into Mark's neck and chest.

The noise from their fall alerted the agents. Agents Stallings and Glasgow tackled Quanda and pulled her off her brother.

"Drop the weapon, LaQuanda!" Agent Glasgow said. To his partner, he said. "Get some help in here. Get a goddamn ambulance in here, now!"

The Marshal that brought her to the room peeped in and took in the scene. What he saw shocked the hell out of him. He saw the blood everywhere. The federal agent lying on top of the female prisoner. A bloody weapon and a dead male prisoner. All he could do was take his hand and make the sign of the cross. "Mary mother of God!"

Anthony Fields

CHAPTER 42

After going through the process at D.C. Jail, Vito was taken to a housing unit.

"Southside!" The CO shouted to an old woman that sat in a bubble that overlooked the whole 3rd floor.

At the end of the hall were three units. Vito read the signs above each one. They read Southeast 3, South 3, and Southwest 3.

The CO handed everybody a card and then he checked his list. "Collins…Gaffney…Williams…Jones and…Taylor. Y'all going right here. Southwest, y'all got five. Open one gate" The CO turned to the remaining men and said, "Y'all going across the hall. Southeast 3, y'all got eight coming in. Open the gate."

Vito thought about Baltimore City Jail and how different it was from the one he was now in. Then he thought about what the cop had said to him at the hospital. To himself, Vito said, *Fuck these D.C. niggas.*

Miller, you in cell fifty. That's on the top right tier."

Vito saw that there were only a few dudes on the floor when he headed to his cell. *Them niggas must be the trustees.* Before he got there, the door to cell fifty opened and a dude stepped out.

"Step back in your cell, fifty cell." The female CO said.

Vito walked in the cell and looked at the dude now sitting at the desk. *Yo black as shit.* "What's up, yo?"

"Ain't shit, moe. What's up with you?"

"Fifty cell close your door." A voice shouted.

Vito looked around like everybody there was crazy. His celly quickly figured that Vito wasn't from there because the gold teeth gave him away.

"You gotta close the door here, moe. They don't close by themselves."

"A'ight, yo. My bad." Vito closed the cell door. Then he made up his bed and laid down. He was reading all the writing on the walls when sleep overtook him.

Kevin Claiborne swept the top left tier, but his thoughts were somewhere else. When he got to the end of the tier, he stopped at thirteen cell and called out to his homie. "B.F.!"

B.F. walked up to the door. "What's up, Kay Kay?"

"The dude that you was talking about earlier, the Baltimore nigga?"

"Yeah, what about him?" B.F. asked.

"He just came in the block. They put him in fifty cell."

B.F. smiled. "Good looking out, big boy. I got him."

* * *

When the cell doors popped early the next morning, Vito ripped a strip of bed sheet and put it around his dreads before leaving the cell. When he did, he saw what looked to be over a hundred dude all over the place in the unit. Dudes were working out, jogging, playing cards, dominoes, watching TV and playing basketball in a small gym. When he saw the twelve phones spaced out on the wall, Vito decided that he needed to call home and tell his peoples to contact his lawyer, "Who got that phone next, yo?"

"My mans and nem." The dude on the first phone responded.

Vito went around to all twelve phones and found out there was a line on each one. He knew what was up, though and he had to respect it. *These D.C. niggas set trippin'.* He couldn't be mad because they did the same thing where he was from.

B.F., Whop, Yukon, and Moe Styles leaned on the rail of the top tier and watched the Baltimore dude with the long dreads. He was in the common area trying to get on a phone.

"This joint got too many cameras, moe. Them joints everywhere in here." B.F. said to his men. "What's the best blind spot in here?"

"The shower or the cell." Moe Styles answered. "But the cameras will catch you going to either spot."

"Man, we can go down there and just gut lova, fuck them cameras and all that shit. I don't give a fuck." Yukon Ron added.

238

In the Blink of an Eye

B.F. knew that his man Ron was dead serious and he respected his gangsta, but now was not the time for it.

"The object to committing crimes these days it tryna get away with it. If you would've known that a few months ago, your ass wouldn't even be in here."

"No bullshit!" Whop agreed.

They talked about every possible scenario before settling for the best one. Yukon went to fifty cell and posted up inside of it. Whop went to the back of the top tier and started doing push-ups. Moe went to the front of the tier and sat down on the steps. B.F. stood right in front forty-nine cell and watched Vito. He needed him to come to his cell.

Thirty minutes later he got his wish.

Vito's stomach started to bubble something vicious. *I shouldn't have eaten that breakfast. The grits and eggs weren't agreeing with his stomach. I gotta shit.* Vito walked up the steps heading for his cell and had to squeeze past the light skinned dude with the long dark cornrow braids. "Excuse me, yo."

"My fault, cuz." The dude said and stood up to let him pass.

Vito saw the dude standing in front of the cell next to his. The dude was dark skinned with shoulder length dreads and a full beard. *These niggas look like Jamaicans around this bitch.* Smiling to himself, Vito gave the dude a head nod as he walked up and passed him.

Before going in the cell, Vito looked behind him and saw the dude with the long braids coming down the tier, but paid him no mind until he said, "Aye main man, where your celly at?"

"I don't know…" That was as far as he got before something was put around his neck. Vito felt himself being pulled backward into the cell. He fought to turn around, but whatever was around his neck tightened with every movement. The dark-skinned dude with the dreads and full beard stepped in front of him. The oxygen in his body wasn't making it to his brain so he was starting to get dizzy. Without saying anything the two dudes in front of him pulled out knives.

His eyes got large as he summoned every ounce of strength in his body to fight off his attackers. But he was outnumbered and overpowered. A lone tear fell down his face as he felt the first knife penetrate him, then the second. Then they seemed to be everywhere at once...

***

"This is Maria Wilson, for City Under Siege Fox News, reporting to you live from the D.C. jail. About two hours ago while conducting the 4 p.m. count, Correctional staff discovered the mutilated body of suspected murderer Valentine 'Vito' Miller, lying under the bunk in his cell. D.C. Jail authorities report that Vito Miller appeared to be strangled and stabbed to death. D.C. Police are on the scene here inside the facility. There are no suspects in custody. The director of the D.C. Department of Correction Devon Brown has issued an immediate lockdown of the facility as a result of the killing...

In other news, today...a twenty-five-year-old man was killed inside the District Courthouse today. Federal authorities identify the man as Mark Lavelle Jasper. A female is in custody for the murder. Sources close to the scene identify the woman as LaQuanda Jasper, the victim's sister. How she was able to smuggle a weapon into the courthouse and kill her brother is still under investigation..."

Eliot 'L.B.' Johnson listened to the caller on the other end of his phone and then smiled. He closed the flip phone and walked outside.

George Foreman, double checked their papers to make sure that everything was proper. The passports, tickets, and everything else was in order. One of the bags was filled with money and his account in the Bahamas had whatever amount he needed just in case the money in the bag wasn't enough. George wasn't staying around to wait for the Feds to grab him. It was time to leave. He knew that he had to go, but one day he'd return. One day. George looked up in time to see L.B. come out of the house.

"You ain't gonna believe this," L.B. said.

"Believe what?" George replied.

L.B. told him about the phone call he'd receive and all about the newscast.

George smiled, and then he laughed. He kept laughing all the way to the Ford Expedition that waited for him in the driveway.

"What so funny?" The man driving the truck asked.

George looked over at Chico and said, "You ain't gonna believe this one."

Anthony Fields

In the Blink of an Eye

CHAPTER 43

One year later…

"Have a seat in the waiting room, Ms. Buchanan, Doctor Chrisette will be with you shortly. She's running a little behind schedule in one of her surgeries."

"Thank you," Rhoda said to the receptionist and walked over to the chairs in the waiting room. Her temples were throbbing, so she pulled out a bottle of pain pills and popped one dry. Since the surgery to try and fix her eye, her headaches were constant. Her doctor said that she would experience migraine headaches for the rest of her life. Rhoda lifted her Dior sunglasses and swiped at the tear forming at the corner of her right eye. The tear was caused by the solution that she had to spray on her eye to keep it moist. When given the option of wearing an eyepatch for the rest of her life or getting a glass eye. Rhoda chose the latter. The glass eye would serve as a constant reminder of everything she experienced in the last five years. And the fact that she had almost been killed. That she would never forget because the one man that she loved more than her own life, was gone. His life was taken the day that her eye was.

Rhoda went into her Dior bag and pulled out the new bestselling Street novel by Eyone Williams. HellRazor Honeys 3 was the talk of the town and she couldn't want to start reading it. The first ten pages of the book brought on too much nostalgia, so Rhoda closed it. The title alone was enough to evoke images of the NHBC. The cover of the book reminded her of Quanda.

Rhoda thought about the last visit she had with Quanda before Quanda was shipped to Bruceton Mills, West Virginia.

"Rho," Quanda had said. "Everything has come full circle for us. I remember when George used to always say that but I never understood what he meant until now. Our past, present, and future is all right here, right now. And I embrace that. I embrace my own mortality and the fact that I'm gonna burn in hell for what I did to my brother. I still cry for him, Rho. I cry for him and my

243

brother Mike. I cry for my grandmother who had to bury my brother and lose her granddaughter, too. I cry for Sparkle, Billie, Vita, and Cinnamon. I cry for you, too. Rho. But most of all I cry for me. I lost my parents when I was young. I was forced to grow up, too fast. I never had a childhood, Rho. I never knew innocence or shame. I sold my body to help a brother that didn't give a shit about me. I've seen too much pain. I've lost too much. Look at this, Rho. We were doing good, girl. Couldn't a bitch in the city get in any one of our business? We were living, girl. Cars, clothes, jewelry, shoes, bank account, credit cards, insurance, youth, good looks, and our bodies. But now look at us, Rho. We are the only ones left. And my good looks are fading…shit after I do this fifteen years, I'll probably be busted up.

"Look at you, Rho. Still beautiful…even though you lost an eye to the game. But our girls…our girls are gone, Rho. Never to return. Who the fuck knew that Chico blamed Billie for her mother's sin nineteen years ago? And look what happened to Sparkle? One bad move created a hundred just like it. It all spun out of control and cost her, her life. Then Star turned out to be the police. I let emotion and lust distract me from seeing the real truth. The signs were there, I just couldn't see the writing on the wall. And then there's Rock. What was his crime? The man made it through twenty-five years in jail only to come home and live for eight months. All he tried to do was love you and honor Roscoe. Look what happened to him. I've learned a lot since I been in jail, Rho. People say that prison is the black man's university. Well, that goes for the black woman, too.

"The most important thing I've learned, Rho, is this. Material possessions don't mean shit. All the cars, clothes, shoes, money, people you meet, parties, clubbing, all that shit don't mean nothing in the grand scheme of things. That shit is frivolous. It comes and goes. Your whole life you work to obtain riches, houses, friendships, money, and all the other shit I just named. But then in the blink of an eye, it's gone. Rock, Star, Cinnamon, Vita, Billie, Sparkle, my brother Mark, my parents, even you and me. We can all disappear in the blink of an eye…"

In the Blink of an Eye

Rhoda wiped at her eyes again, but this time they were her tears. The words that Quanda had said to her that day touched her heart and pierced her soul. Everything that Quanda had said was true and she knew it. In the blink of an eye...everything had changed. If you blinked too long you missed it. And nothing that anybody could do would change that. The past was gone forever. It was then that Rhoda thought about the postcard she had received from George Foreman. It was sent to her at the hospital with no return address. It read:

"Time is free, but it's priceless. You can use it, but you can't own it. You can spend it, but you can't keep it. Once you've lost it, you can never get it back..."

It took a while for her to really understand it's meaning, but eventually, she did. The word on the street was that George had left the country. He was running from the same indictment that had snagged Quanda. Nobody was ever arrested in Sparkle's murder and Chico had disappeared without a trace.

Rhoda never did find out what happened to Star. But she did get a bouquet of flowers at the hospital one day, with a card that said, *"Get well...Love S!"* She couldn't confirm it, but Rhoda felt in her heart that the flowers were from Star.

"Rhoda Buchanan."

Hearing her name snapped Rhoda out of her reverie. She walked up to the receptionist, who said, "There you are, Doctor Chrisette will see you now."

Rhoda walked in the back to Doctor Chrisette's office and knocked on the door.

"Come in."

"Hello, Doc, you ready for me?"

Doctor Chrisette, finished writing something in her notepad, and then she looked up at Rhoda. "Go ahead and get undressed Ms. Buchanan."

Rhoda had been waiting for this day for over six months. She had made the decision as soon as she had left D.C. jail visiting Quanda. After undressing and putting on the flimsy hospital gown, Rhoda walked into the room that was marked 'Surgery'. Doctor Chrisette was busy prepping herself.

"Lie down on that table."

Rhoda did as she was told. She was nervous but determined.

"Ms. Buchanan, are you one hundred percent sure that you want to surgically remove that tattoo?" Doctor Chrisette asked.

Rhoda looked down at her breasts and saw the naked image of Vita sitting on several stacks of money, while holding a link chain and pendant that read, 'NHBC'.

She laid her head back and said, "Yeah, I'm sure."

THE END!

Submission Guideline

Submit the first three chapters of your completed manuscript to ldpsubmissions@gmail.com, subject line: Your book's title. The manuscript must be in a .doc file and sent as an attachment. Document should be in Times New Roman, double spaced and in size 12 font. Also, provide your synopsis and full contact information. If sending multiple submissions, they must each be in a separate email.

Have a story but no way to send it electronically? You can still submit to LDP/Ca$h Presents. Send in the first three chapters, written or typed, of your completed manuscript to:

LDP: Submissions Dept
Po Box 944
Stockbridge, Ga 30281

DO NOT send original manuscript. Must be a duplicate.

Provide your synopsis and a cover letter containing your full contact information.

Thanks for considering LDP and Ca$h Presents.

Anthony Fields

Coming Soon from Lock Down Publications/Ca$h Presents

BOW DOWN TO MY GANGSTA
By **Ca$h**
TORN BETWEEN TWO
By **Coffee**
BLOOD OF A BOSS **VI**
SHADOWS OF THE GAME II
TRAP BASTARD II
By **Askari**
LOYAL TO THE GAME **IV**
By **T.J. & Jelissa**
IF LOVING YOU IS WRONG... **III**
By **Jelissa**
TRUE SAVAGE **VIII**
MIDNIGHT CARTEL IV
DOPE BOY MAGIC IV
CITY OF KINGZ III
By **Chris Green**
BLAST FOR ME **III**
A SAVAGE DOPEBOY III
CUTTHROAT MAFIA III
DUFFLE BAG CARTEL VI
HEARTLESS GOON VI
By **Ghost**
A HUSTLER'S DECEIT III
KILL ZONE **II**
BAE BELONGS TO ME III
A DOPE BOY'S QUEEN III

In the Blink of an Eye

By **Aryanna**
COKE KINGS V
KING OF THE TRAP III
By **T.J. Edwards**
GORILLAZ IN THE BAY V
3X KRAZY III
De'Kari
THE STREETS ARE CALLING II
Duquie Wilson
KINGPIN KILLAZ IV
STREET KINGS III
PAID IN BLOOD III
CARTEL KILLAZ IV
DOPE GODS III
Hood Rich
SINS OF A HUSTLA II
ASAD
KINGZ OF THE GAME VI
Playa Ray
SLAUGHTER GANG IV
RUTHLESS HEART IV
By Willie Slaughter
FUK SHYT II
By Blakk Diamond
TRAP QUEEN
RICH $AVAGE II
By Troublesome
YAYO V
GHOST MOB II

Anthony Fields

Stilloan Robinson
CREAM III
By Yolanda Moore
SON OF A DOPE FIEND III
HEAVEN GOT A GHETTO II
By Renta
FOREVER GANGSTA II
GLOCKS ON SATIN SHEETS III
By Adrian Dulan
LOYALTY AIN'T PROMISED III
By Keith Williams
THE PRICE YOU PAY FOR LOVE III
By Destiny Skai
I'M NOTHING WITHOUT HIS LOVE II
SINS OF A THUG II
TO THE THUG I LOVED BEFORE II
By Monet Dragun
LIFE OF A SAVAGE IV
MURDA SEASON IV
GANGLAND CARTEL IV
CHI'RAQ GANGSTAS IV
KILLERS ON ELM STREET IV
JACK BOYZ N DA BRONX II
A DOPEBOY'S DREAM II
By **Romell Tukes**
QUIET MONEY IV
EXTENDED CLIP III
THUG LIFE IV
By **Trai'Quan**

In the Blink of an Eye

THE STREETS MADE ME III
By **Larry D. Wright**
IF YOU CROSS ME ONCE II
ANGEL III
By **Anthony Fields**
FRIEND OR FOE III
By **Mimi**
SAVAGE STORMS III
By **Meesha**
BLOOD ON THE MONEY III
By J-Blunt
THE STREETS WILL NEVER CLOSE II
By K'ajji
NIGHTMARES OF A HUSTLA III
By King Dream
IN THE ARM OF HIS BOSS
By Jamila
HARD AND RUTHLESS III
MOB TOWN 251 II
By Von Diesel
LEVELS TO THIS SHYT II
By Ah'Million
MOB TIES III
By SayNoMore
BODYMORE MURDERLAND III
By Delmont Player
THE LAST OF THE OGS III
Tranay Adams
FOR THE LOVE OF A BOSS II

251

Anthony Fields

By C. D. Blue
MOBBED UP II
By King Rio

Available Now

RESTRAINING ORDER **I & II**
By **CA$H & Coffee**
LOVE KNOWS NO BOUNDARIES **I II & III**
By **Coffee**
RAISED AS A GOON I, II, III & IV
BRED BY THE SLUMS I, II, III
BLAST FOR ME I & II
ROTTEN TO THE CORE I II III
A BRONX TALE I, II, III
DUFFLE BAG CARTEL I II III IV V
HEARTLESS GOON I II III IV V
A SAVAGE DOPEBOY I II
DRUG LORDS I II III
CUTTHROAT MAFIA I II
By **Ghost**
LAY IT DOWN **I & II**
LAST OF A DYING BREED I II
BLOOD STAINS OF A SHOTTA I & II III
By **Jamaica**
LOYAL TO THE GAME I II III
LIFE OF SIN I, II III

252

In the Blink of an Eye

Anthony Fields

BLOOD OF A BOSS **I, II, III, IV, V**

SHADOWS OF THE GAME

TRAP BASTARD

By **Askari**

THE STREETS BLEED MURDER **I, II & III**

THE HEART OF A GANGSTA I II& III

By **Jerry Jackson**

CUM FOR ME I II III IV V VI VII

An **LDP Erotica Collaboration**

BRIDE OF A HUSTLA **I II & II**

THE FETTI GIRLS **I, II& III**

CORRUPTED BY A GANGSTA I, II III, IV

BLINDED BY HIS LOVE

THE PRICE YOU PAY FOR LOVE I II

DOPE GIRL MAGIC I II III

By **Destiny Skai**

WHEN A GOOD GIRL GOES BAD

By **Adrienne**

THE COST OF LOYALTY I II III

By Kweli

A GANGSTER'S REVENGE **I II III & IV**

THE BOSS MAN'S DAUGHTERS I II III IV V

A SAVAGE LOVE **I & II**

BAE BELONGS TO ME I II

A HUSTLER'S DECEIT I, II, III

WHAT BAD BITCHES DO I, II, III

SOUL OF A MONSTER I II III

KILL ZONE

A DOPE BOY'S QUEEN I II

254

In the Blink of an Eye

By **Aryanna**
A KINGPIN'S AMBITON
A KINGPIN'S AMBITION **II**
I MURDER FOR THE DOUGH
By **Ambitious**
TRUE SAVAGE I II III IV V VI VII
DOPE BOY MAGIC I, II, III
MIDNIGHT CARTEL I II III
CITY OF KINGZ I II
By **Chris Green**
A DOPEBOY'S PRAYER
By **Eddie "Wolf" Lee**
THE KING CARTEL **I, II & III**
By **Frank Gresham**
THESE NIGGAS AIN'T LOYAL **I, II & III**
By **Nikki Tee**
GANGSTA SHYT **I II &III**
By **CATO**
THE ULTIMATE BETRAYAL
By **Phoenix**
BOSS'N UP **I , II & III**
By **Royal Nicole**
I LOVE YOU TO DEATH
By Destiny J
I RIDE FOR MY HITTA
I STILL RIDE FOR MY HITTA
By **Misty Holt**
LOVE & CHASIN' PAPER
By **Qay Crockett**

255

Anthony Fields

TO DIE IN VAIN

SINS OF A HUSTLA

By **ASAD**

BROOKLYN HUSTLAZ

By **Boogsy Morina**

BROOKLYN ON LOCK I & II

By **Sonovia**

GANGSTA CITY

By **Teddy Duke**

A DRUG KING AND HIS DIAMOND I & II III

A DOPEMAN'S RICHES

HER MAN, MINE'S TOO I, II

CASH MONEY HO'S

THE WIFEY I USED TO BE I II

By Nicole Goosby

TRAPHOUSE KING **I II & III**

KINGPIN KILLAZ I II III

STREET KINGS I II

PAID IN BLOOD **I II**

CARTEL KILLAZ I II III

DOPE GODS I II

By **Hood Rich**

LIPSTICK KILLAH **I, II, III**

CRIME OF PASSION I II & III

FRIEND OR FOE I II

By **Mimi**

STEADY MOBBN' **I, II, III**

THE STREETS STAINED MY SOUL I II

By **Marcellus Allen**

256

In the Blink of an Eye

WHO SHOT YA **I, II, III**

SON OF A DOPE FIEND I II

HEAVEN GOT A GHETTO

Renta

GORILLAZ IN THE BAY **I II III IV**

TEARS OF A GANGSTA I II

3X KRAZY I II

DE'KARI

TRIGGADALE I II III

Elijah R. Freeman

GOD BLESS THE TRAPPERS I, II, III

THESE SCANDALOUS STREETS I, II, III

FEAR MY GANGSTA I, II, III IV, V

THESE STREETS DON'T LOVE NOBODY I, II

BURY ME A G I, II, III, IV, V

A GANGSTA'S EMPIRE I, II, III, IV

THE DOPEMAN'S BODYGAURD I II

THE REALEST KILLAZ I II III

THE LAST OF THE OGS I II

Tranay Adams

THE STREETS ARE CALLING

Duquie Wilson

MARRIED TO A BOSS... I II III

By Destiny Skai & Chris Green

KINGZ OF THE GAME I II III IV V

Playa Ray

SLAUGHTER GANG I II III

RUTHLESS HEART I II III

By Willie Slaughter

Anthony Fields

FUK SHYT

By Blakk Diamond

DON'T F#CK WITH MY HEART I II

By Linnea

ADDICTED TO THE DRAMA I II III

IN THE ARM OF HIS BOSS II

By Jamila

YAYO I II III IV

A SHOOTER'S AMBITION I II

By S. Allen

TRAP GOD I II III

RICH $AVAGE

By Troublesome

FOREVER GANGSTA

GLOCKS ON SATIN SHEETS I II

By Adrian Dulan

TOE TAGZ I II III

LEVELS TO THIS SHYT

By Ah'Million

KINGPIN DREAMS I II III

By Paper Boi Rari

CONFESSIONS OF A GANGSTA I II III

By Nicholas Lock

I'M NOTHING WITHOUT HIS LOVE

SINS OF A THUG

TO THE THUG I LOVED BEFORE

By Monet Dragun

CAUGHT UP IN THE LIFE I II III

By Robert Baptiste

In the Blink of an Eye

259

Anthony Fields

By K'ajji

CREAM I II

By Yolanda Moore

NIGHTMARES OF A HUSTLA I II

By King Dream

CONCRETE KILLA I II

By Kingpen

HARD AND RUTHLESS I II

MOB TOWN 251

By Von Diesel

GHOST MOB II

Stilloan Robinson

MOB TIES I II

By SayNoMore

BODYMORE MURDERLAND I II

By Delmont Player

FOR THE LOVE OF A BOSS

By C. D. Blue

MOBBED UP

By King Rio

In the Blink of an Eye

BOOKS BY LDP'S CEO, CA$H

TRUST IN NO MAN

TRUST IN NO MAN 2

TRUST IN NO MAN 3

BONDED BY BLOOD

SHORTY GOT A THUG

THUGS CRY

THUGS CRY 2

THUGS CRY 3

TRUST NO BITCH

TRUST NO BITCH 2

TRUST NO BITCH 3

TIL MY CASKET DROPS

RESTRAINING ORDER

RESTRAINING ORDER 2

IN LOVE WITH A CONVICT

LIFE OF A HOOD STAR

Anthony Fields